The Soft Voice of the Serpent

The Soft Voice of the Serpent

AND OTHER STORIES BY

NADINE GORDIMER

THE VIKING PRESS · NEW YORK

Certain stories included in this collection originally appeared in *Harper's Magazine, The New Yorker, The Virginia Quarterly,* and *The Yale Review.*

Compass books Edition
ISSUED IN 1962 BY THE VIKING PRESS, INC.
625 MADISON AVENUE, NEW YORK 22, N.Y.

DISTRIBUTED IN CANADA BY
THE MACMILLAN COMPANY OF CANADA LIMITED

PRINTED IN THE U.S.A. BY THE COLONIAL PRESS INC.

CONTENTS

The Soft Voice of the Serpent

The Soft Voice of the Serpent

He was only twenty-six and very healthy and he was soon strong enough to be wheeled out into the garden. Like everyone else, he had great and curious faith in the garden: "Well, soon you'll be up and able to sit out in the garden," they said, looking at him fervently, with little understanding tilts of the head. Yes, he would be out . . . in the garden. It was a big garden enclosed in old dark, sleek, pungent firs, and he could sit deep beneath their tiered fringes, down in the shade, far away. There was the feeling that there, in the garden, he would come to an understanding; that it would come easier, there. Perhaps there was something in this of the old Eden idea; the tender human adjusting himself to himself in the soothing impersonal presence of trees and grass and earth, before going out into the stare of the world.

The very first time it was so strange; his wife was wheeling him along the gravel path in the sun and the shade, and he felt exactly as he did when he was a little boy and he used to bend and hang, looking at the world upside down, through his ankles. Everything was vast and open, the sky, the wind blowing along through the swaying, trembling greens, the flowers shaking in vehement denial. Movement . . .

The Soft Voice of the Serpent

A first slight wind lifted again in the slack, furled sail of himself; he felt it belly gently, so gently he could just feel it, lifting inside him.

So she wheeled him along, pushing hard and not particularly well with her thin pretty arms—but he would not for anything complain of the way she did it or suggest that the nurse might do better, for he knew that would hurt her—and when they came to a spot that he liked, she put the brake on the chair and settled him there for the morning. That was the first time and now he sat there every day. He read a lot, but his attention was arrested sometimes, quite suddenly and compellingly, by the sunken place under the rug where his leg used to be. There was his one leg, and next to it, the rug flapped loose. Then looking, he felt his leg not there; he felt it go, slowly, from the toe to the thigh. He felt that he had no leg. After a few minutes he went back to his book. He never let the realization quite reach him; he let himself realize it physically, but he never quite let it get at *him*. He felt it pressing up, coming, coming, dark, crushing, ready to burst—but he always turned away, just in time, back to his book. That was his system; that was the way he was going to do it. He would let it come near, irresistibly near, again and again, ready to catch him alone in the garden. And again and again he would turn it back, just in time. Slowly it would become a habit, with the reassuring strength of a habit. It would become such a habit never to get to the point of realizing it, *that he never would realize it*. And one day he would find that he had achieved what he wanted: *he would feel as if he had always been like that*.

Then the danger would be over, for ever.

In a week or two he did not have to read all the time; he could

2

let himself put down the book and look about him, watching the firs part silkily as a child's fine straight hair in the wind, watching the small birds tightroping the telephone wire, watching the fat old dove trotting after his refined patrician gray women, purring with lust. His wife came and sat beside him, doing her sewing, and sometimes they spoke, but often they sat for hours, a whole morning, her movements at work small and unobtrusive as the birds', he resting his head back and looking at a blur of sky through half-closed eyes. Now and then her eye, habitually looking inwards, would catch the signal of some little happening, some point of color in the garden, and her laugh or exclamation drawing his attention to it would suddenly clear away the silence. At eleven o'clock she would get up and put down her sewing and go into the house to fetch their tea; crunching slowly away into the sun up the path, going easily, empowered by the sun rather than her own muscles. He watched her go, easily. . . . He was healing. In the static quality of his gaze, in the relaxed feeling of his mouth, in the upward-lying palm of his hand, there was annealment. . .

One day a big locust whirred dryly past her head, and she jumped up with a cry, scattering her sewing things. He laughed at her as she bent about picking them up, shuddering. She went into the house to fetch the tea, and he began to read. But presently he put down the book and, yawning, noticed a reel of pink cotton that she had missed, lying in a rose bed.

He smiled, remembering her. And then he became conscious of a curious old-mannish little face, fixed upon him in a kind of hypnotic dread. There, absolutely stilled with fear beneath his glance, crouched a very big locust. What an amusing face the thing had! A lugubrious long face, that somehow suggested a

3

bald head, and such a glum mouth. It looked like some little person out of a Disney cartoon. It moved slightly, still looking up fearfully at him. Strange body, encased in a sort of old-fashioned creaky armor. He had never realized before what ridiculous-looking insects locusts were! Well, naturally not; they occur to one collectively, as a pest—one doesn't go around looking at their faces.

The face was certainly curiously human and even expressive, but looking at the body, he decided that the body couldn't really be called a body at all. With the face, the creature's kinship with humans ended. The body was flimsy paper stretched over a frame of matchstick, like a small boy's homemade airplane. And those could not be thought of as legs—the great saw-toothed back ones were like the parts of an old crane, and the front ones like—like one of her hairpins, bent in two. At that moment the creature slowly lifted up one of the front legs, and passed it tremblingly over its head, stroking the left antenna down. Just as a man might take out a handkerchief and pass it over his brow.

He began to feel enormously interested in the creature, and leaned over in his chair to see it more closely. It sensed him and beneath its stiff, plated sides, he was surprised to see the pulsations of a heart. How fast it was breathing. . . . He leaned away a little, to frighten it less.

Watching it carefully, and trying to keep himself effaced from its consciousness by not moving, he became aware of some struggle going on in the thing. It seemed to gather itself together in muscular concentration: this co-ordinated force then passed along its body in a kind of petering tremor, and ended in a stirring along the upward shaft of the great back legs. But the locust remained where it was. Several times this wave of effort currented through it and was spent, but the next time it ended surprisingly in a few hobbling, uneven steps, undercarriage—airplanelike again—trailing along the earth.

Then the creature lay, fallen on its side, antennae turned stretched out toward him. It groped with its hands, feeling for a hold on the soft ground, bending its elbows and straining. With a heave, it righted itself, and as it did so, he saw—leaning forward again—what was the trouble. It was the same trouble. His own trouble. The creature had lost one leg. Only the long upward shaft of its left leg remained, with a neat round aperture where, no doubt, the other half of the leg had been jointed in.

Now as he watched the locust gather itself again and again in that concentration of muscle, spend itself again and again in a message that was so puzzlingly never obeyed, he knew exactly what the creature felt. Of course he knew that feeling! That absolute certainty that the leg was there: one had only to lift it. . . . The upward shaft of the locust's leg quivered, lifted; why then couldn't he walk? He tried again. The message came; it was going through, the leg was lifting, now it was ready—now! . . . The shaft sagged in the air, with nothing, nothing to hold it up.

He laughed and shook his head: He *knew* . . . Good Lord, *exactly* like— He called out to the house—"Come quickly! Come and see! You've got another patient!"

"What?" she shouted. "I'm getting tea."

"Come and look!" he called. "Now!"

". . . What is it?" she said, approaching the locust distastefully.

"Your locust!" he said. She jumped away with a little shriek.

"Don't worry—it can't move. It's as harmless as I am. You must have knocked its leg off when you hit out at it!" He was laughing at her.

"Oh, I didn't!" she said reproachfully. She loathed it but she loathed to hurt, even more. "I never even touched it! All I hit was air . . . I couldn't possibly have hit it. Not its leg off."

"All right then. It's another locust. But it's lost its leg, anyway. You should just see it. . . . It doesn't know the leg isn't there. God, I know exactly how that feels. . . . I've been watching it, and honestly, it's uncanny. I can see it feels just like I do!"

She smiled at him, sideways; she seemed suddenly pleased at something. Then, recalling herself, she came forward, bent double, hands upon her hips.

"Well, if it can't move . . . ," she said, hanging over it.

"Don't be frightened," he laughed. "Touch it."

"Ah, the poor thing," she said, catching her breath in compassion. "It can't walk."

"Don't encourage it to self-pity," he teased her.

She looked up and laughed. "Oh you—" she parried, assuming a frown. The locust kept its solemn silly face turned to her. "Shame, isn't he a funny old man," she said. "But what will happen to him?"

"I don't know," he said, for being in the same boat absolved him from responsibility or pity. "Maybe he'll grow another one. Lizards grow new tails, if they lose them."

"Oh, *lizards*," she said. "—But not these. I'm afraid the cat'll get him."

"Get another little chair made for him and you can wheel him out here with me."

"Yes," she laughed. "Only for him it would have to be a kind of little cart, with wheels."

"Or maybe he could be taught to use crutches. I'm sure the farmers would like to know that he was being kept active."

"The poor old thing," she said, bending over the locust again. And reaching back somewhere into an inquisitive childhood she picked up a thin wand of twig and prodded the locust, very gently. "Funny thing is, it's even the same leg, the left one." She looked round at him and smiled.

"I know," he nodded, laughing. "The two of us . . ." And then he shook his head and, smiling, said it again: "The two of us."

She was laughing and just then she flicked the twig more sharply than she meant to and at the touch of it there was a sudden flurried papery whirr, and the locust flew away.

She stood there with the stick in her hand, half afraid of it again, and appealed, unnerved as a child, "What happened. What happened."

There was a moment of silence.

"Don't be a fool," he said irritably.

They had forgotten that locusts can fly.

locust to serpent
as blacks spoil idealic
society in S. Africa.

H is thin strong bony legs passed by at eye level every morning as they lay, stranded on the hard smooth sand. Washed up thankfully out of the swirl and buffet of the city, they were happy to lie there, but because they were accustomed to telling the time by their nerves' response to the different tensions of the city—children crying in flats, lorries going heavily, and bicycles jangling for early morning, skid of tires, sound of frying, and the human insect noise of thousands talking and walking and eating at midday—the tensionless shore keyed only to the tide gave them a sense of timelessness that, however much they rejoiced mentally, troubled their habit-impressed bodies with a lack of pressure. So the sound of his feet, thudding nearer over the sand, passing their heads with the deep sound of a man breathing in the heat above the rolled-up faded trousers, passing away up the beach and shrinking into the figure of an Indian fisherman, began to be something to be waited for. His coming and going divided the morning into three; the short early time before he passed, the time when he was actually passing, and the largish chunk of warm midday that followed when he had gone.

After a few days, he began to say good morning, and looking

up, they found his face, a long head with a shining dark dome surrounded with curly hair given a stronger liveliness by the sharp coarse strokes of gray hairs, the beautiful curved nose handed out so impartially to Indians, dark eyes slightly blood-shot from the sun, a wide muscular mouth smiling on strong uneven teeth that projected slightly like the good useful teeth of an animal. But it was by his legs they would have known him; the dark, dull-skinned feet with the few black hairs on the big toe, the long hard shaft of the shin tightly covered with smooth shining skin, the pull of the tendons at his ankle like the taut ropes that control the sails of a ship.

They idly watched him go, envious of his fisherman's life not because they could ever really have lived it themselves, but because it had about it the frame of their holiday freedom. They looked at him with the curious respect which people feel for one who has put a little space between himself and the rest of the world. "It's a good life," said the young man, the words not quite hitting the nail of this respect. "I can just see *you* . . . ," said the girl, smiling. She saw him in his blue creased suit, carrying a bottle of brandy wrapped in brown paper, a packet of bananas, and the evening paper.

"He's got a nice open face," said the young man. "He wouldn't have a face like that if he worked as a waiter at the hotel."

But when they spoke to him one morning when he was fish-ing along the surf for chad right in front of them, they found that he like themselves was only on holiday from a more com-plicated pattern of life. He worked five or six miles away at the sugar refinery, and this was his annual two weeks. He spent it fishing, he told them, because that was what he liked to do with his Sundays. He grinned his strong smile, lifting his chin out to sea as he swung his spoon glittering into the coming wave. They stood by like children, tugging one another back when he cast his line, closing in to peer with their hands behind their backs when he pulled in the flat silver fish and pushed the heads into the sand. They asked him questions, and he answered with a kind of open pleasure, as if discounting his position as a man of skill, a performer before an audience, out of friendliness. And they questioned animatedly, feeling the knowledge that he too was on holiday was a sudden intimacy between them, like the discovery between strangers that they share a friend. The fact that he was an Indian troubled them hardly at all. They almost forgot he *was* an Indian. And this too, though they did not know it, produced a lightening of the heart, a desire to do conversational frolics with a free tongue the way one stretches and kicks up one's legs in the sun after confinement in a close dark room.

"Why not get the camera?" said the girl, beginning to help with the fish as they were brought in. And the young man went away over the sand and came back adjusting the complications of his gadget with the seriousness of the amateur. He knelt in the wet sand that gave beneath his weight with a wet grinding, trying to catch the moment of skill in the fisherman's face. The girl watched quietly, biting her lip for the still second when the camera blinked. Aware but not in the least self-conscious of the fact that he was the subject, the Indian went on with his fishing, now and then parenthetically smiling his long-toothed smile.

The tendrils of their friendship were drawn in sharply for

a moment when, putting his catch into a sack, he inquired naturally, "Would you like to buy one for lunch, sir?" Down on his haunches with a springy strand of hair blowing back and forth over his ear, he could not know what a swift recoil closed back through the air over his head. He wanted to sell something. Disappointment as much as a satisfied dig in the ribs from opportunist prejudice stiffened them momentarily. Of course, he was not in quite the same position as themselves, after all. They shifted their attitude slightly.

"Well, we live at the hotel, you see," said the girl.

He tied the mouth of the sack and looked up with a laugh. "Of course!" he smiled, shaking his head. "You couldn't cook it." His lack of embarrassment immediately made things easy.

"Do you ever sell fish to the hotel?" asked the young man. "We must keep a lookout for it."

"No—no, not really," said the Indian. "I don't sell much of my fish—mostly we eat it up there," he lifted his eyebrows to the hills, brilliant with cane. "It's only sometimes I sell it."

The girl felt the dismay of having mistaken a privilege for an imposition. "Oh well," she smiled at him charmingly, "that's a pity. Anyway, I suppose the hotel has to be sure of a regular supply."

"That's right," he said. "I only fish in my spare time."

He was gone, firmly up the beach, his strong feet making clefts in the sand like the muscular claws of a big strong-legged bird.

"You'll see the pictures in a few days," shouted the girl. He stopped and turned with a grin. "That's nothing," he said.

The Catch

"Wait till I catch something big. Perhaps soon I'll get something worth taking."

He was "their Indian." When they went home they might remember the holiday by him as you might remember a particular holiday as the one when you used to play with a spaniel on the beach every day. It would be, of course, a nameless spaniel, an ownerless spaniel, an entertaining creature existing nowhere in your life outside that holiday, yet bound with absolute intimacy within that holiday itself. And as an animal becomes more human every day, so every day the quality of their talk with the Indian had to change; the simple question-and-answer relation that goes with the celluloid pop of a ping-pong ball and does so well for all inferiors, foreigners, and children became suddenly a toy (the Indian was grown-up and might smile at it). They did not know his name, and now, although they might have asked the first day and got away with it, it was suddenly impossible, because he didn't ask them theirs. So their you's and he's and I's took on the positiveness of names, and yet seemed to deepen their sense of communication by the fact that they introduced none of the objectivity that names must always bring. He spoke to them quite a lot about Johannesburg, to which he assumed they must belong, as that was his generalization of city life, and he knew, sympathetically, that they were city people. And although they didn't live there, but somewhere near on a smaller pattern, they answered as if they did. They also talked a little of his life; or rather of the processes of the sugar refinery from which his life depended. They found it fascinating.

"If I were working, I'd try and arrange for you to come and

see it," he said, pausing, with his familiar taking his own time, and then looking directly smiling at them, his head tilted a little, the proud, almost rueful way one looks at two attractive children. They responded to his mature pleasure in them with a diffusion of warm youth that exuded from their skin as sweat is released at the touch of fear. "What a fascinating person he is!" they would say to one another, curious.

But mostly they talked about fishing, the sea, and the particular stretch of coast on which they were living. The Indian knew the sea—at home the couple would have said he "loved" it—and from the look of it he could say whether the water would be hot or cold, safe or nursing an evil grievance of currents, evenly rolling or sucking at the land in a fierce backwash. He knew, as magically to them as a diviner feeling the pull of water beneath the ground, where the fish would be when the wind blew from the east, when it didn't blow at all, and when clouds covered in from the hills to the horizon. He stood on the slippery rocks with them and saw as they did, a great plain of heaving water, empty and unreadable as infinity; but *he* saw a hard greedy life going on down in there, shining plump bodies gaping swiftly close together through the blind green, tentacles like dark hands feeling over the deep rocks. And he would say, coming past them in his salt-stiff old trousers that seemed to put to shame clothes meekly washed in soap and tap water, "Over there at the far rocks this morning."

They saw him most days; but always only in the morning. By afternoon they had had enough of the beach, and wanted to play golf on the closely green course that mapped inland through the man-high cane as though a barber had run a pair of clippers through a fine head of hair, or to sit reading old hotel magazines on the porch whose windows were so bleared with salt air that looking through them was like seeing with the opaque eyes of an old man. The beach was hot and faraway; one day after lunch when a man came up from the sand and said as he passed their chairs, "There's someone looking for you down there. An Indian's caught a huge salmon and he says you've promised to photograph it for him,"—they sat back and looked at one another with a kind of lazy exasperation. They felt weak and unwilling, defeating interest.

"Go on," she said. "You must go."

"It had to be right after lunch," he grumbled, smiling.

"Oh go on," she insisted, head tilted. She herself did not move, but remained sitting back with her chin dropped to her chest, whilst he fetched the camera and went jogging off down the steep path through the bush. She pictured the salmon. She had never seen a salmon: it would be pink and powerfully agile; how big? She could not imagine.

A child came racing up from the beach, all gasps. "Your husband says," saying it word for word, "he says you must come down right away and you must bring the film with you. It's in the little dressing-table drawer under his handkerchiefs." She swung out of her chair as if she had been ready to go. The small boy ran before her all the way down to the beach, skidding on the stony path. Her husband was waving incoherently from the sand, urgent and excited as a waving flag. Not understanding, she began to hurry too.

"Like this!" he was shouting. "Like this! Never seen anything like it! It must weigh eighty pounds—," his hands sized out a great hunk of air.

"But where?" she cried impatiently, not wanting to be told, but to see.

"It's right up the beach. He's gone to fetch it. I'd forgotten the film was finished, so when I got there, it was no use. I had to come back, and he said he'd lug it along here." Yet he hadn't been able to leave the beach to get the film himself; he wanted to be there to show the fish to anyone who came along; he couldn't have borne to have someone see it without him, who had seen it first.

At last the Indian came round the paw of the bay, a tiny black stick-shape detected moving alive along the beached waterline of black drift-sticks, and as he drew nearer he took on a shape, and then, more distinctly, the shape divided, another shape detached itself from the first, and there he was— a man hurrying heavily with a huge fish slung from his shoulder to his heels. "O-o-h!" cried the girl, knuckle of her first finger caught between her teeth. The Indian's path wavered, as if he staggered under the weight, and his forearms and hands, gripping the mouth of the fish, were bent stiff as knives against his chest. Long strands of gray curly hair blew over from the back of his head along his bright high forehead, that held the sun in a concentric blur of light on its domed prominence.

"Go and help him," the girl said to her husband, shaming him. He was standing laughing proudly, like a spectator watching the winner come in at a race. He was startled he hadn't gone himself: "Shall I?" he said, already going.

They staggered up with the fish between them, panting heavily, and dropped the dead weight of the great creature with a scramble and thud upon the sand. It was as if they had rescued someone from the sea. They stood back that they might feel the relief of their burden, and the land might receive the body. But what a beautiful creature lay there! Through the powdering of sand, mother-of-pearl shone up. A great round glass eye looked out.

"Oh, get the sand off it!" laughed the girl. "Let's see it properly."

Exhausted as he was, he belonged to the fish, and so immediately the Indian dragged it by the tail down to the rill of the water's edge, and they cupped water over it with their hands. Water cleared it like a cloth wiping a film from a diamond; out shone the magnificent fish, stiff and handsome in its mail of scales, glittering a thousand opals of color, set with two brilliant deep eyes all hard clear beauty and not marred by the capability of expression which might have made a reproach of the creature's death; a king from another world, big enough to shoulder a man out of the way, dead, captured, astonishing.

The child came up and put his forefinger on its eye. He wrinkled his nose, smiling and pulling a face, shoulders rising. "It can't see!" he said joyously. The girl tried it; smooth, firm, resilient eye; like a butterfly wing bright under glass.

They all stood, looking down at the fish, that moved very slightly in the eddy of sand as the thin water spread out softly round its body and then drew gently back. People made for them across the sand. Some came down from the hotel; the piccanin caddies left the golf course. Interest spread like a net, drawing in the few, scattered queer fish of the tiny resort, who avoided one another in a gesture of jealous privacy. They came to stand and stare, prodding a tentative toe at the real fish, scooped out of his sea. The men tried to lift it, making terse suggestions about its weight. A hundred, seventy, sixty-five, they said with assurance. Nobody really knew. It was a wonderful fish. The Indian, wishing to take his praise modestly, busied himself with practical details, explaining with serious charm, as if he were quoting a book or someone else's experience, how such a fish was landed, and how rarely it was to be caught on that part of the coast. He kept his face averted, down over the fish, like a man fighting tears before strangers.

"Will it bite? Will it bite?" cried the children, putting their hands inside its rigid white-lipped mouth and shrieking. "Now that's enough," said a mother.

"Sometimes there's a lovely stone, here," the Indian shuffled nearer on his haunches, not touching but indicating with his brown finger a place just above the snout. He twisted his head to find the girl. "If I find it in this one, I'll bring it for you. It makes a lovely ring." He was smiling to her.

"I want a picture taken with the fish," she said determinedly, feeling the sun very hot on her head.

Someone had to stand behind her, holding it up—it was too heavy for her. It was exactly as tall as she was; the others pointed with admiration. She smiled prettily, not looking at the fish. Then the important pictures were to be taken: the Indian and his fish.

"Just a minute," he said, surprisingly, and taking a comb out of his pocket, carefully smoothed back his hair under his guiding hand. He lifted the fish by the gills with a squelch out of the wet sand, and some pictures were taken. "Like this?" he kept saying anxiously, as he was directed by the young man to stand this way or that.

He stood tense, as if he felt oppressed by the invisible presence of some long-forgotten backdrop and palmstand. "Smile!" demanded the man and the girl together, anxiously. And the sight of them, so concerned for his picture, released him to smile what was inside him, a strong, wide smile of pure achievement, that gathered up the unequal components of his face—his slim fine nose, his big ugly horse-teeth, his black crinkled-up eyes, canceled out the warring inner contradictions that they stood for, and scribbled boldly a brave moment of whole man.

After the pictures had been taken, the peak of interest had been touched; the spectators' attention, quick to rise to a phenomenon, tended to sink back to its level of ordinary, more dependable interests. Wonderment at the fish could not be sustained in its purely specific projection; the remarks became more general and led to hearsay stories of other catches, other unusual experiences. As for the Indian, he had neglected his fish for his audience long enough. No matter how it might differ as an experience, as a fish it did not differ from other fish. He worried about it being in the full hot sun, and dragged it a little deeper into the sea so that the wavelets might flow over it. The mothers began to think that the sun was too hot for their children, and straggled away with them. Others followed, talking about the fish, shading the backs of their necks with their hands. "Half-past two," said someone. The sea glittered with broken mirrors of hurtful light. "What do you think you'd get for it?" asked the young man, slowly fitting his camera into its case.

"I'll get about two-pound-ten." The Indian was standing with his hands on hips, looking down at the fish as if sizing it up.

So he *was* going to sell it! "As much as that?" said the girl in surprise. With a slow, deliberate movement that showed that the sizing up had been a matter of weight rather than possible profit, he tried carrying the fish under his arm. But his whole body bent in an arc to its weight. He let it slither to the sand.

"Are you going to try the hotel?" she asked; she expected something from the taste of this fish, a flavor of sentiment.

He smiled, understanding her. "No," he said indulgently, "I might. But I don't think they'd take it. I'll try somewhere else. They might want it." His words took in vaguely the deserted beach, the one or two tiny holiday cottages. "But where else?" she insisted. It irritated her although she smiled, this habit of other races of slipping out of one's questioning, giving vague but adamant assurances of sureties which were supposed to be hidden but that one knew perfectly well did not exist at all. "Well, there's the boardinghouse at Bailey's River—the lady there knows me. She often likes to take my fish."

Bailey's River was the next tiny place, about a mile away over the sands. "Well, I envy them their eating!" said the girl, giving him her praise again. She had taken a few steps back over the sand, ready to go; she held out her hand to draw her husband away. "When will I see the picture?" the Indian stayed them eagerly. "Soon, soon, soon!" they laughed. And they left him, kneeling beside his fish and laughing with them.

"I don't know how he's going to manage to carry that great thing all the way to Bailey's," said the young man. He was steering his wife along with his hand on her little nape. "It's only a mile!" she said. "Ye-es! But—?" "Oh, they're strong. They're used to it," she said, shaking her feet free of the sand as they reached the path.

When they got back to the hotel, there was a surprise for them. As though the dam of their quiet withdrawal had been fuller than they thought, fuller than they could withstand, they found themselves toppling over into their old stream again, that might run on pointlessly and busy as the brook for ever and ever. Three friends from home up country were there, come on an unexpected holiday to a farm a mile or two inland. They had come to look them up, as they would no doubt come every day of the remainder of the holiday; and there would be tennis, and picnic parties, and evenings when they would laugh riotously on the verandah round a table spike with bottles and glasses. And so they were swept off from something too quiet and sure to beckon them back, looking behind them for the beckon, but already twitching to the old familiar tune. The visitors were shown the hotel bedroom, and walked down the broken stone steps to the first tee of the little golf course. They were voracious with the need to make use of everything they saw; bouncing on the beds, hanging out of the window, stamping on the tee, and assuring that they'd be there with their clubs in the morning.

After a few rounds of drinks at the close of the afternoon, the young man and his wife suddenly felt certain that they had had a very dead time indeed up till now, and the unquiet gnaw of the need to "make the best"—of time, life, holidays, anything —was gleefully hatched to feed on them again. When someone suggested that they all go into Durban for dinner and a cinema, they were excited. "All in our car!" the girl cried. "Let's all go together."

The women had to fly off to the bedroom to prepare themselves to meet the city, and whilst the men waited for them, talking quieter and closer on the verandah, the sun went down behind the cane, the pale calm sea thinned into the horizon and turned long straight shoals of light foam to glass on the sand, pocked, further up, by shadow. When they drove off up the dusty road between the trees they were steeped in the first dark. White stones stood out; as they came to the dip in the road where the sluit ran beneath, they saw someone sitting on the boulder that marked the place, and as they slowed and bumped through, the figure moved slightly with a start checked before it could arrest their attention. They were talking. "What was that?" said one of the women, without much interest. "What?" said the young man, braking in reflex. "It's just an old Indian with a sack or something," someone else broke off to say. The wife, in the front seat, turned:

"Les!" she cried. "It's him, with the fish!"

The husband had pulled up the car, skidded a little sideways on the road, its two shafts of light staring up among the trees. He sat looking at his wife in consternation. "But I wonder what's the matter?" he said. "I don't know!" she shrugged, in a rising tone. "Who is it?" cried someone from the back.

"An Indian fisherman. We've spoken to him on the beach. He caught a huge salmon today."

"We know him well," said the husband; and then to her: "I'd better back and see what's wrong." She looked down at her handbag. "It's going to make us awfully late, if you hang about," she said. "I won't hang about!" He backed in a long jerk, annoyed with her or the Indian, he did not know. He got out, banging the door behind him. They all twisted, trying to see through the rear window. A silence had fallen in the back of the car; the woman started to hum a little tune, faded out. The wife said with a clear little laugh: "Don't think we're crazy. This Indian is really quite a personality. We forgot to tell you about the fish—it happened only just before you came. Everyone was there looking at it—the most colossal thing I've ever seen. And Les took some pictures of him with it; I had one taken too!"

"So why the devil's the silly fool sitting there with the thing?"

She shrugged. "God knows," she said, staring at the clock.

The young husband appeared at the window; he leaned conspiratorially into the waiting faces, with an unsure gesture of the hand. "He's stuck," he explained with a nervous giggle. "Can't carry the thing any further." A little way behind him the figure of the Indian stood uncertainly, supporting the long dark shape of the fish. "But why didn't he sell it?" said the wife, exasperated. "What can *we* do about it."

"Taking it home as a souvenir, of course," said a man, pleased with his joke. But the wife was staring, accusing, at the husband. "Didn't he try to sell it?" He gestured impatiently. "Of course. But what does it matter? Fact is, he couldn't sell the damn thing, and now he can't carry it home." "So what do you want to do about it?" her voice rose indignantly. "Sit here all night?" "Shh," he frowned. He said nothing. The others kept the studiedly considerate silence of strangers pretending not to be present at a family argument. Her husband's silence seemed to be forcing her to speak. "Where does he live?" she said in resigned exasperation. "Just off the main road," said the husband, pat.

She turned with a charmingly exaggerated sense of asking a favor. "Would you mind awfully if we gave the poor old thing a lift down the road?" "No. No. . . . Good Lord, no," they said in a rush. "There'll be no time to have dinner," someone whispered.

"Come on and get in," the young man called over his shoulder, but the Indian still hung back, hesitant. "*Not* the fish!" whispered the wife urgently after her husband. "Put the fish in the boot!"

They heard the wrench of the boot being opened, the thud of the lid coming down again. Then the Indian stood with the young husband at the door of the car. When he saw her, he smiled at her quickly.

"So your big catch is more trouble than it's worth," she said brightly. The words seemed to fall hard upon him; his shoulders dropped as if he suddenly realized his stiff tiredness; he smiled and shrugged.

"Jump in," said the husband heartily, opening the door of the driver's seat and getting in himself. The Indian hesitated, his hand on the back door. The three in the back made no move.

"No, there's no room there," said the girl clearly, splintering the pause. "Come round the other side and get in the front." Obediently the fisherman walked round through the headlights —a moment of his incisive face against the light—and opened the door at her side.

She shifted up. "That's right," she said, as he got in.

His presence in the car was as immediate as if he had been drawn upon the air. The sea-starched folds of his trousers made a slight harsh rubbing noise against the leather of the seat, his damp old tweed jacket smelled of warm wool, showed fuzzy against the edge of light. He breathed deeply and slowly beside her. In her clear voice she continued to talk to him, to ask him about his failure to sell the fish.

"The catch was more trouble than it was worth," he said once, shaking his head, and she did not know whether he had just happened to say what she herself had said, or whether he was consciously repeating her words to himself.

She felt a stab of cold uncertainty, as if she herself did not know what she had said, did not know what she had meant, or might have meant. Nobody else talked to the Indian. Her husband drove the car. She was furious with them for leaving it all to her: the listening of the back of the car was as rude and blatant as staring.

"What shall you do with the salmon now?" she asked brightly, and "I'll probably give it away to my relations," he answered obediently.

When they got to a turnoff a short distance along the main road, the Indian lifted his hand and said quickly, "Here's the place, thank you." His hand sent a little whiff of fish into the air. The car scudded into the dust at the side of the road, and as it did so, the door swung open and he was out.

He stood there as if his body still held the position he had carefully disciplined himself to in the car, head hunched a bit, hands curled as, if he had had a cap, he might perhaps have held it before him, pinned there by the blurs of faces looking out at him from the car. He seemed oddly helpless, standing whilst the young husband opened the boot and heaved the fish out.

"I must thank you very much," he kept saying seriously. "I must thank you."

"That's all right," the husband smiled, starting the car with a roar. The Indian was saying something else, but the revving of the engine drowned it. The girl smiled down to him through the window, but did not turn her head as they drove off.

"The things we get ourselves into!" she said, spreading her

skirt on the seat. She shook her head and laughed a high laugh. "Shame! The poor thing! What on earth can he do with the great smelly fish now?"

And as if her words had touched some chord of hysteria in them all, they began to laugh, and she laughed with them, laughed till she cried, gasping all the while, "But what have I said? Why are you laughing at me? What have I said?"

In the warm stupor of early Sunday afternoon, when the smell of Sunday roast still hangs about the house, and the servants have banged the kitchen door closed behind them and gone off, gleaming and sweaty in tight Sunday clothes, to visit at the Location, the family comes out dreamily, slackly, to lie upon the lawn. The hour has drained them of will; they come out at the pull of some instinct, like that which sends animals creeping away to die. They lie, suspended in the hour, with the cushions and books about them. The big wheels have turned slower and slower; now they cease to turn, and hang motionless. Only the tiny wheels turn still; silent and busy and scarcely noticeable, the beetles climbing in the grass blades, the flowers fingered gently by small currents, as they lift, breathing up to the sun. The little world is still running, where the birds peck, stepping daintily on their twigs of claws in the flower beds.

"Have you got Micky there?" The voice came clearly from the bedroom window and it almost made her wince, it almost penetrated, but there was no resistance to it: in the fluid, heavy, resurgent air the steel blade of sound slid through and was lost. Her head, drooping near the drooping, bee-heavy, crumpled paper chalices of the poppies, lifted half-protestingly, her lazy hand brushed the gray specks of insects which flecked the pages of Petrarch's "Laura in Death." In her mind's eye, she saw Micky, head to tail, asleep, somewhere near . . . On the grass, at her back, at her side; somewhere . . . She grunted and waved in assent, already back in the book, in the mazy spell of steady warmth and flowers fixed in the hypnosis of the sun, and grass blades, seen from their own level, consumed in dark blazing light along the edges. The pulses slackened and the blood ran sweet and heavy in the veins; the print danced and the mind almost swooned. It swerved away, off into thoughts half-formed, that trailed and merged.

good

In one of the neighboring houses that enclosed the garden on three sides, some poor child began to practice the piano. The unsure notes came hesitantly across the air, a tiny voice that disturbed the afternoon no more than would a fly, buzzing about the ear of a sleeping giant. The Sunday paper lay about. The father lay rolled on to his back, suddenly asleep in the defenseless fashion of the middle-aged, with his mouth half-open and the stretched folds of his neck relaxed like the neck of an old turkey. The little boy had grass in his hair, that was itself like winter grass, pale and rough. The others read, dozed, dreamed, and lay on their backs, the sky and the trees and the house and the bright dots of poppies reflected in their eyes as in an old-fashioned convex mirror—the kind of mirror that in Victorian days reflected the room it looked down upon as another world into which one might climb, like *Alice Through the Looking-glass*. There it was, the shining white house, the shining green fir, the shining blue sky, in the little round mirror of each eye.

Yuk.

She read on, lost, drowsing, flicking minute creatures from

the pages, scratching mechanically at her leg, where the grass pricked her.

And the next moment it was gone; the beautiful lassitude turned sick and sour within her, the exquisite torpor hung heavy around her neck, she struggled free of the coils of the dead afternoon. "But I was sure . . . ," she said, stunned; feeling beaten down before the figure of her mother. Her mother stood, almost too much to bear, purposeful and hard as reality, demanding and urgent. Her glance was too insistent, it came like a pain, piercing the spell. "Well, there you are . . . ," the mother spoke with scornful resignation, angrily, "I might have known you wouldn't bother to look."

"But I thought . . ."

"Yes, of course 'you thought'—surely it wasn't asking too much of you to see whether the dog was with you? Well, it's done now, and the poor little bird's bleeding and half torn to bits and still alive, too."

The girl sat up. She was dizzy. The afternoon suddenly sang and was orange-colored. The great wheels started turning, the world creaked and groaned and rushed into confusion and activity, the clamor started up again.

Yesterday they had found a bird—an injured dove, its wing damaged by some small boy's catapult. Once before they had found a hurt bird, and had kept it in a cage and fed it until it was able to fly again, and so this time they brought out the old cage and put the sullen soft gray dove inside with food and water, confident that with care it would soon be healed. Now this afternoon, the mother—always mindful of the small responsibilities that everyone else so easily forgot after the first ardor of sympathy—had gone out to the shed to see how the bird was progressing, and seeing it sulking, puffed up resentfully in a corner of its cage, had decided to let it out to peck about the back garden for a while, intending to return it to the cage if it were still unable to fly. But of course Micky, who eyed the doves upon the wall longingly, and chased them ineffectually when they alighted upon the path or the grass, must be kept out of the way. The mother had made sure that Micky was safely on the front lawn with the family. She had called out of the bedroom window. . . .

"I was sure he was here," the girl repeated. "I felt sure he was here. I thought . . ."

"I had a feeling he'd gone round there after the bird, and when I went out, sure enough, there he was worrying it as if it were a bone."

"Little beast . . . ," the girl shuddered.

"It's alive, poor creature, too.—I'm sure I don't know what's to be done for it now." The mother kept her accusing gaze on the girl, washing her hands of the whole affair.

"You didn't kill it . . . ?" the girl asked, almost pleadingly.

"*I* can't kill the thing," she said. She had always done everything unpleasant for her children; she had always stood between them and the ugliness of life: death, sickness, despair.

The girl looked for something in her mother's face and this time did not find it.

Suddenly she wished, wished she could have the last half-hour back, she wanted it over again, desperately, childishly, uselessly, so that she might look up from her book and say: No, Micky isn't here.

In a kind of sulky horror she got up and started to walk round the side of the house. "Where?" she said drearily, pausing and turning. Her hair was rumpled and grass clung to her clothes, her right cheek was flushed with sun. "Just near the hedge," said the mother.

She tried to prepare herself, to imagine what the bird would look like, but her mind turned away from the thought. It was upset, too lately, roughly woken to serve her. The narcotic sun stared hatefully upon her and she sickened from it, as a man turns from the smell of liquor he has drunk too freely the night before. She did not *care* about the bird; she did not want to be bothered with it. She wanted to go away into the house, or out, somewhere, and pretend it hadn't happened. If you ignored something, put it utterly from you, and went on to the next thing, it was as if it had never happened. If she walked away now, life would grow over the incident, covering it, hiding it smoothly.

I am weak, she said, self-pitying.

I'll have to kill it.

Something lifted and turned over inside her as she realized the thought. Fear prickled right over her body, from her head to her toes.

Then she came out round the screen of the hedge and into the shade of the hedge and she looked upon the ground, that was damp and mossy in patches, and she could not see the bird. She looked here and there, and poked at a drift of dead leaves with her foot, but she did not find it.

And then she turned and there it was, lying in a stony hollow just behind her. There it was, and it was not a bird, it was a flattened mess of dusty feathers, torn and wet with the dog's saliva, oozing dark blood from wounds that lay hidden, making sodden the close soft down of—ah, what was it, was it the breast, the tail; what part was recognizable in the crushed wad of that small body. . . .

Only the head. And as she saw the head a thrill of such vivid, terrifying, utter anguish contracted in her that she felt that some emotion she had never used before had been called up from her soul. It was unbearable. It was the emotion that bursts the human heart. The emotion from which men hide their heads in despair. For the head of the bird lay sunken in the last humility, down upon its broken breast; the beak rested piteously in the feathers, and the eyes were closed strangely, resignedly, in the final martyrdom of suffering. A passionate desperation of agony had passed over that small gray head, had blazed up in the little being of the bird, making it great, bigger than itself, and breaking it, bringing its head down upon its broken breast.

She felt that nothing could expiate this, ever; nothing, nothing; no tears, no sorrowing, no compensation of other joys could wipe out this thing that existed in life.

She saw that the bird still lived; that it was; that it experienced the awfulness of its own annihilation. And cowardly and trembling, knowing that each moment she delayed out of cowardice it suffered to the full, she slowly drew off her sandal. Very slowly, almost whimpering, she lifted the sandal and brought it down upon the bird's head. She had not known it would be so terrible—that beneath the blow of the sandal she would feel the shape of the small gray head, the particular horror of the resistance of the delicate-boned skull and the softness of the outer covering of feathers, all at once, at the moment of contact. And in an agonized instant life asserted itself vainly and for the last time in the tiny creature, and it half-raised itself, opening the thin mute beak in a wild flutter. Wildly she brought the sandal down again; once, twice, three times. The bird was dead.

And now it was nothing; it was a dead bird.

She put her sandal on again, feeling the dust on her bare foot uncomfortable against the inner sole.

She looked at the bird. How strange a thing that was—she had killed, had battered the life out of something. She thought: killing is a strange thing; it is terrible, until you do it, right up to the moment of doing it.

She had read so many times of murder, and it had meant nothing to her; it was as emotionally incomprehensible to her as a passionate love affair would be to a child of seven. But now with a slow cold trickle of fear that ran—and could not be checked, could not be fought—through her soul, leaving its cold awful imprint, a dark knowledge came to her. She felt it open, a Lethean flower of knowledge, that she feared and did not want, chilling her soul with a strange cold sap. It came coldly because it was a dreadful cold thing, the understanding of the fulfillment of the will to kill. I could kill anything now, she thought, and the words seemed light and easy. They were the words of no-feeling, and she was afraid of them. She was deadened under the weight of this cold knowledge, that would never leave her now, once it was discovered. Ah, the hopelessness, the awfulness of knowing. . . . The passion of pity she had felt for the bird was nothing compared with this; gladly, gladly would she feel that again. But she could not; only the calm reasonableness of the clear thought: I could kill anything now.

She came round to the front garden, breathing warmly, with her face drawn in a wry frown. They watched her from the lawn. "Well, what happened?" they asked, watching her face. "I killed it. It's dead," she said.

"Ugh . . . How awful . . . How could you?"

"It was the kindest thing to do," said someone else sensibly. "She had to put the poor thing out of its misery—what else could she do?" The mother got up and went round to the back to dispose of the body.

She went inside because she could not bear the lazy, sprawling sun, that blazed as horribly now as an electric light left burning right on into daylight. She washed, and combed her hair, and let the water run over her hands. And later, in the evening, she went out, and laughing and talking in a group of those social acquaintances who are vaguely referred to as "friends," she said with a grimace—"I had to do something ghastly this afternoon —I had to kill a bird." "How brave of you!" said the young man, laughing, with mock heroic emphasis. "For a girl—yes," said another, spearing an olive on a colored toothpick. "Women are terrified of squashing a beetle. God knows, they can be cruel and ruthless in their own devious subtle fashions—but when it comes to killing any sort of little creature, they're the most craven cowards." "Well, I did," she said stoutly, carelessly; and laughing like a woman of spirit, she took the olive from him and popped it into her mouth.

The Hour and the Years

It was one of those South African days which bear the characteristics of no particular season: still, very clear, with the dry sunlight like fine dust sloping down from the walls of the houses and sparkling on the sandy road; it might have been spring, summer, or autumn. Shouts and voices came floating up from distant streets. The dog Candia barked and the terrier down the road answered in his short, clipt yelps, and—like an orchestra striking up—other dogs, to north, south, east, and west, took up the theme, added comment.

Going into her bedroom to fetch her shopping bag, she caught sight of her face in the mirror and saw that where Sydney had kissed her good-by, on her cheek, there was a faint yellow smear of egg yolk. She felt a momentary depression. He used to kiss her good-by on the mouth when he left in the morning, and his mouth had always tasted of his breakfast egg. Now the mark of the egg was on her cheek. She was not conscious of having avoided his mouth, of having presented her cheek instead. She must have turned away involuntarily.

She picked up Sydney's blue suit, which was lying on the bed, carefully folded, with a note pinned to it: "Send to cleaners." (He had reminded her twice, first at breakfast and then again as he left the house, but he liked to leave notes explaining things, he liked "to be sure.") Putting the suit in her bag, she went out and down into the road, Candia leaping, bowing, and snuffling about her feet.

When she was first married, she had told Sydney that she would like a dog, a Sealyham, and he had ordered one for her; but a day or two later he had arrived home with the big gray mongrel. "There's a dog for you!" he had said. "There's a proper watchdog, to look after things."

She left Sydney's suit at the dry cleaner's and went on to the butcher's, enjoying the sense of bustle, the robust simple stir of life along the shops: the women with their bundles of provisions; the earthy scent of vegetables from the greengrocer's, where the pavement was untidy with scraps of lettuce and the feathery tops of carrots; the cool sweet smell of the chemist's; the thin little girls sent to buy milk, coming out of the dairy balancing brimming jugs, tense as tightrope walkers in a circus.

She bought a pound of chops, some cheese, and after a moment of indecision, two punnets of strawberries, because today was what she had come to think of as "Lewis' day."

Once a week her husband's brother, young Lewis, came to lunch with her, usually bringing a friend. This had become a standing arrangement, grown up out of the pleasant mutual sense of fun that isolated Lewis and her in silent, lighthearted, sympathetic comradeship from the deadly boredom of family gatherings. In the house of her parents-in-law she was a stranger, not because they did not make her welcome, but merely because they were unlike her, and she found her visits there dull—even Sydney became one of them, was absorbed into the colorless quality of their talk—and only Lewis, wryly smiling

35

at her across the table, was an assurance that the visit would end, that there was someone else as bored as herself to help her turn the boredom into a conspiracy of kindly contempt for the others.

Lewis had brought quite a variety of young men to their lunches—some once, others several times, and one, a great friend of his, had made a regular thing of it, coming week after week. This boy Paul was exceptional: gentle, unself-conscious, intelligent, with the most extraordinary facility for adaptation, so that he could roam into the kitchen and discuss various aspects of housekeeping without in any way seeming any less a most masculine and attractive man, and return to the dining room and, with the customary young male dignity, take up a political discussion with Lewis.

The three of them had seemed so much at ease together that she was surprised, amused, and certainly flattered, in an unbelieving sort of way, when Lewis told her that Paul had decided to discontinue the weekly "party" because he felt that if he kept coming he might begin to become "fond of her."

"Nonsense!" she had laughed, protesting. She only half-believed it; it was just an excuse! "Of course he must come again. Tell him not to worry." And she marveled at it in a disinterested sort of way; he had seen her domestic, flushed, smelling of cooking, her face shiny from bending over the stove, heard her talking of her husband, knew her settled and absorbed, and yet he thought her attractive?

That was more than three months ago, and during the last week or two he had begun coming with Lewis again. There was no sense of constraint about him; the whole thing had fizzled out, as if it had never been mentioned. He had forgotten it, probably saw her now as she really was, and she was glad.

The advent of Lewis and a friend for luncheon each week was one of the small pleasures upon which she hinged her days. She had never been able to cure herself of the childish need to have "something to look forward to"; and the knowledge that Lewis' day had come round again gave her a pleasant, well-ordered feeling. Her shopping completed, she whistled to the dog and went back up the road towards the house. She sighed when she saw it—it was not the sort of house she had wanted. At first Sydney had treated it as a joke; there had been a tacit agreement that they would build a house to suit themselves as soon as they could afford it and do so without offense to Sydney's parents, who had given them this house in the first place. But later she had discovered that Sydney only wanted a place where he could eat, sleep, and put his feet up, and he didn't care what it was like.

At noon the telephone rang.

It was Lewis, to tell her that he was stranded in an outlying suburb, his car broken down, and there certainly wasn't a hope of his being able to come up for lunch. Unfortunately, he'd asked Paul to come up too; and now he couldn't get in touch with him because he might be in any of a dozen places. "Tell him I'm sorry," he said, "tell him I'm awfully sorry." "Oh!" she said, disappointed, "And I've got strawberries, what a shame. . . ."

She could smell the faint, sharp fragrance of strawberry juice on her hands as she held the receiver. She had been washing the fruit when the telephone interrupted her, feeling a vague sense of reckless guilt at the sight of the growing pile in the glass bowl, because she knew that buying strawberries before they were fully in season was one of the petty extravagances which she allowed herself on the grounds that they were too small to amount to anything, but which nevertheless ate away a great hole in her housekeeping allowance each month.

She rang off and went back to the kitchen. And now there'll only be the two of us to eat them, she thought. There were far too many for two people. And she didn't want Sydney to know about them, so she couldn't serve the remainder for dessert at dinner. Well, perhaps the two of us will manage the lot, after all.

She felt suddenly high-spirited, lifted with a pleasant sense of diversion at the unexpected twist in the day. She finished cleaning the strawberries and went out onto the verandah. Midday held the road in thrall. The stones winked and flashed, a silent code. The sun seemed to be emanating from the walls of the houses. In the next-door garden, a small syringa bloomed early in the shelter of a wall. The strong, concentrated sweetness of white blossoms was suddenly borne over to her on some invisible movement of air; it enveloped her as the petals of a flower enclose and intoxicate a bee within a world of scent, exquisite, penetrating, strong and almost blinding, as if someone had suddenly taken the stopper out of a perfume bottle right under her nose. She felt dazzled, queer, and then very peaceful. She turned from the brightness of the sun back into the house and, going into her bedroom, sat for a moment or two, motionless, at her dressing-table, before slowly and carefully beginning to comb her hair.

Later she sat on the verandah sewing, and at last she saw

Paul turning the corner and coming up the road in the sun, with his head down. When he reached the gate she rose, and he smiled, clanging the gate behind him, and said, in the bright tone people use for greetings: "Am I late? I'm so sorry —but I had an idea Lewis might call for me, so I hung about a bit, waiting."

"I know," she said. "He 'phoned to tell me. The car broke down and he couldn't come. He was worried about not being able to let you know."

He lifted his eyebrows in surprised concern. He was coming up the steps onto the verandah. They were talking comfortably, and she felt that, like the turn of a key in a lock, everything was easy now; why, now that he was here, it was no effort to entertain him on her own.

He sat down on a canvas chair beside her. He was breathing a little fast, from the pull up the road. "Ah!" he said, lifting his head, "Ah, it's lovely. . . . It is you, isn't it? I've never smelt perfume like it."

"Oh, the scent!" she laughed. "It's the syringa, next door. Not me."

"Is it really? I thought it was some wonderful perfume you were wearing."

She shook her head, and he smiled at her, his slow, sweet smile, in which he showed his bottom teeth, like a child.

They sat for a few minutes, smoking and talking quietly.

When they went in they were blinded by the light of the sun they had left, and the little dining room was a strange, dark place, shot with stars and trailing meteors of orange, green, and purple. As usual, Paul was entirely unself-conscious, going to the kitchen to fetch the glasses which the native girl had forgotten to put on the table, and quite naturally taking over the task of carving the cold ox tongue.

Yet she was looking at him for the first time. The other times he had come she had merely glanced at him, seen him in flashes, in relation to whatever he had been saying in contribution to the general conversation. Now she read the complete, individual language of his face; it was very vivid, like a face reproduced in a dream: not merely an arrangement of features, but the embodiment of all one had ever known about that face, all the moods, faults, charms contained in the image. She had experienced this moment before with others, sometimes people whom she had known superficially for years. It was like coming face to face with a picture which one has always seen obliquely.

How young he looks, she thought. And yet he cannot be so very young, he's older than Lewis, nearly as old as Sydney, I suppose. But it goes, she thought sadly, it goes, that wonderful youngness, that cleanness that is something more than soap and water and has nothing to do with purity—they can lead the wildest lives when they are so young, and still look like beautiful children. It's an illusion, a gloss, and it dries away. Sydney has lost it, thickened, become a man with a red face, with stolid, uncreative hands, perpetually half-curled.

There was a curious sense of growing awareness in her; what was it? A feeling of apprehension, of a need to pause, and think. . . . But she went on talking. She told him about the strawberries. They laughed, urged one another to eat more. "What about your husband?" he asked, pausing in contrition. "Shouldn't we leave some for him?"

"Ah, no," she lied, "You see, he doesn't eat them." And a slow surge of color burned up over her face; all at once she felt a terrible, shameful embarrassment for those small meannesses, the carping, niggling faults of her husband, about which this young man did not know, could not dream. He was looking at her, puzzled, uncertain of her expression. So she smiled at once.

"You're lonely here, sometimes?"

"Yes—but not often; I'm usually kept busy in the house."

"I always think that women must be so much more resourceful than men—they have more leisure, a less disciplined sort of life. And yet they don't seem to get bored."

Their voices were polite, expressing trivialities, commonplace reserved opinions such as people might talk in a bus. Yet the more rigidly their speech kept its distance, the stronger the tension between them grew.

She felt that though he sat across the table from her, she could feel him breathing close to her, see the detail of the shining brown pupils of his eyes. She was aware of the faint, warm essence breathed from the pores of the skin on his cheeks.

Her hands faltered about the dishes; time moved too fast, the necessity for talk prevented the pause she must have in which to collect herself. The steady stream of talk bore her along, half-unwilling, intrigued and afraid—oh, afraid!—and fascinated by the novelty of fear, trying to remember Sydney, her home, who she was, the peace of respectability, aghast that these things should suddenly have lost their power to recall her to herself.

Her elbow overturned the pepper-pot, and a cloud of the dark powder puffed up into her face and made her sneeze. Tears ran down her face, she gasped between spasms, and he quickly poured a glass of water and came over to her to hold the glass while she drank. His hand brushed her forearm as he lifted the glass; it seemed to sear the skin, so that she was aware of that small area, stung to life above the numbness of her limbs and body.

The irritation ceased; she sneezed one last time. "Bless you," he said. She had not heard it since she was a child; it was one of those old, old superstitions, faithfully observed by children, like touching wood whenever an ambulance passes, or pledging honor with "cross my heart and hope to die." She smiled at the recollection.

They left the table and went along the passage to the living room.

All about her were the familiar objects of her daily life. Suddenly she saw them pitilessly, the furniture she hadn't wanted, the pictures she didn't like, the carpet they had persuaded her to buy because it was serviceable, Sydney's pile of trade journals on the bureau, covered with penciled calculations, and the inevitable warning, underlined: *"Do not disarrange."* And outside, Candia barked at the postman. Tears of resentment rushed savagely to her throat; she hadn't wanted that dog!

She sat down on the sofa, and he lit her cigarette. Once again she felt that he was much nearer to her than he really was, that his face drew close and enveloping, like a face brought forward by a camera on the screen.

She felt choked by the nearness of him, she saw his ears, his brown eyes, the firm skin of his chin.

Pictures, books, chairs stared back at her: dead. She was away and above the room, looking down upon it from afar; waves of excitement, of detachment, washed between her and the familiar objects. The cigarette trembled in her cold hand. She thought of her husband, her mother, as one thinks of people across a bridge of years. The past morning might have been part of another life.

I have lost it all, she thought clearly; it has gone, everything will be changed from this moment.

And danger, change, and the unknown opened up before her like a chasm, no landmarks and only a dark wind, with the wild tang of a strange sea, blowing all sense and thought out of her, sending a streak of fear like lightning through her.

She was telling him about a book she was reading. It was a Naval autobiography, with illustrations, and she opened it to show him a picture of the sinking of the *Scharnhorst*. He rose to take it from her, and she saw his foot half turn, as if to proceed back to his chair, and then pause.

He kissed her.

She saw that his eyes were full of distress. Then he kissed her again. His mouth was gentle and insistent and she knew that he had been thinking about kissing her for a long time. Now that he was really close to her, that terrible oppressive sense of his nearness was gone. There was nothing strange in the feel of his cheek on her face.

Timidly she put up her hand and passed her fingers unevenly along the line of his jaw. He looked at her deeply, with a face so troubled that she felt with him a momentary weight of guilt, as if they had cut themselves off from the world. He took her in his arms and kissed her again.

His first spoken words seemed to crystallize the dreamlike quality of their actions into reality. It was true. It was happening. It was not some wishful imaginative dissolution into intimacy taking place in the secrecy of the mind, behind the cold barriers of common sense. They had smashed them; she felt them melt away at the first touch; they were nothing, those barriers, nothing, only words: marriage, wife, convention. . . . Amazed, she turned to him and smiled, and they were in one world, a tenuous, trembling, membranous world, which enclosed them and hung about them like the shining rainbow walls of a bubble.

Then: a howl of agony, opening at a crescendo peak and seesawing down through a series of piercing yelps to a whimper. . . .

They stirred as if in sleep; they heard it and they did not. It was repeated, again and again. The heavy fragrance of syringa hung coiled about them like a snake. Slowly, she struggled, broke through. She shut her eyes, as if to shake off a momentary dizziness. She swallowed.

There was a silence between them, alert. Like water lapping up in steadily encroaching circles over the shore, the room, the existence of the road without, the realization that they were strangers, flowed back to them. "It's Candia," she said, startled at the sound of her own voice. The howling continued. "It's hurt?" he said. There was a queer, blank look on his face. "I must go," she said with an effort. "I must go."

They half-ran out to the verandah, dazed and shocked as people dragged from their beds in the middle of the night. It was horrible, this rude contact with the glare of sunlight and other people's faces. They saw a knot of neighbors in the road below. She ran down ahead of him, through the gate.

A small boy made his way through the crowd, carrying the

big gray dog in his arms, its long hind legs trailing on the ground. "'S hurt," he said. "Went right over its stomach."

"Oh!" she said, shuddering. She took the dog gently from him.

It was whimpering softly now, and blood trickled from its jaw. "What happened?" said Paul. He was feeling carefully over the dog's body, trying to discover the extent of the injury. "Oh, I saw the whole thing," the boy was eager to explain. "The bicycle came round the corner, and the native was shouting something to a girl over there, he had his head round, he wasn't looking, and your dog ran out into the road, barking and snapping at the wheels, and then the boy lost his balance and swung out. Went right over its stomach."

There was an unseeing glaze over the dog's eyes. Paul shook his head. "We'd better get it in." She kneeled down in the road, supporting the dog on her thighs. She felt so strange, so strange. As if she had come down from a distant planet, amongst these peering neighbors. She murmured solicitously over the dog, but she felt nothing.

They carried the dog between them into the house, and she moved about attending to it, scarcely knowing what she did, her hands performing a ritual, by instinct, detached from herself. Paul worked with her, frozen as herself.

Once as he bent over the dog beside her, she saw with astonishment his mouth, the shine of the wet soft rosy membrane just inside his lips. It was the unknown, mysterious mouth of a stranger. She strove to remember it, but there was only a terrible negativeness in place of the feeling.

When they had done what they could for the dog, they made a comfortable bed for it in the kitchen. She gathered up the iodine, cotton-wool, and bandages, and they went into the bathroom to wash their hands. "You think it will be all right?" she asked.

"I don't know," he said. "It's difficult to say. So long as there isn't some internal hemorrhage we don't know about." She took the towel which he had been using, folded it mechanically, and put it back on the rail. He looked at her with a curious struggling sadness. She wished to speak, to say something real to him, but she could not.

"I had better be getting along," he said. He lifted his sleeve to look at his watch. "It's rather late—I must get back, I suppose."

There was a pause.

"I'm sorry. . . . ," he said gently, very low. They were both afraid of this; they wanted it said and over. Her head moved in an awkward little movement of distress. She turned suddenly, as if she had just remembered something, and walked quickly out of the bathroom.

In silence they walked to the front door. "Well, good-by . . . ," he said. She smiled with her mouth, felt her lips lift back dryly. "Good-by." The strong scent of the syringa blew over, battered against her. The gate screeched behind him. He turned uncertainly, half-met her eyes, and then went away up the road.

She knew and dreaded that presently she would come back to life and feel again. She was filled with horror at the thought of facing up to her life, of finding that everything still went on, while she was utterly changed. She wandered about the house in a muffled distress which separated her even from herself. She knew the numb detachment of the dispossessed.

She went into the kitchen and spoke to the native girl, and the girl did not know. She saw at last, with the release of a final, piercing despair, her husband coming home from his office. He walked in and immediately became engrossed in the injured dog; Sydney did not know.

She lived from day to day in fascinated disbelief at the continuation of her life just as it had always been. Time passed. The great sea of commonplace washed over that hour.

Nothing happened.

Yet several times during her life she returned to her thin faith in the power of events; she expected to be changed.

Later, when she had children, she thought that they would bring about some dramatic readjustment in her marriage, but it remained the same, no better, no worse. She drifted into a gentle resignation, almost succeeded in forgetting that she had wanted so much for it to be different. There was only a gradual emergence from one year into the next, each event slowly conforming to, becoming lost in, the familiar pattern.

But she kept her half-superstitious conviction that change loomed, somewhere, that several times she had stood on the brink of change, and only some small inexplicable disharmony had turned it aside, let it slip silently past.

She saw Paul twice again. Once, getting out of a train, he brushed past and did not see her. And another time, when she was in Durban on a holiday. She was with her sisters, and he had his wife with him: a dark, pretty girl, strange as a doll.

The stranger that was Paul was vaguely familiar, like meeting someone seen once before in a snapshot.

The Train from Rhodesia

*T*he train came out of the red horizon and bore down toward them over the single straight track.

The stationmaster came out of his little brick station with its pointed chalet roof, feeling the creases in his serge uniform in his legs as well. A stir of preparedness rippled through the squatting native vendors waiting in the dust; the face of a carved wooden animal, eternally surprised, stuck out of a sack. The stationmaster's barefoot children wandered over. From the gray mud huts with the untidy heads that stood within a decorated mud wall, chickens, and dogs with their skin stretched like parchment over their bones, followed the piccanins down to the track. The flushed and perspiring west cast a reflection, faint, without heat, upon the station, upon the tin shed marked "Goods," upon the walled kraal, upon the gray tin house of the stationmaster and upon the sand, that lapped all around, from sky to sky, cast little rhythmical cups of shadow, so that the sand became the sea, and closed over the children's black feet softly and without imprint.

The stationmaster's wife sat behind the mesh of her verandah. Above her head the hunk of a sheep's carcass moved slightly, dangling in a current of air.

They waited.

The train called out, along the sky; but there was no answer; and the cry hung on: I'm coming . . . I'm coming . . .

The engine flared out now, big, whisking a dwindling body behind it; the track flared out to let it in.

Creaking, jerking, jostling, gasping, the train filled the station.

Here, let me see that one—the young woman curved her body further out of the corridor window. Missus? smiled the old boy, looking at the creatures he held in his hand. From a piece of string on his gray finger hung a tiny woven basket; he lifted it, questioning. No, no, she urged, leaning down toward him, across the height of the train, toward the man in the piece of old rug; that one, that one, her hand commanded. It was a lion, carved out of soft dry wood that looked like spongecake; heraldic, black and white, with impressionistic detail burnt in. The old man held it up to her still smiling, not from the heart, but at the customer. Between its Vandyke teeth, in the mouth opened in an endless roar too terrible to be heard, it had a black tongue. Look, said the young husband, if you don't mind! And round the neck of the thing, a piece of fur (rat? rabbit? meerkat?); a real mane, majestic, telling you somehow that the artist had delight in the lion.

All up and down the length of the train in the dust the artists sprang, walking bent, like performing animals, the better to exhibit the fantasy held toward the faces on the train. Buck, startled and stiff, staring with round black and white eyes. More lions, standing erect, grappling with strange, thin, elongated warriors who clutched spears and showed no fear in their slits of eyes. How much, they asked from the train, how much?

Give me penny, said the little ones with nothing to sell. The dogs went and sat, quite still, under the dining car, where the train breathed out the smell of meat cooking with onion.

A man passed beneath the arch of reaching arms meeting gray-black and white in the exchange of money for the staring wooden eyes, the stiff wooden legs sticking up in the air; went along under the voices and the bargaining, interrogating the wheels. Past the dogs; glancing up at the dining car where he could stare at the faces, behind glass, drinking beer, two by two, on either side of a uniform railway vase with its pale dead flower. Right to the end, to the guard's van, where the stationmaster's children had just collected their mother's two loaves of bread; to the engine itself, where the stationmaster and the driver stood talking against the steaming complaint of the resting beast.

The man called out to them, something loud and joking. They turned to laugh, in a twirl of steam. The two children careered over the sand, clutching the bread, and burst through the iron gate and up the path through the garden in which nothing grew.

Passengers drew themselves in at the corridor windows and turned into compartments to fetch money, to call someone to look. Those sitting inside looked up: suddenly different, caged faces, boxed in, cut off, after the contact of outside. There was an orange a piccanin would like. . . . What about that chocolate? It wasn't very nice. . . .

A young girl had collected a handful of the hard kind, that no one liked, out of the chocolate box, and was throwing them to the dogs, over at the dining car. But the hens darted in, and swallowed the chocolates, incredibly quick and accurate, before they had even dropped in the dust, and the dogs, a little bewildered, looked up with their brown eyes, not expecting anything.

—No, leave it, said the girl, don't take it. . . .

Too expensive, too much, she shook her head and raised her voice to the old boy, giving up the lion. He held it up where she had handed it to him. No, she said, shaking her head. Three-and-six? insisted her husband, loudly. Yes baas! laughed the boy. *Three-and-six?*—the young man was incredulous. Oh leave it—she said. The young man stopped. Don't you want it? he said, keeping his face closed to the boy. No, never mind, she said, leave it. The old native kept his head on one side, looking at them sideways, holding the lion. Three-and-six, he murmured, as old people repeat things to themselves.

The young woman drew her head in. She went into the coupé and sat down. Out of the window, on the other side, there was nothing; sand and bush; a thorn tree. Back through the open doorway, past the figure of her husband in the corridor, there was the station, the voices, wooden animals waving, running feet. Her eye followed the funny little valance of scrolled wood that outlined the chalet roof of the station; she thought of the lion and smiled. That bit of fur round the neck. But the wooden buck, the hippos, the elephants, the baskets that already bulked out of their brown paper under the seat and on the luggage rack! How will they look at home? Where will you put them? What will they mean away from the places you found them? Away from the unreality of the last few weeks? The man outside. But he is not part of the unreality; he is for good now. Odd . . . somewhere there was an idea that he, that living with him, was part of the holiday, the strange places.

Outside, a bell rang. The stationmaster was leaning against the end of the train, green flag rolled in readiness. A few men who had got down to stretch their legs sprang on to the train, clinging to the observation platforms, or perhaps merely standing on the iron step, holding the rail; but on the train, safe from the one dusty platform, the one tin house, the empty sand.

There was a grunt. The train jerked. Through the glass the beer drinkers looked out, as if they could not see beyond it. Behind the fly-screen, the stationmaster's wife sat facing back at them beneath the darkening hunk of meat.

There was a shout. The flag drooped out. Joints not yet co-ordinated, the segmented body of the train heaved and bumped back against itself. It began to move; slowly the scrolled chalet moved past it, the yells of the natives, running alongside, jetted up into the air, fell back at different levels. Staring wooden faces waved drunkenly, there, then gone, questioning for the last time at the windows. Here, one-and-six baas!—As one automatimatically opens a hand to catch a thrown ball, a man fumbled wildly down his pocket, brought up the shilling and sixpence and threw them out; the old native, gasping, his skinny toes splaying the sand, flung the lion.

The piccanins were waving, the dogs stood, tails uncertain, watching the train go: past the mud huts, where a woman turned to look, up from the smoke of the fire, her hand pausing on her hip.

The stationmaster went slowly in under the chalet.

The old native stood, breath blowing out the skin between his ribs, feet tense, balanced in the sand, smiling and shaking his head. In his opened palm, held in the attitude of receiving, was the retrieved shilling and sixpence.

The blind end of the train was being pulled helplessly out of the station.

The young man swung in from the corridor, breathless. He was shaking his head with laughter and triumph. Here! he said. And waggled the lion at her. One-and-six!

What? she said.

He laughed. I was arguing with him for fun, bargaining—when the train had pulled out already, he came tearing after. . . . One-and-six Baas! So there's your lion.

She was holding it away from her, the head with the open jaws, the pointed teeth, the black tongue, the wonderful ruff of fur facing her. She was looking at it with an expression of not seeing, of seeing something different. Her face was drawn up, wryly, like the face of a discomforted child. Her mouth lifted nervously at the corner. Very slowly, cautious, she lifted her finger and touched the mane, where it was joined to the wood.

But how could you, she said. He was shocked by the dismay of her face.

Good Lord, he said, what's the matter?

If you wanted the thing, she said, her voice rising and breaking with the shrill impotence of anger, why didn't you buy it in the first place? If you wanted it, why didn't you pay for it? Why didn't you take it decently, when he offered it? Why did you have to wait for him to run after the train with it, and give him one-and-six? One-and-six!

She was pushing it at him, trying to force him to take it. He stood astonished, his hands hanging at his sides.

But you wanted it! You liked it so much?

—It's a beautiful piece of work, she said fiercely, as if to protect it from him.

You liked it so much! You said yourself it was too expensive—

Oh *you*—she said, hopeless and furious. *You.* . . . She threw the lion on to the seat.

He stood looking at her.

She sat down again in the corner and, her face slumped in her hand, stared out of the window. Everything was turning round inside her. One-and-six. One-and-six. One-and-six for the wood and the carving and the sinews of the legs and the switch of the tail. The mouth open like that and the teeth. The black tongue, rolling, like a wave. The mane round the neck. To give one-and-six for that. The heat of shame mounted through her legs and body and sounded in her ears like the sound of sand pouring. Pouring, pouring. She sat there, sick. A weariness, a tastelessness, the discovery of a void made her hands slacken their grip, atrophy emptily, as if the hour was not worth their grasp. She was feeling like this again. She had thought it was something to do with singleness, with being alone and belonging too much to oneself.

She sat there not wanting to move or speak, or to look at anything, even; so that the mood should be associated with nothing, no object, word or sight that might recur and so recall the feeling again. . . . Smuts blew in grittily, settled on her hands. Her back remained at exactly the same angle, turned against the young man sitting with his hands drooping between his sprawled legs, and the lion, fallen on its side in the corner.

The train had cast the station like a skin. It called out to the sky, I'm coming, I'm coming; and again, there was no answer.

A Watcher of the Dead

When my grandmother died, in 1939, Uncle Jules took over. There was no man about our house; my father, a poor provider, uncomplainingly suffered by my mother, apologetically aware of his own unimportance, had run away and left us eight years before. Uncle Jules was my father's brother, and he seemed to materialize in response to family crises, such as weddings and funerals. In Johannesburg, where we lived, there were numerous other relatives on my father's side, but we did not see them often. Quite suddenly, out of the vague comings and goings of some sort of business (diamond buying? traveling in jewelry?) that kept Uncle Jules out of Johannesburg and sometimes even out of South Africa, he appeared and made all the necessary arrangements.

Although my grandmother was an old lady with the soft-pink color that comes from growing up in rainy England and the friendly, Cockney quickness of speech that comes from being a Londoner, and although she had friends on our street, in the unfashionable part of Johannesburg, who were Scotch and Afrikander and Italian, when she died, she was Jewish; all the other things were gone and she was only Jewish. Her race and the religion she had lightheartedly ignored claimed her for initiation at last, an initiation that we did not understand and that took her away from us as her death, by itself, had not yet done.

I was a girl of sixteen and the eldest of the three children, but to me, as to my brother William and my sister Helen, being Jewish had simply meant that we had a free half hour while the other children at our convent school went to catechism. If Mother had ever known any Jewish customs—and I doubt it— she had forgotten them long before we were born. Jewish funerals are simple and austere—no flowers; just a short service at the graveside, and the plain wooden coffin goes down into the grave. In South Africa, at least, it is not usual for Jewish women to go to funerals, even of their closest friends. Uncle Jules arranged for a rabbi to conduct the service at the cemetery, had the death notice put in the paper, and telephoned all the relatives to tell them when the funeral would be. We could do nothing. We didn't even believe that my grandmother was dead. She had been mashing a banana for Helen, and tasting more than she mashed, when the fork simply failed to reach her mouth. A blood clot, the doctor said, but it seemed to us that she had merely been interrupted and would presently return, saying, "Now, what was I doing when . . ."

The afternoon of the day she died, the family and two embarrassed neighbors sat around the living room, where my grandmother's sword ferns, in the windows, made the light green. Uncle Jules, preoccupied, came and went. At last, he paused and sat down in the brown armchair, alert, drumming with his fingers and biting nervously at the inside of his cheek. His eyebrows gathered in a frown as things to be done passed in review before his mind. Suddenly his eyebrows arched, his mouth pursed, and he said, "We'll have to get a *wacher*."

"A what?" asked William.

"A *wacher*," Uncle Jules said. "I'll have to go and phone the synagogue to . . ." Mumbling to himself, he went to the telephone.

I got up and went out into the passage after him. "What's a *wacher*?" I whispered, catching his coat sleeve.

"Good God! Don't you know?"

"Sh-h-h!" I said, and tugged at him, not wanting my mother to hear.

With a glance toward the room where the others sat, he said softly, "A watcher of the dead."

These words, coming from that matter-of-fact man's mouth, seemed to me like an incantation carelessly repeated by someone who has merely overheard it somewhere and says it again, not knowing what it is that he says. A watcher of the dead. *Who* watches, I wondered, and for what does he watch? For that which has happened to them already? For some sign of where they have gone? What kind of man can watch where there is nothing to watch at all, only what is past, blank, behind, and what is unknown, blank, ahead? A watcher of the dead.

"How long will he stay?" I asked.

"Sunset to sunrise, I think it is," my uncle said. Then he dragged the telephone directory from beneath the magazines that always piled up on top of it on the rickety hall table.

The synagogue sent an elderly gentleman who dwindled from a big stomach, outlined with a watch chain, to thin legs that ended in neat, shabby brown shoes, supple with years of polishing. He wore glasses that made his brown eyes look very big, he had a small beard, and his face was pleasantly pink and planned in folds—a fold beneath each eye, another fold where the cheek skirted the mouth, a fold where the jaw met the neck, a fold where the neck met the collar. There was even a small fold beneath the lobe of each ear, as if the large, useful-looking ears had sagged under their own weight and usefulness over the years.

He took off his hat and put down his cane, and at once busied himself about the room in which my grandmother lay, in the peculiar silence of one who does not breathe, on her own side of the old double bed that she had brought with her when she came to live with us. He moved her body onto the floor, lit a candle, altered the position of a chair. I almost expected him to begin humming softly to himself. My mother stood in the doorway, biting the joint of the first finger of her clenched hand, exactly the way my ten-year-old sister sometimes did. We children did not know that this placing of the body on the floor was a gesture of the Jewish faith, signifying the renunciation of worldly comforts. We said nothing. Even my mother said nothing, but only looked at the figure on the floor, as people look after the retreating bundle of a sick person wheeled away down a hospital corridor to some unimagined treatment in some unimagined room.

A little later, Uncle Jules, who had been out of the house arranging about the funeral, which was to take place next afternoon, came into the living room again. "The what-d'you-call-'em's come," William said.

"The *wacher*? Good!" Uncle Jules said, and dropped his raincoat into a dark corner of the hall.

A Watcher of the Dead

The darkness of the first night—the first night that she was not there—was welling up in all the rooms of the house. As the lights came on, now in this room, then in that; as the family went into bedrooms, into the kitchen, into the bathroom, and, without thinking, touched each room into light, my grandmother began really to be dead. The electric light opened up every shadowy room and found her not there.

Always before at this time in the evening, there had been a smell of frying in the house; the door of my room would fly open and there she would be, saying, "Darling, shall we have chips?" Her cheeks were always pinker when she cooked; the tiny diamond earrings that had grown into her lobes over forty years before came winking alive against her pink ears. She would look anxiously and respectfully at my schoolbooks, waiting for me to make up my mind. Then she would leave me to my studies, and a moment or two later I would hear her talking to Helen in the hall.

My grandmother had lived with us and kept house for us ever since my father disappeared. Mother ran a little stationery shop and came home every night, like the man of the family, to hear from my grandmother what had happened during the day and to make the decisions and check the bills. It was just as it had been with my father. My grandmother did not like to have to make up her mind. She had never had to while my grandfather was alive; she had never lived, as my mother had lived, with a man who abdicated all authority, a man to lean on whom would have been to fall against empty air. She had trembled joyfully in the shadow of her husband all his life, and she respected my mother enormously.

Though it didn't show, I realized later, out of my knowledge of my own life as a woman, that there was a wistfulness in my mother's acceptance of her mother's respect. My little grandmother was feminine as a dove, with her full bosom, in her gray dress; vain of her two new hats, winter and summer; moved easily to tears by the Shirley Temple films she and Helen followed around the small suburban cinemas; remembering from fifty years back the happy, vulgar, innocent music-hall songs we children loved to hear. Mother cherished her, in the true sense of the word, as a man cherishes a woman, a woman a child, but also saw in her something that she herself did not have—the easy tears, the gentle weakness, the submission to sex.

Uncle Jules went into my grandmother's room to speak to the watcher, and we children, unable to settle down anywhere, even in our own rooms, went in search of my mother, who was in the kitchen getting dinner. All day long she had been doing something; I could not have said what it was that she was doing, but she moved about, there were objects in her hands, and her eyes were lowered in concentration. She was busy at the kitchen table when we went into the kitchen, and the cat was arching itself plaintively against her legs, begging for food. Our house was small, and all on one floor, and Uncle Jules had hardly gone into my grandmother's room when I heard him coming back along the passage.

"Haven't you given him anything?" he asked urgently.

My mother looked at Uncle Jules and said, "What does he want?"

"He doesn't *want* anything. But, good Lord, it's always done." My uncle felt that he must not get exasperated and was unsure what feeling he *could* display toward my mother. All attitudes are equally embarrassing and affronting before the fact of death.

"Should I cook him something?" asked my mother.

"No, no, you must have something for him to drink. It's usual. A bottle of brandy. They're always given a bottle of brandy."

"What?" said my mother.

"Haven't you got a bottle of brandy, or something, in the house?" Uncle Jules asked patiently. "Surely you've got *something.*"

"Oh, yes," said my mother. "He's going to drink brandy? You mean to tell me he's going to drink brandy tonight?"

My Uncle smiled and shrugged his head on one side. "Well," he said, "it's the custom. It's always done."

"There's a bottle not opened yet," my mother said. "It's put away. I'll get it." She went out of the kitchen. The cat stalked around and around the table leg. In a moment, my mother was back. "Is this all right?" she asked anxiously, handing a new bottle of brandy to my uncle.

"Of course, of course," he said. "What should he expect—Napoleon?" From his expression, it was clear that he felt he had said the wrong thing again. He sighed and left the kitchen, carrying the bottle of brandy by its neck.

"Here you are, then, my cat," said my mother, taking a pat of ground meat out of the refrigerator and sitting down on the kitchen chair, so that the cat might feed easily from her hand. In a brief series of gobbles, the meat disappeared; the cat went on licking at the empty fingers. My mother began to cry, her face pulled awry, looking more like Helen than ever, and tears ran down into her mouth. Helen, William, and I stood still, on the other side of the kitchen table, afraid to touch her.

"I don't want her to be with him! I don't want her to be with him!" my mother said. Nobody answered, nobody spoke or moved.

Presently, she got up and blew her nose and went over to the sink to wash her hands.

The family and Uncle Jules sat beneath the round yellow ceiling light, gathered at table for supper. Everything tasted very good; everyone was very gentle and attentive. Love rose into consciousness between us children and within us; William's hand, passing the butter, was my hand; my little sister's hair, resting along her back, was my hair. This was an exciting discovery, and the more exciting for being a shared one. We could not share it with my mother, though. She sat, serving, spiritually and physically alone at the head of the table.

Afterward, we trooped into the living room and sat in silence, William and Helen pretending to read, Mother and I merely sitting. Uncle Jules stared down between his knees at the floor. An hour or two ago, there had come the knowledge of my grandmother *not there*—lack, absence, the *goneness* of someone well loved, familiar. Now there was something, someone, again. I felt the presence of our dead grandmother, like a stranger in the room nearby.

Before my mother went to bed, she walked into the room where my grandmother lay, and we children followed. The watcher, who had taken off his glasses and was resting his eyes, got up from his chair. There was something of the air of a museum attendant about him; I felt that he might say, "Now, is there anything in particular you would like to see? Any information you wish?"

My mother went over to my dead grandmother and bent down and touched her hair.

"Excuse me," said the old gentleman. With a thrill of fear, I remembered the notices they put on exhibits: "Please do not touch!"

"What?" asked my mother.

"It is not allowed," the old gentleman said regretfully.

"I'm not doing anything," my mother said. "I've come to kiss my mother good night."

"It is not allowed—to touch the dead," said the watcher.

My mother stood bent over the dead woman, with her head turned to him. Her look seemed to draw a line around herself and her mother that the old gentleman, blinking without his glasses, quietly within his rights, didn't dare to cross. I knew he could not take one step nearer to my mother, to the place where my grandmother lay. He moved his hands with the apologetic, imploring denial of the small official. And, like all small officials, he clutched at the authority behind him. "It's against the Jewish religion," he said with a shrug and a smile of distress.

My mother drew a deep breath and then said sharply, "But she didn't die of anything contagious! I couldn't get anything from her!"

The watcher looked shocked. His attitude toward death was abstract, the abstraction of the professional; my mother's approach was individual, the approach of the amateur. He shrugged once more.

"Why? Why?" insisted my mother. And before he could

answer, she asked again, "Why? Why shouldn't I?" She was excited and angry, with the impossible, aggressive anger that feeds on itself and does not even want to be placated. I thought she might stamp her feet, grind her teeth.

"There's no reason, is there? *Is* there?" she repeated, shrilly.

I felt sick and my heart beat terribly fast. "But, Mother," I said, "he can't help it. It's not *his* fault." I looked at my grandmother, so deep asleep.

My mother's eyes flashed pure venom at the watcher, who stood there tugging at one ear, like a simple, obstinate mule who doesn't even know, or pretends he doesn't know, that all the shoving, pushing, and shouting of the mule driver is directed at him. "No," she said, her voice trembling. "I know it isn't his fault." And I saw that because it wasn't his fault, because he couldn't help it, she hated him. She wanted to flay him for his innocence.

In the power of her inconsolable rage, she swept to the door. Then she remembered, and turned for one look at my grandmother, alone on the floor, and, with a terrible shock of sorrow, found that she had forgotten her, that she had lost her last moment with her, lost it in anger.

Lying in my bed in the dark, I felt that perhaps in the morning the watcher, the poor old gentleman with the well-polished shoes, would be dead, too—killed silently and innocently in his chair by the rage of my mother's grief.

But in the morning all things are different. In the morning, unbelievably and reassuringly, my mother was cooking a big breakfast of kippers and fried eggs. "Bring me the brass tray from the breakfast room," she said. "He'll want something to eat early, before he goes, poor old thing. He's not so young, to be sitting in a chair all night."

I looked at her. Her face, over the stove, was quiet.

Her hands moved slowly and were very cold to the touch. She arranged the tray and carried it into the breakfast room and put it before the old gentleman. He sat patiently at the table, with his napkin tucked into the V of his waistcoat, while she poured tea for him. The flaps beneath his eyes were more pronounced; he ate steadily, like an obedient child. When he had finished, he wiped his mouth very thoroughly, put the crumpled napkin by his place, and thanked her.

He went out to get his hat and stick, and she stood, her hand on the teapot, looking after him. Uncle Jules paid the watcher his two-guinea fee, and the old gentleman left, carrying a neat paper parcel that must have been the bottle of brandy—opened or intact, one could not tell.

My mother took the breakfast tray out to the kitchen and I followed her. She looked very tired; a nerve jumped beneath her left eye. "Poor old thing," she murmured gently. "He must be old, you know."

"Mmm. And being up all night—" I said.

A pallid smile lifted the corner of her mouth, which looked dry and thin. "He had eaten an apple," she said. "There was the skin of an apple curled on a bit of newspaper beside him. Shame! He'd been eating an apple. I only just remembered, now, seeing it there."

"But didn't he—" I said, hardly knowing what I was saying but beginning to understand.

"Asleep," she said. "Asleep all the time. Fast asleep."

There was a moment of silence—kitchen silence, composed

of the small hissings of the cooking pots, the scraping of a knife, the drizzling tap. "Mother," I said, "did you—" Her back was to me—perhaps she did not even hear me—and I never asked her what I had started to ask her.

I have never asked her to this day. At the time, I thought, shocked, she means this morning; it was this morning that she went into the room and found him. I could see, as if I had been there, the dark, withdrawn house, the room of the dead, with the candle burning, the old man asleep, with his chin sunk sidewise into its own folds, the green coil of apple peeling, with the faint scent of vanished apple in the room, and my mother, alone with my grandmother for the last time.

*T*here was a beach on the South Coast of Natal where there was time for the sand to record every footstep. At the end of the day, there they were, interlaced perhaps, but clear with the stamp of the foot that impressed them; the quick, kicked-up track of a running child, the fancy dapple of the big dog's paws, the even clefts left by the hard bony feet of an Indian fisherman. They asserted authority over the beach as little as a flag, stuck by an explorer into a mound of snow, over the white, baffling supremity of the Pole. The beach, the sea, the madly singing bushes were the live, the real, the supreme here; the light dabs of human feet had not stepped out a beautiful background for a frieze of figures, running, cavorting and clowning, but had merely succeeded in feeling lightly over one curve, one convolution of a composition so enormous that they would never be able to feel out the whole of it. There was white sand all around the few, far, faint footsteps, sand drying thin-crusted and bright in the wind, looped from rocks to rocks along each inlet, mile after mile.

It was here that they had brought her when she was two years old, to sit in a hat of plaited mealie leaves with her feet plastered over with a mound of heavy wet sand. It was here that she fought and struggled and screamed against the touch of the sea, until the feel of it, rising cool and enclosing against the small of her little back, and the scent of it prickling her nose with froth woke a new pleasure in her, and as she was brought back year after year, seemed to egg her on to show off, to dive and tumble and scream. It was at this beach, or another like it, that she first discovered a hint of the activity of the sea, the strange thick wet rubbery foliage, the red flowers buttoned along the undersides of rocks, the silent fish and lethargic dabs of mucus living in perfect shells, the hundreds of shells individually fashioned and colored to a whim. All this delicate craftsmanship, done by the sea. She had discovered it led by her native nanny along the tiny low-tide beaches where between the rocks, the wash turned over hundreds of thousands of shells with the sound of money gently clinking, and sucked back away gustily whilst they sprang into wet color under the sun. The nanny collected brown-backed cowrie shells like tiny tortoises to trim milk jug covers, but the child stuffed her pockets with whatever they would hold. When she got back to her room and turned them all out upon the bed, her pockets were wet with a curious heavy salt wetness. It was the glitter come off the shells. Now they lay with the sand upon the bedcover, dull as any china. A few winkles that she had found room for were crusted disgustingly in their little towers, dead.

She threw the lot out of the window.

But next day and next year she was back hunched down with her knees up to her chin again, gathering up the unbelievable satin pink shimmer of the mother-of-pearl oyster shells, wet from the sea.

When she grew up she traveled, but more stirring than all the dead palaces, the mountains and cities, pictures and monuments, the ballet, the theater, the opera and the stirring talk of café philosophers; eliciting from her the tug of a warm crude response rooted in the kernel around which her adult layers of taste, discernment and appreciation had folded, was the sight of small boys in southern ports who swam out to the ship and dived for passengers' coins. She hung with the rail pressing into her stomach, flinging her coins as far and hard as her excitement. And she seemed to feel the thin rim of the coin cutting down hard through the enormous green weight of water, and the bubbles flying from the boy's ears as he went after it and beat it to the bottom. The sea was so immense, so weighted in favor, able to hide whole ships and never return them, yet the boy got the mere fleck of a penny back from it. He beat the sea to the bottom. One day when they were far out, she went to the rail and dropped a penny, away from her hand into ten thousand miles of endless gray water. Gone, lost, taken by the sea and too infinitesimal to be taken account of.

"Wishing, my dear young lady?" said a delicate old gentleman, passing by. And she smiled the brilliant smile of accession to other people's impressions that we all gratefully employ to distract the world from ourselves. He took the sunburst of a smile and put it away with his collection of the characteristics of young women.

In America the nature of the sea's fascination for her was mistaken for a physical zest something like that she had felt when, almost a baby and still learning to distinguish different sensory discoveries, she had been dipped into a new and buoyant element, less staid than air. They rushed her to Florida beaches and sent her scudding over the backs of long rollers balanced on a piece of fragile board, watching her face for the furious pleasure which they awaited as their triumph. They laid her on a sprung-rubber chaise longue under a fringed canopy, to absorb the sting of sun and the abrasive of salt in close company with thousands who flocked to the benefits of another kind of Ganges. Offering them the sunburst, she supposed it must be what she enjoyed. But when, in a determination to give her everything they had contracted the sea to offer in the way of a kick, they took her deep-sea fishing off Florida Sound, enjoyment of a very personal kind came up and seized her as she landed a great fish, heaving with life, out of the depths of the sea. They wanted to take photographs of her, holding it tail to shoulder. But she wanted it stuffed, she called, throwing it in tight triumph where it could not jump back into the sea.

After that, wherever she went she fished, and the record of the beautiful, shiny, gaping creatures she had hooked out of the sea grew almost at the pace of her collection of hundreds of thousands of shells, picked up alone on beaches all over the world, and thrown into boxes and old pillowcases. At home now she had a special aquarium built, and in it she tried to persuade salt-water fish and sea plants to grow as they did for the sea. But transported by airplane in special containers, and deluded by lights and artificial currents in the big box of water, they refused to adapt themselves to the slightest degree. Every time she returned to the white beaches where hundreds of anemones closed themselves away at her touch in every pool, and fish so small and finely made that you could see their threads of skeletons through the opalescent flesh flickered in easy survival through raging tides and the menace of bigger creatures, she smiled at the triumph of the sea. The sea kept its treasures to itself. Threw them carelessly upon the beach in the knowledge that the abundance was never-ending, that there would always be more, more, more; in the confidence that whoever took them away would find that he had taken nothing: the very discarded shells and stones that children gathered left the color for which they had been prized behind them on the beach; the seaweed broken from the slowly waving mesh became an unrecognizable putrid stickiness; the splendid fish, once out and on land, gross and stupid enough only to be eaten.

It was about this time that she met a man whose idea of her was so much what she wanted herself to be that she fell deeply in love with him. He was young and he was beautiful, and through him, she felt herself vulnerable for the first time. She did not want him to fly; she was suddenly afraid for him to swim out beyond the breakers. He had soaked up her life like a sponge, and she looked forward to living in the interstices of his being for the rest of her time. Her friends were neglected, her books unread, her aquarium a greenish and dried-up piece of clutter.

They wanted to marry as soon as possible, but before they could hollow a warm place for themselves in their world, there was a business obligation in Rhodesia he had to fulfill. She could not decide which would be more pleasure: to go with him, or to wait for him for two short weeks in certainty in some place that she loved. He decided for the latter, and she took the added pleasure of accepting his deciding for her. It was suddenly all quite perfect; she would go down to the deserted South Coast village where she had been so often before. She would play in the sun on the sand (he found her delight in rock-pools and shells and quaint sea-things an astonishing and precious streak of child in a person so definitely molded by the world) and he would come to her there.

What else was there to decide? His forehead was wrinkled, arranging it all. Oh, a ring! She must have his ring to signal that she was waiting for him. What kind of a ring did she want? What about a sapphire?

Oh no! she said swiftly with the happiness of inspiration. A pearl! A big pink pearl.

Of course, a pearl would be just the thing for her!

Lying flat on a smooth black rock watched by unseen black crabs petrified by the very displacement of air her motionless body caused, her happiness grew round the rosy pearl as the pearl had itself grown round a tiny piece of grit. Luster on luster, warmth on warmth, the pearl on her finger was the core of her life, the fact of love round which the future gathered itself. And as the human self, watchful of stingier times perhaps ahead, nets in all possible satisfactions attending a happiness which is already great enough in itself, she added a delicate but strong nuance to her happiness by the knowledge that here, lying with the softness of the sea air touching at her armpits, with her happiness beating steadily inside her, the symbol of that happiness which she wore in the pink pearl on her finger was also the most beautiful possession of the sea. The sea made nothing more lovely than a pearl. And though no longer belonging to the sea, the pearl was as lovely as it had ever been. All that was best, fullest, at the peak and most perfect welled up to the brim of her life. And the most precious treasure of the sea hung on her finger. She smiled slowly the long slow relaxed smile that seemed to pass from her face to the warm rock beneath her, and set forever in the seams of that rock, in the sand of that shore, on the shore of that sea.

The days themselves passed with a slowness that she treasured, for she could wait. Waiting had become a positive state, the balance of a drop ready to fall. All day long she wandered on the beach watching her footsteps fill with ooze, and lay for afternoons high on the rock with her hand dipping the lapping water as a bird. She was too full to want anything: to want to fish, or explore the life of the pools, or endear herself to the big old dog by throwing a piece of driftwood for him. She lay with her eyes half-shuttered against the sky, and sometimes, although she was silent, she thought she felt herself singing. Sometimes she fell asleep. And when she woke up she saw circles and splotches of dark, and as she lifted her stiff head, the sea and the sky lurched as if from the porthole of a boat on a rough passage.

One afternoon she woke from a quick light sleep and saw, as she rested, from the corner of her eye, something pinkish move on a rock just across the pool from the one on which she lay. It might have been a crab, but it didn't seem to be. She sat up to get a better view. It moved again. She smiled to herself, in that warm weakness for all life which her own present joy in life engendered. Getting on her haunches and clambering to the edge of her rock, she put her hand out to steady herself and leaned out over the pool to see. The water glittered up at her. The brightness was replaced with blackness. Dizzy, she caught out at what seemed to be a point of rock, a piece of triangular dark. With a surprised intake of breath like a child tumbling, she fell into the pool.

The pool was very shallow, shallow enough for a child to

paddle in, and she lay for a moment with one arm over the rock on which she had struck her head, the sand clouding up into the water, the tiny crabs scuttling away from the risen water-line. Then her body slid down, the water hid her face and the drop of blood, from the scratch made on her chin by a fragment of shell, stained the water faintly like a tiny drop of cochineal. The water hardly covered her back. But later in the afternoon the tide rose, and the waves climbed over the rocks into the pool and turned her over and over, handling her curiously.

All night long the sea lifted and laid, lifted and laid her body, until there was no part of her that was not touched by the sea. And in the morning, when the tide ran out with the rising of the sun, she lay quietly, sheltered, in the pool, and a soft current rippled beneath her floating hand, playing her fingers delicately as a reed instrument, threading in and out with the softest touch possible about the cold finger on which the pearl still shone, very beautiful in the water.

When I went to school at Mrs. Keyter's I used to sit next to the old push-up-and-down window that looked out on the yard. But it was too high for me to see out. I was in the front row at the end, right under the corner of Mrs. Keyter's eye, but I could watch her too; the rough wood of our benches, clawed along the grain with scrubbing and deeply indented with furrows tooled by pencils and pocketknives, rubbed smooth with dirt and the glistening waterways of sweat that play mapped out on our palms, nipped at my thighs; the children breathed over their scribblers; the three-legged alarm ticked on the cupboard; without lifting my head, my pencil lead cold to my tongue, my hand as if shielding what I had written, I sat doing nothing, watching her.

Her left hand went slowly up to the side of her chin, and began to pull at the hair. The hair was a single bristle, albino, that caught the light. Her thumb and first finger tried to nip it, to get a grip between the two nails. But it slipped through, seemed to be not there. Yet when the pad of her first finger felt for it again, there it was—the prick of it. She tried again.

A little aureole of red rose round the invisible hair; made

clumsy with impatience, the thumb and first finger sometimes pinched the skin in a quick white pleat that went redder again.

Then her head turned swiftly and she picked up a ruler or a pencil with a click against her table: stir. Like bubbles breaking up to the surface, the attention of the children rose; glazed eyes lifted, heads bobbed, the calm concentration rippled with refractions, bright, choppy. —My head bent furiously to finish the work I had not even begun. When the ruler came down against the table and the voice opened: "Now—" A spurt of panic sent my pencil black and hasty over the empty lines. "Everybody finished?" —It was a high, slow, questioning voice that only made statements. The jostle of the other children's released attention buffeted my harassed mind. "Close your books." QUESTION 1, she was chalking on the blackboard, in sweeping strokes as if she used a brush. Then the a, in parenthesis, enclosing like claws. . . .

Although I have forgotten what it was like to be a child, I can always remember this. And remembering it is like opening up an old seam, worked out and closed off long ago; feeling your way along the dark, low passages there are smells, objects you stumble over, the sudden feel under your hand of a surface you know. Round the side of the house there were dank stones under the hedge, pincushions of moss between them; putting up your hand to leave the room, you could go round there in summer and sit on the cool stones. A light grayish dust bloomed everything in the schoolroom; chalk blew like pollen from the old towel with which the children took it in turns to clean the blackboard. Mrs. Keyter's hand, resting on your book as she bent to explain something made a smooth dry sound on the paper; if it touched you it was dry as fine sea-sand. But outside, the yard where we screamed at playtime was red-earthed and damp because over it all was a great apricot tree, and in the apricot tree, an owl.

The owl belonged to Mark, Mrs. Keyter's little boy. He went to her school along with the rest of us. And along with the rest of us he left when he was nine or ten and old enough to go to a real school with bells and uniforms and proper classrooms. We went back to see her sometimes, during our first year or two at the Government school; and then we began to have nothing to say to her, and in our gyms and badges, with fountain pens sticking out of our blazer pockets, we smiled at the little house with the black-and-white linoleum down the passage, the bare-board schoolroom with the unsteady scrubbed benches and forms.

We forgot about her altogether at thirteen or fourteen. Except to meet her in the street, with the trapped, embarrassed grin of children for their former teachers; a kind of momentary paralysis of self-confidence, as if in the eyes of the teacher the child reads always its own guilt, a secret the other will never forget. Mrs. Keyter trotted quietly on, her paper shopping bag swinging from the small dry hand, her greenish coat flapping. She had mild tired eyes deep beneath a hat that was always the same shape.

Perhaps it was always the same hat; the Keyters were peculiar people, our mothers said. Mrs. Keyter still kept her little school, year after year, taking other people's third and fourth children. She herself had never had another child. And it seemed that they led a very odd life, without friends, without change since the days when *we*, the eldest children, the same age as her Mark, had been small. Keyter was a black-haired handsome man with black eyes under brows that guarded them heavily, and he was some sort of minor official at the post office. He had been there ever since anyone could remember. "—My but he was a handsome young man all the same—," my mother used to say. We giggled disbelief. He had once had a sweeping mustache and worn dress trousers with braid down the sides at a Masonic dance. "Mind you, he was surly. There was something morose about him, he danced with you as if he didn't know you were there." —We had been afraid of Mr. Keyter when we went to Mrs. Keyter's school; "Mark's father" was a phrase of threat to Mark, we knew, and if we met him in a doorway, we stood dead still, our ribs blowing in and out our only movement, unable to speak. He seldom spoke either. He went by as he might have stepped over a mouse.

Now our parents didn't go to Masonic gatherings anymore, but were members of a country club and played golf; they had cocktail parties and Rotary dinners. We no longer lived in the township where we had been just down the road from Mrs. Keyter's little school. With the money that had come suddenly —like the reward pouring out of a slot machine when luck presses the innocent-looking but right button—from gold shares or the sale of squares of weedy ground in the town made suddenly valuable by new gold mines thrown up like mole-workings all around us, our parents had built new houses. Most families owned an American car.

But the Keyters found no new pleasures and those they had had sank into disuse. He went to work and walked home again. She taught school in the mornings, walked into town to do her household shopping in the afternoons. She kept her head down, not submissively, but as if she minded her own business and wanted other people to mind theirs. They kept the same old house in the same old street—how close the houses were together! How had we ever breathed there?—and the grass grew tall round the garage in which were housed an old kitchen table and some spare forms not in use in the schoolroom. People said they had lost on the share market. How else could it be that they lived so quietly, so dully? They had never got on well together (so people said). How on earth had he come to marry her, in the first place? She was not the sort to marry. And he was a disagreeable creature; what had made her marry him? They never went out together, yet out of school hours, when her high, reasonable voice and the following chant of the children sang out, no one had ever heard anything but silence issuing from that small house on the street. There was a rumor that they did not speak. They had not spoken to one another for several years—a native girl who had worked for them had told it to someone else's servant.

The one link that kept the Keyters alive to the community, made them belong still, was their son Mark. Or rather Mrs. Keyter's Mark; his father had never paid any attention to him when he was a baby or a small boy, now that he was growing up they had for one another the strangeness of daily intimates who do not know one another. It was Mrs. Keyter and Mark.

Mark was a big, black-haired handsome boy, as big as a grown man at fourteen. He had his father's face, his father's body, his father's walk. But it was as if the father's body had been snatched up and put on—any old outward form will do—by a wild, careless, loving streak of life. Keyter's heavy handsomeness was fired up and tossed around by Mark; a wonderful deep color spread like visible energy from the neck of his old jersey, up from his curiously healthy bright ears, up his cheeks. In winter it was quick and rosy, in summer warm and mellow as the sun-colored skin of a fruit. His dark eyes were always lit up, as if he had been running. —In fact that was the total impression of him; you had caught him in the splendid moment of activity.

Mark went to boarding school in the Free State, and he matriculated, of course, about the same time as we did. Mrs. Keyter, who, as our old teacher, was interested in what we were going to do, told us that he was to take a degree in engineering.

But he never came to the University. Three of us met him on the train the day we had been in to Johannesburg to register as students. We were sitting close together over timetables and suggested reading lists for the courses on which we had decided, when the train door opened at a siding and Mark jumped in. He was carrying one of those tin lunch cases with a wire handle. He was working at a steel foundry.

When we came home with our piece of news, our mothers countered it with another: old Keyter had gone to live at the Cape. Since when? Transferred down there since the beginning of the month, someone said. —Well, they were a queer bunch. . . . We shrugged. Our own affairs were fascinatingly absorbing just at that time; there is perhaps nothing in family life, except a marriage of one of the daughters, so happily fingered-over as the aura which surrounds the first child to be sent up to a university. Everyone from the servant to the grandmother must reach out to touch it; a faint nimbus of distinction, like a smear of phosphorescence rubbed on through contact, glimmers from them as well.

So it was not until much later that we heard that Mark's father had denied any interest in furthering Mark's education at the University, and, completely withdrawing his support, had gone off to live as he wished at the coast. It was at examination time at the end of the first year, when my mother had been greatly impressed by my distracted air and the strip of light showing under my door until two o'clock in the morning, and meeting Mrs. Keyter, had kept her talking in lower and lower tones outside the grocer's. My mother is such a determined giver of confidences that the burden of her unburdening must in the end completely disarm the most reticent; it becomes impossible to withhold at least some return of confidence without appearing hurtfully mistrusting and positively insulting. So Mrs. Keyter, with her eyes gently smiling faraway in her head and her coat hanging flatter to her slighter body, told in a low voice of statement how Mr. Keyter had refused to help her let Mark become an engineer. She could not afford to do it on her own. Now he was her young workman, coming home to her; she smiled. He didn't mind it so much; the work was—well . . . He couldn't be expected to take much interest in it. But perhaps, who knows, Mr. Keyter might change his mind later? That was what she told Mark. But he's young of course, and he feels bitter about it. . . .

My mother came home tight-lipped and wide-nostriled. She'd talk about him politely and call him "Mr. Keyter" if he belonged to her! —That poor woman, sticking to such a creature. No feeling even for his own child. What a shame. Mrs.

Keyter became "old Mrs. Keyter": the epithet of compassion, nothing to do with age; she was no older than my mother. On the infrequent occasions when Mr. Keyter was spoken of, people prefixed "old" to his name too; scornfully, the dismissal, the condemnation by society of an unnatural father. "Old Keyter? Oh, he's mad . . . ," my mother would say with impatience, having to find a name for something she could not understand.

But Mark did not have to stay in his black overalls at the steel foundry long.

The war came and at once he left and joined the air force. He occurs in every war. He must have been at Waterloo, at Balaklava, at Ladysmith, at Gallipoli; an archetype of great physical beauty, energy, gaiety, magnificent in an officer's uniform, some germ that springs up to life from the morbid atmosphere of war like those extraordinary orchid-fungi that appear overnight out of the sodden soil of dark hidden places. He is the manifestation of the repellent fascination of war; wonderful enough to be worthy of sacrifice as an offering—at the same time too much a tantalization of what life might be like to be given without a pang and a doubt. Utterly innocent himself, everyone who looks at him gains a spurious nobility. Your heart beats with excitement and at the same time tears rim your eyes.

When Mark came home on leave and walked out of the broken gate of his mother's little house he seemed to fill the street. The two dirty little girls who played in the gutter opposite stood looking out from under their brows as he passed. The rheumatic old retriever who had belonged to the people up the road for ten years came out to sniff at his shoes and not remember him. He was an officer. His uniform lay on him like the plumes of a cock. His cap cut a slanting line above the line of his eyes: black, deep, friendly, male—not cajoling, but simply drawing to the surface like a blush, a melting of response from everyone who met them. And the smile; with pleasure at the sight of it was mixed envy: how could anyone feel such a smile inside himself? What capacity for joys did it shine off?

There's Mark Keyter! people would say. He's a lovely boy—! the old ladies said with astonishment. He's grown a fine man, the men remarked reflectively. The young women said nothing: —I saw Mark today. There was no knowing what women felt at the sight of him; the shopgirls—perhaps they had known him as children; I'm Lily Burgess . . . Kathleen Pretorius . . . Meg . . . they might offer suddenly, shyly, as they tied the string round the parcel. And he would lean across the counter, smile with surprise—there was a curious little blush, just round the eyes, when he smiled, very warm—and ask and answer the usual questions of past acquaintance, laughing, pleasant. Beside him was his mother, to whom he belonged. Small, stooped, in the greens, browns and grays that had faded on her for years, she went about with him, handing her parcels up to his arms, talking to him in her questioning voice, listening quietly with a smile beneath her lowered hat as they walked. She seemed to take on a gently vigorous frailty, like a god resting in the sight of his creation.

If no woman in our town knew more of Mark than the lift of his handsome head beside his mother in the cinema, or the quickness of his legs along the street, we knew that in the town near the airport where he was stationed he took all the tributes to which his attractions entitled him. When you met other men who had been stationed at the same place and you mentioned

Mark's name, they laughed and jerked their heads knowingly. "They fight over him. He's always got some new girl on the string. Some of the chaps' wives, too, wouldn't say no to a crooked finger from Keyter. And he doesn't care a damn. —But he's a good chap— Who could blame him? Anybody else with his advantages would be a fool not to do the same." Then, of course, Mark got married; in every woman in wartime there rises the instinct to mate with a man like Mark. He married one of the pretty girls and brought her home to visit, to Mrs. Keyter's old house behind the dying hedge. "She's a dear girl," Mrs. Keyter told my mother. "Young people must marry quickly in these times."

And then there was a baby. It was a boy, and Mrs. Keyter went down for the christening. Several people saw photographs of the tiny thing, brought out of a leather case in her handbag. She twisted her head to smile over them once again whilst you were looking at them. She carried around with her a roll of knitting in a fawn silk scarf. She seemed armed against her aloneness, her solitary comings and goings, the clamor of the pupils and the silence of her empty afternoons.

When the baby was three or four months old Mark was sent away to a fighter command in Egypt; it was surprising that he had been kept in South Africa as long as he had. I was buying some bulbs in the local florist's one morning soon after when Mrs. Keyter came in and stood waiting beside the little ledge where the florist kept a pen and ink and the printed cards for greetings and the black-bordered cards for wreaths. She stood with her handbag held in front of her between her two hands rather the way a person does who comes steeled to an interview for a job, or some sort of interrogation. . . . She had her tongue pressing her lower lip and she did not seem to see me for a moment; then she looked sideways with a start and smiled slowly. "They're lovely, aren't they?" —with the slight self-consciousness of the past child for the teacher, I indicated a great bucket of chrysanthemums. But she cut past that. Ignoring it, turning straight to me as a woman she said: "I'm so annoyed; it's wrong of them. Mark has been reported missing, and people keep sending me flowers. —As if someone were dead, flowers and messages of sympathy. I'm going to tell the florist please not to send any more." The lids of her familiar sunken eyes were infinitely finely wrinkled, delicate as the fine shining skin cast by some newly emerged insect. Under them her eyes held me with reasonableness. I brought an edge of hysteria to it with the over-vehemence of my agreement. I felt that *she* must be looking at *me* curiously; I was the one whose face must be watched for the appearance of disaster, like a rash. I know that I left that shop stupidly, backing away as if from some fearful sight.

Mark Keyter was never found. As well expect to have returned to you a garland you have dropped into the sea. Because he was never reported killed he died slowly; for some people— with a shrug, after two or three months; for others, only at the end of the war, when they realized he wasn't back; for his mother, nobody knows when. And because of this, his legend was without the fitting close it should have had. No stir of mourning for his youth and beauty rose because everybody found its loss at a different time. And then again because of that there is no starting-point for his memory; we do not know when absence became nonexistence, we cannot say: Mark Keyter died here, and build up a pyre of recollection on that spot. We talked about him now and then for a year or two, and then we stopped talking of him.

Mrs. Keyter has kept on teaching school. She did stop for a short while—round about the time of Mark's death, it must have been—but now she has been at it again for a long time. Old Keyter came back, too. Not directly after Mark was reported missing, but soon. He has become a recluse; he never goes out, except at night. My brother saw him once turn round suddenly under a street lamp. He said that the old man is as handsome as ever, and that for that instant, he felt again exactly as we did when we were children, and we met him in a doorway. We seldom see Mrs. Keyter; only my mother does, of course—she bumps into everybody. When I got back from my trip to Europe last month and came home to stay with the family for a few weeks, she reproached me: "You know, it would be nice if you went to see old Mrs. Keyter for a minute while you're here. She's always asking after you. Whenever I've seen her, she's wanted to know where you were, and what you were doing. Poor old thing, she's got so little in her own life. She's very thrilled just now, mind you—she's got Mark's little boy with her."

The only way you can escape from the necessity of taking up the everyday life that waits for you again is to go round visiting people, telling over and over the fortnight in Paris, the Rembrandts in Holland, the plays in London. I had seen everybody; the dwindling end of my return began to open out on days that would have to be taken up and lived. . . . Then I remembered

Mrs. Keyter; mother, I haven't been round to see Mrs. Keyter!
—I went that same afternoon, justified in the assumption of a
guilt.

When I stood at the old green front door with the red glass
fleur-de-lis inset, standing ajar into the hall, I smiled to see the
sameness of that house. A patch of new wire net shone water-
marked like moiré on the old rusted verandah screening; the
black-and-white linoleum jumped up and down before your
eyes. Through the hall archway came the same Mrs. Keyter, the
gentle, precise, enquiring walk, the soft enquiring laugh—the
pleasure of surprise as she took my hand in hers. We went into
the living room that was still evidently the schoolroom as well;
while we talked and she sat on the edge of her chair with her
head tilted, nodding sympathetic noises in her throat, my eyes
as they moved in animation caught the curling map of Africa,
the stack of beaded counting boards, the blackboard turned
against the wall. It was like not being able to prevent oneself
seeing the words of someone else's letter, left before one on a
table. I wanted to look and look around that room. I wanted to
get up and go and touch things. The amused, half-patronizing
wish to renew contact with what you have succeeded in leaving
far, far behind; confinements that seem too small, too frail ever
to have bounded you.

Hanging on the wall amongst the old spotted prints (a dead
fly was caught under the glass of one) there was a clear studio
portrait of Mark in his officer's cap. I said: "Mother tells me
you've got Mark's little boy with you for a while—"

Out of her eyes, that seemed as if sleeping (I remembered her
eyes that day at the florist's), life, the grip of living people on
everyday things came and currented that quiet, inert body, long

ago folded away into resignation like a set of neat, faded clothes. Inner joy and content showed miraculously in a face that no longer thought itself capable of expressing such emotions, should they still exist anywhere.

"For good," said Mrs. Keyter.

It was more than joy; it was the tender acceptance of a miracle by someone without hope. I was filled with a light-hearted relief, the selfish relief of not having to feel sorry for someone else, of not having to be guilty of one's own happiness. Mrs. Keyter was not imprisoned in the pale disappointments of her unrewarded age, her loss of lover and son, the one by failure of relationship, the other by death. It did not matter that she was old, poor and shabby. For she in her turn held something cupped in her life; the quick, fluttering being of a child. She went out to call him from the yard. I smiled after her, at ease.

She was gone five minutes; ten. It was quiet in that room.

It had always had a watching air, that room, the watching air of a clock.

Suddenly, the wind of my life that roared through my ears with voices, places, experiences, attainments, dropped—; I fell through in the space, the silence; through time; I found myself becalmed in the waiting, the emptiness of childhood. It was a most curious feeling; a tingling in my hands. I sat breathing the dryness of chalk; there was chalk filming the table in front of me, chalk beneath my palm on the arm of the old leather chair, chalk, chalk, silting the floorboards and all the surfaces, high and low, rubbed by hands every day, or hidden away out of reach for years on the tops of cupboards. Chalk dried the blood. People powder away. There was a torpor of life as if I crouched, with secret stiff hands acting a lie, watching a small, dry chalk-ingrained hand go up to a face to finger a hair. A single colorless hair. Nothing has changed. It repeated itself with horror. *Nothing has changed.* In poverty and drabness nothing changes. Wood does not wither. Chalk does not rot. What is dead and dry lives on forever and is forever dead.

I looked up with a start. A small boy had come into the room. He stood just in the doorway, eating a piece of cake. He stood obediently, a child who has been sent. "Hullo," I said quickly, and remembered that I didn't know his name. "Have you come to say hullo to me?" "Yes," he said, going on eating. "And what's your name?" "Charles," he said. He was looking at the last piece of cake as if he wanted to impress himself with the finality of the bite to come. He was a thin little boy with dirty knees, not like Mark at all. He had a pale neck like a stem, and his eyes, pale blue, lifted round and round the room away from me. The chapped nobs of his wrists stuck out far beyond the sleeves of a stern dark gray jersey. He had finished the cake. He had finished the lingering crumbs round his mouth. He stood there, quietly. Fortunately, Mrs. Keyter came in at that moment for I could not think of anything to say to him. She came in smiling her distant gentle smile, like a far-off sun whose warmth one cannot feel, and she put her hands on the narrow yoke of his shoulders. "Grandma," he said in his little hoarse voice, "Can I have anuller piece—"

The hands were drawn with chalk, as a washerwoman's hands are drawn with years of water.

When I came out of the gate into the early twilight a streetlight went on suddenly just outside. It caught Mark's little boy in the shadow of the gatepost, hunched back against it with one small foot turned in slightly before him, the other lifted resting back on the crumbling concrete. He had a pocketful of stones and he was throwing them, slowly, one by one, at the pole.

Is There Nowhere Else Where We Can Meet?

*I*t was a cool gray morning and the air was like smoke. In that reversal of the elements that sometimes takes place, the gray, soft, muffled sky moved like the sea on a silent day.

The coat collar pressed rough against her neck and her cheeks were softly cold as if they had been washed in ice water. She breathed gently with the air; on the left a strip of veld fire curled silently, flameless. Overhead a dove purred. She went on over the flat straw grass, following the trees, now on, now off the path. Away ahead, over the scribble of twigs, the sloping lines of black and platinum grass—all merging, tones but no color, like an etching—was the horizon, the shore at which cloud lapped.

Damp burnt grass puffed black, faint dust from beneath her feet. She could hear herself swallow.

A long way off she saw a figure with something red on its head, and she drew from it the sense of balance she had felt at the particular placing of the dot of a figure in a picture. She was here; someone was over there. . . . Then the red dot was gone, lost in the curve of the trees. She changed her bag and parcel from one arm to the other and felt the morning, palpable, deeply cold and clinging against her eyes.

Is There Nowhere Else Where We Can Meet?

She came to the end of a direct stretch of path and turned with it round a dark-fringed pine and a shrub, now delicately boned, that she remembered hung with bunches of white flowers like crystals in the summer. There was a native in a red woolen cap standing at the next clump of trees, where the path crossed a ditch and was bordered by white-splashed stones. She had pulled a little sheath of pine needles, three in a twist of thin brown tissue, and as she walked she ran them against her thumb. Down; smooth and stiff. Up; catching in gentle resistance as the minute serrations snagged at the skin. He was standing with his back toward her, looking along the way he had come; she pricked the ball of her thumb with the needle-ends. His one trouser leg was torn off above the knee, and the back of the naked leg and half-turned heel showed the peculiarly dead, powdery black of cold. She was nearer to him now, but she knew he did not hear her coming over the damp dust of the path. She was level with him, passing him; and he turned slowly and looked beyond her, without a flicker of interest, as a cow sees you go.

The eyes were red, as if he had not slept for a long time, and the strong smell of old sweat burned at her nostrils. Once past, she wanted to cough, but a pang of guilt at the red-weary eyes stopped her. And he had only a filthy rag—part of an old shirt?—without sleeves and frayed away into a great gap from underarm to waist. It lifted in the currents of cold as she passed. She had dropped the neat trio of pine needles somewhere, she did not know at what moment, so now, remembering something from childhood, she lifted her hand to her face and sniffed: yes, it was as she remembered, not as chemists pretend it in the bath salts, but a dusty green scent, vegetable rather than flower. It was clean, unhuman. Slightly sticky too; tacky on her fingers. She must wash them as soon as she got there. Unless her hands were quite clean, she could not lose consciousness of them, they obtruded upon her.

She felt a thudding through the ground like the sound of a hare running in fear and she was going to turn around and then he was there in front of her, so startling, so utterly unexpected, panting right into her face. He stood dead still and she stood dead still. Every vestige of control, of sense, of thought, went out of her as a room plunges into dark at the failure of power and she found herself whimpering like an idiot or a child. Animal sounds came out of her throat. She gibbered. For a moment it was Fear itself that had her by the arms, the legs, the throat; not fear of the man, of any single menace he might present, but Fear, absolute, abstract. If the earth had opened up in fire at her feet, if a wild beast had opened its terrible mouth to receive her, she could not have been reduced to less than she was now.

There was a chest heaving through the tear in front of her; a face panting; beneath the red hairy woolen cap the yellowish-red eyes holding her in distrust. One foot, cracked from exposure until it looked like broken wood, moved, only to restore balance in the dizziness that follows running, but any move seemed toward her and she tried to scream and the awfulness of dreams came true and nothing would come out. She wanted to throw the handbag and the parcel at him, and as she fumbled crazily for them she heard him draw a deep, hoarse breath and he grabbed out at her and—ah! It came. His hand clutched her shoulder.

Now she fought with him and she trembled with strength as they struggled. The dust puffed round her shoes and his scuffling toes. The smell of him choked her. —It was an old pajama jacket, not a shirt —His face was sullen and there was a pink place where the skin had been grazed off. He sniffed desperately, out of breath. Her teeth chattered, wildly she battered him with her head, broke away, but he snatched at the skirt of her coat and jerked her back. Her face swung up and she saw the waves of a gray sky and a crane breasting them, beautiful as the figurehead of a ship. She staggered for balance and the handbag and parcel fell. At once he was upon them, and she wheeled about; but as she was about to fall on her knees to get there first, a sudden relief, like a rush of tears, came to her and instead, she ran. She ran and ran, stumbling wildly off through the stalks of dead grass, turning over her heels against hard winter tussocks, blundering through trees and bushes. The young mimosas closed in, lowering a thicket of twigs right to the ground, but she tore herself through, feeling the dust in her eyes and the scaly twigs hooking at her hair. There was a ditch, knee-high in blackjacks; like pins responding to a magnet they fastened along her legs, but on the other side there was a fence and then the road. . . . She clawed at the fence—her hands were capable of nothing—and tried to drag herself between the wires, but her coat got caught on a barb, and she was imprisoned there, bent in half, whilst waves of terror swept over her in heat and trembling. At last the wire tore through its hold on the cloth; wobbling, frantic, she climbed over the fence.

And she was out. She was out on the road. A little way on

there were houses, with gardens, postboxes, a child's swing. A small dog sat at a gate. She could hear a faint hum, as of life, of talk somewhere, or perhaps telephone wires.

She was trembling so that she could not stand. She had to keep on walking, quickly, down the road. It was quiet and gray, like the morning. And cool. Now she could feel the cold air round her mouth and between her brows, where the skin stood out in sweat. And in the cold wetness that soaked down beneath her armpits and between her buttocks. Her heart thumped slowly and stiffly. Yes, the wind was cold; she was suddenly cold, damp-cold, all through. She raised her hand, still fluttering uncontrollably, and smoothed her hair; it was wet at the hairline. She guided her hand into her pocket and found a handkerchief to blow her nose.

There was the gate of the first house, before her.

She thought of the woman coming to the door, of the explanations, of the woman's face, and the police. Why did I fight, she thought suddenly. What did I fight for? Why didn't I give him the money and let him go? His red eyes, and the smell and those cracks in his feet, fissures, erosion. She shuddered. The cold of the morning flowed into her.

She turned away from the gate and went down the road slowly, like an invalid, beginning to pick the blackjacks from her stockings.

The Amateurs

They stumbled round the Polyclinic, humpy in the dark with their props and costumes. "A drain!" someone shouted, "Look out!" "Drain ahead!" They were all talking at once.

The others waiting in the car stared out at them; the driver leaned over his window: "All right?"

They gesticulated, called out together.

"—Can't hear. Is it O.K.?" shouted the driver.

Peering, chins lifted over bundles, they arrived back at the car again. "There's nobody there. It's all locked up."

"Are you sure it was the Polyclinic?"

"Well, it's very nice, I must say!"

They stood around the car, laughing in the pleasant little adventure of being lost together.

A thin native who had been watching them suspiciously from the dusty-red wash set afloat upon the night by the one street light, came over and mumbled, "I take you. . . . You want to go inside?" He looked over his shoulder to the Location gates.

"Get in," one young girl nudged the other towards the car. Suddenly they all got in, shut the doors.

"I take you," said the boy again, his hands deep in his pockets.

97

At that moment a light wavered down the road from the gates, a bicycle swooped swallow-like upon the car, a fat police-boy in uniform shone a torch. "You in any trouble there, Sir?" he roared. His knobkerrie swung from his belt. "No, but we've come to the wrong place—"

"You having any trouble?" insisted the police-boy. The other shrank away into the light. He stood hands in pockets, shoulders hunched, looking at the car from the street light.

"We're supposed to be giving a play—concert—tonight, and we were told it would be at the Polyclinic. Now there's nobody there," the girl called impatiently from the back seat.

"Concert, Sir? It's in the Hall, Sir. Just follow me."

Taken over by officialdom, they went through the gates, saluted and stared at, and up the rutted street past the Beer Hall, into the Location. Only a beer-brazen face, blinking into the car lights as they passed, laughed and called out something half-heard.

Driving along the narrow, dark streets, they peered white-faced at the windows, wanting to see what it was like. But curiously, it seemed that although they might want to see the Location, the Location didn't want to see them. The rows of low two-roomed houses with their homemade tin and packing-case lean-tos and beans growing up the chicken wire, throbbed only here and there with the faint pulse of a candle; no one was to be seen. Life seemed always to be in the next street, voices singing far off and shouts, but when the car turned the corner— again, there was nobody.

The bicycle wobbled to a stop in front of them. Here was the hall, here were lights, looking out like sore eyes in the moted air, here were people, more part of the dark than the light, standing about in straggling curiosity. Two girls in flowered head-scarves stood with their arms crossed leaning against the wall of the building; some men cupped their hands over an inch of cigarette and drew with the intensity of the stub-smoker.

The amateur company climbed shrilly out of their car. They nearly hadn't arrived at all! What a story to tell! Their laughter, their common purpose, their solidarity before the multifarious separateness of the audiences they faced, generated once again that excitement that so often seized them. What a story to tell!

Inside the Hall, the audience had been seated long ago. They sat in subdued rows, the women in neat flowered prints, the men collared-and-tied, heads of pens and pencils ranged sticking out over their jacket pockets. They were a specially selected audience of schoolteachers, who, with a sprinkling of social workers, two clerks from the administrative offices and a young girl who had matriculated, were the educated of the rows and rows of hundreds and hundreds who lived and ate and slept and talked and loved and died in the houses outside. Those others had not been asked, and were not to be admitted because they would not understand.

The ones who had been asked waited as patiently as the children they taught in their turn. When would the concert begin?

In an atmosphere of brick-dust and bright tin shavings behind the stage, the actors and actresses struggled to dress and paint their faces in a newly built small room intended to be used for the cooking of meat at Location dances. The bustle and sideburns of a late Victorian English drawing room went on; a young woman whitened her hair with talcum powder and pinned a great hat like a feathery ship upon it. A fat young man sang, with practiced nasal innuendo, the latest dance tune, whilst he adjusted his pince-nez and covered his cheerful head with a clerical hat.

"You're not bothering with make-up?" A man in a wasp-striped waistcoat came down from the stage.

A girl looked up from her bit of mirror, face of a wax doll.

"Your ordinary street make-up'll do—they don't know the difference," he said.

"But of course I'm making-up," said the girl, quite distressed. She was melting black grease paint in a teaspoon over someone's cigarette lighter.

"No need to bother with mustaches and things," the man said to the other men. "They won't understand the period anyway. Don't bother."

The girl went on putting blobs of liquid grease paint on her eyelashes, holding her breath.

"I think we should do it properly," said the young woman, complaining.

"All right, all right." He slapped her on the bustle. "In that case you'd better stick a bit more cotton-wool in your bosom—you're not nearly pouter-pigeon enough."

"For God's sake, can't you open the door, somebody," asked the girl. "It's stifling."

The door opened upon a concrete yard; puddles glittered, one small light burned over the entrance to a men's lavatory. The night air was the strong yellow smell of old urine. Men from the street slouched in and out, and a tall slim native dressed in the universal long-hipped suit that in the true liberalism of petty gangsterdom knows no color bar or national exclusiveness, leaned back on his long legs, tipped back his hat and smiled on teeth pretty as a girl's.

"I'm going to close it again," said the fat young man grimly.

"Oh, no one's going to eat you," said the girl, picking up her parasol.

They all went backstage, clambered about, tested the rickety steps; heard the murmur of the audience like the sea beyond the curtain. "You'll have to move that chair a bit," the young woman was saying, "I can't possibly get through that small space." "Not with that behind you won't," the young man chuckled fatly. "Now remember, if you play well, we'll put it across. If you act well enough, it doesn't matter whether the audience understands what you're saying or not." "Of course— look at French films." "It's not that. It's not the difficulty of the language so much as the situations. . . . The manners of a Victorian drawing room—the whole social code—how can they be expected to understand. . . ."—the girl's eyes looked out behind the doll's face.

They began to chaff one another with old jokes; the clothes they wore, the slips of the tongue that twisted their lines: the gaiety of working together set them teasing and laughing. They stood waiting behind the makeshift wings, made of screens. Cleared their throats; somebody belched.

They were ready.

When would the concert begin?

The curtain screeched back on its rusty rings; the stage opened on Oscar Wilde's *The Importance of Being Earnest*.

At first there was so much to *see*; the mouths of the audience

parted with pleasure at the sight of the fine ladies and gentlemen, dressed with such color and variety; the women?—gasp
at them; the men?—why laugh at them, of course. But gradually
the excitement of looking became acceptance, and they began
to listen, and they began not to understand. Their faces remained alight, lifted to the stage, their attention was complete,
but it was the attention of mystification. They watched the
players as a child watches a drunken man, attracted by his bab-
bling and his staggering, but innocent of the spectacle's cause or
indications.

The players felt this complete attention, the appeal of a great
blind eye staring up at their faces, and a change began to work
in them. A kind of hysteria of effort gradually took hold of
them, their gestures grew broader, the women threw great
brilliant smiles like flowers out into the half-dark over the footlights, the men strutted and lifted their voices. Each frowning
in asides at the "hamming" of the other, they all felt at the same
time this bubble of queerly anxious, exciting devilment of over-
emphasis bursting in themselves. The cerebral acid of Oscar
Wilde's love scenes was splurged out by the oglings and winks
of musical comedy, as surely as a custard pie might blot the
thin face of a cynic. Under the four-syllable inanities, under
the mannerisms and the posturing of the play, the bewitched
amateurs knocked up a recognizable human situation. Or perhaps it was the audience that found it, looking so closely, so
determined, picking up a look, a word, and making something
for themselves out of it.

In an alien sophistication they found there was nothing *real*
for them, so they made do with the situations that are tradi-
tionally laughable and are unreal for everyone—the strict

dragon of a mother, the timid lover, the disdainful young girl. When a couple of stage lovers exited behind the screens that served for wings, someone remarked to his neighbor, very jocular: "And what do they do behind there!" Quite a large portion of the hall heard it and laughed at this joke of their own.

"Poor Oscar!" whispered the young girl, behind her hand. "Knew it wouldn't do," hissed the striped waistcoat. From her position at the side of the stage the young girl kept seeing the round, shining rapt face of an elderly schoolteacher. His head strained up towards the stage, and a wonderful, broad, entire smile never left his face. He was asleep. She watched him anxiously out of the corner of her eye, and saw that every now and then the movement of his neighbor, an unintentional jolt, would wake him up: then the smile would fall, he would taste his mouth with his tongue, and a tremble of weariness troubled his guilt. The smile would open out again: he was asleep.

After the first act, the others, the people from outside who hadn't been asked, began to come into the hall. As if what had happened between the players and the audience inside had somehow become known, given itself away into the air, so that suddenly the others felt that *they* might as well be allowed in, too. They pushed past the laconic police-boys at the door, coming in in twos and threes, barefoot, bringing a child by the hand or a small hard bundle of a baby. They sat where they could, stolidly curious, and no one dared question their right of entry, now. The audience pretended not to see them. But they were, by very right of their insolence, more demanding and critical. During the second act, when the speeches were long, they talked and passed remarks amongst themselves; a baby was allowed to wail. The schoolteachers kept their eyes on the stage, laughed obediently, tittered appreciatively, clapped in unison.

There was something else in the hall, now; not only the actors and the audience groping for each other in the blind smile of the dark and the blind dazzle of the lights; there was something that lived, that continued uncaring, on its own. On a seat on the side the players could see someone in a cap who leaned forward, eating an orange. A fat girl hung with her arm round her friend, giggling into her ear. A foot in a pointed shoe waggled in the aisle; the people from outside sat irregular as they pleased; what was all the fuss about anyway? When something amused them, they laughed as long as they liked. The laughter of the schoolteachers died away: they knew that the players were being kept waiting.

But when the curtain jerked down on the last act, the whole hall met in a sweeping excitement of applause that seemed to feed itself and to shoot off fresh bursts as a rocket keeps showering again and again as its sparks die in the sky. Applause came from their hands like a song, each pair of palms taking strength and enthusiasm from the other. The players gasped, could not catch their breath: smiling, just managed to hold their heads above the applause. It filled the hall to the brim, then sank, sank. A young woman in a black velvet head-scarf got up from the front row and came slowly up onto the stage, her hands clasped. She smiled faintly at the players, swallowed. Then her voice, the strange, high, minor-keyed voice of an African girl, went out across the hall.

"Mister Mount and his company, Ladies and Gentlemen"— she turned to the players—"we have tried to tell you what you have done here, for us tonight"—she paused and looked at them all, with the pride of acceptance—"we've tried to show you, just now, with our hands and our voices what we think of this wonderful thing you have brought to us here in Athalville Location." Slowly, she swung back to the audience: a deep, growing chant of applause rose. "From the bottom of our hearts, we thank you, all of us here who have had the opportunity to see you, and we hope in our hearts you will come to us again *many times*. This play tonight not only made us see what people can do, even in their spare-time after work, if they *try*; it's made us feel that perhaps we could try and occupy our leisure in such a way, and learn, ourselves, and also give other people pleasure —the way everyone in this whole hall tonight"—her knee bent and arm outstretched, she passed her hand over the lifted heads —"everyone here has been made *happy*." A warm murmur was drawn from the audience; then complete silence. The girl took three strides to the center of the stage. "I ask you," she cried out, and the players felt her voice like a shock, "is this perhaps the answer to our Juvenile Delinquency here in Athalville? If our young boys and girls"—her hand pointed at a brown beardless face glazed with attention—"had something like this to do in the evenings, would so many of them be at the Police Station? Would we be afraid to walk out in the street? Would our mothers be crying over their children?—Or would Athalville be a better place, and the mothers and fathers full of pride? Isn't this what we need?"

The amateurs were forgotten by themselves and each other, abandoned dolls, each was alone. No one exchanged a glance. And out in front stood the girl, her arm a sharp angle, her nostrils lifted. The splash of the footlights on her black cheek caught and made a sparkle out of a single tear.

The Amateurs

Like the crash of a crumbling building, the wild shouts of the people fell upon the stage; as the curtain jerked across, the players re-collected themselves, went slowly off.

The fat young man chuckled to himself in the back of the car. "God, what we didn't do to that play!" he laughed.

"What'd you kiss me again for?" cried the young woman in surprise. "—I didn't know what was happening. We never had a kiss there, before—and all of a sudden"—she turned excitedly to the others—"he takes hold of me and kisses me! I didn't know what was happening!"

"They liked it," snorted the young man. "*One* thing they understood anyway!"

"Oh, I don't know—" said someone, and seemed about to speak.

But instead there was a falling away into silence.

The girl was plucking sullenly at the feathered hat, resting on her knee. "We cheated them; we shouldn't have done it," she said.

"But what could we *do*?" The young woman turned shrilly, her eyes open and hard, excitedly determined to get an answer: an answer somewhere, from someone.

But there was no answer.

"We didn't know what to do," said the fat young man uncertainly, forgetting to be funny now, the way he lost himself when he couldn't remember his lines on the stage.

A Present for a Good Girl

n an afternoon in September a woman came into the jeweler's shop. The two assistants, whose bodies had contrived, as human bodies doggedly will, to adapt the straight, hard stretch of the glass showcases to a support, sagged, hips thrust forward, elbows leaning in upon their black crepe-de-Chine-covered stomachs, and looked at her without a flicker, waiting for her to go. For they could see that she did not belong there. No woman in a frayed and shapeless old Leghorn hat, carrying a bulging crash shopping bag decorated in church bazaar fashion with wool embroidery, and wearing stained old sandshoes and cheap thick pink stockings that concertinaed round her ankles, could belong in the jeweler's shop. They knew the kind; simple, a bit dazed, shortsighted, and had wandered in mistaking it for the chemist's, two doors up. She would peer round stupidly, looking as if she had stumbled into Aladdin's cave, and when she saw the handsome canteens of cutlery, with their beautifully arranged knives spread like a flashing keyboard in their velvet beds, and the pretty little faces of the watches in their satin cases, and the cool, watery preening of the cut glass beneath its special light, she would mumble and shamble herself out again. So they stood, unmoved, waiting for her to go.

But, uncomfortably, she didn't go. She advanced right in, half-defiantly, half-ingratiatingly—she gave a little sniff to herself as if to say: Come on, now! Well, why *shouldn't* I—and put the shopping bag down on the counter. Then she gave the hat a pull, and stood waiting, not looking at the young ladies.

But still they did not move. Their half-closed eyes rested with faint interest upon the crash shopping bag, as upon some fossil discovery.

The third assistant, who was sitting at a table threading wedding rings in order on a velvet rod, pushed the rings aside and got up, thinking with as much crossness as lethargy could muster, Well, someone must see what the old creature wants.

"Yes?" she said.

It was all ready in the woman's mouth; as a child comes threshing up out of water with bulging cheeks, and lets out all its mouthful of breathlessness and enthusiasm in one great gasp, she said: "Good afternoon, Miss, there's a green bag in the window, Miss—in the corner, right down near the front. I want to get one for my daughter, she's always talking about a green one—and I wondered, you see, it's really only for Christmas, but I thought . . ."—and her pupils, that seemed to swim like weak small fish in the colorless wetness of her eyes with their underlids drooping down in a reddish peak, darted wildly. Like a beggar exhibiting valuable sores, she smiled on a mouth of gaps and teeth worn like splinters of driftwood.

"You want the green handbag in the window?" asserted the assistant, looking up, then down.

"Well, how much is it?" said the woman, in the coy tone of a confessed secret, screwing up one eye.

But the young assistant would not be drawn into such intimacy.

"I'll have a look . . . ," she said, resigned to wasting her time, and came out from behind the counter. Slow and measured, she unfastened the window catches, leaned in, and drew out the bag. The old woman pressed forward over the counter, her tongue feeling anxiously along the dark canyons of her teeth. She leaned on her elbow and her left hand, with the bones and great knobs that punctuated each joint sliding beneath tough slack skin like that of a tortoise, had taken up a curious pose, hanging indolent from the wrist, like the hand of a Louis XVI dandy pinching up snuff. "Mmm," she said, fumbling the air round the bag, wanting to touch it. She breathed hard down her nose, and whilst the assistant parted the bright locked fangs of the zipper and felt for the price-tag inside, the girl held her breath against the fusty sourness of the old woman's breath.

"Four-fifteen," said the assistant at last.

"Four-fifteen, four-fifteen," nodded the woman, sucking in her lower lip.

"Ninety-five shillings," said the assistant, hand on hip.

"Ah," said the woman, lifting her eyebrows under the flop of the zany hat, as if that explained away any difficulty. "It's got a mirror?" she asked.

"Yes," said the assistant ironically. You can't afford it, said the hand on her hip.

"Oh, I'm sure she'll like it," chatted the woman, fidgeting with the pockets and gadgets of the leather interior. "She loves green, you know. Everythink must be green. All her dresses and everythink. When I tell her it's supposed to be unlucky, she just says, Mum, you're old-fashioned. She's always wanted a green bag—"

"Then you should certainly take it for her, madam," said the assistant. Another minute or two and the old thing would be gone, muttering she'd see . . . she'd speak to her husband . . .

"You see, I thought I'd get it for her for Christmas," said the woman. She played with the knobbly string of yellow beads that stood up like boulders on the bony plateau of her chest.

"Yes, better take it when you see it." Habit prompted the assistant, "It might be gone, if you wait. You can put it away till Christmas."

"Oh well, I couldn't take it *now*—" she said. "You see I haven't got the money on me now."

"Well, we could put it aside for you until tomorrow," said the assistant.

The woman stood blinking at her subserviently, with the smirk of cunning innocence worn by the beggar whilst you read his tattered "testimonial." "You see, dear," she said in a hushed small voice, "I thought perhaps you'd let me pay off for it, like." Her face was drawn into a question.

"Can't do that, Miss Pierce," chimed in the other two assistants at once, like the representatives of some great power waking up halfway through a conference in time to boom a veto on some mewling little voice they haven't even heard. "Mr. Cano isn't in."

"You see, the manager isn't in at the moment," offered the assistant.

"Oh, I don't expect you to let me *take* it—" protested the woman, smiling at the young ladies as if they had just done her the most charming favor. "I just wanted to pay somethink down on it, then you could keep it here for me, and I'd come in every week and pay somethink more off it."

She grinned at them all like a cornered urchin.

"I see," said the girl Miss Pierce, not prepared for this.

"You can't do it without Mr. Cano's permission," stated the other two. "You can't do it without him."

"All right, all right, I know," said Miss Pierce. "—How much did you want to pay now?" she asked the woman.

Subdued with tension, the old creature grappled down in the shopping bag and dragged up a thin purse. "I could let you have ten bob," she said.

"And how long to pay the balance?"

"Well, until Chr— until just about the fifteenth of December."

"It's out of the question, Miss Pierce," said one of the others in a high voice.

The girl heard it behind her; in front of her the old woman grinned on her bad teeth, like a dog continuing to wag its tail even at the person who approaches to take away the bone that enchants it.

"All right," said the girl suddenly.

Silently the woman took a ten-shilling note from the flat stomach of her purse, and waited in silence whilst the receipt was made out. The moment she had the receipt in her possession, and was folding it away in the purse and the purse away in the crash bag, a mood of lighthearted talkativeness seized her. She opened up into confidential mateyness like a Japanese paper flower joyously pretending to be a flower instead of a bit of paper as it swells with water.

A Present for a Good Girl

She spoke only of her daughter. What her daughter always said, and what she always told her daughter.

"You must know my daughter—" she said, pooh-poohing the remote notion that the girl mightn't. "*You know*, dear, she's the cashier at the Grand Lyceum—fair girl, got a very good figure . . . ?"—She had a peculiar way of speaking; each "d" was a little step before which her voice hesitated, then hastily tripped over.

"Yes," murmured Miss Pierce, who was actually quite a frequent patron of the cinema in question, but who was never reduced to buying her own seat, and so had never seen the cashier. "Yes, I think I have seen—"

"Wears a lot of green? Got a quiet way of talking?" went on the woman. "Of course you know her. It's a good job, you know. She's a clever girl—sharp as a needle. She's been a good daughter to me, I must say. Not like some. That's why I'm glad I got that bag for her. She's been wanting a green one for a long time; I seen her, when we've been walking along, stopping to look in the shop window. And when I've asked her, she's said, no, nothin', just looking generally. But I knew what it was all right; sure enough, somewhere in the window there was always bound to be a green bag. . . ."

When she had shambled out with her flattened heels leaning over the sides of the old sandshoes, the two assistants stood looking at Miss Pierce. "Well, don't say *we* said it was all right. You know Mr. Cano—"

"Peculiar-looking woman," reproached the other one. "Did you see the way she was dressed! She looks to me as if she drinks, too."

"Well, why don't you ever do anything, anyway? Why do

you always wait for me to come forward?" flashed out Miss
Pierce, in a sudden temper.

Two weeks went by and then the woman came in, with an air
of wanting to get her ten-shilling note safely paid in before it
"went" on other things. She asked to see the bag again, and repeated to her fellow conspirator, Miss Pierce, the details of her
daughter's taste, color preferences, and mental powers. To get
rid of the woman, the girl pretended to have taken particular
note of the fair-haired cashier the last evening she had visited
the Grand Lyceum. The mother became almost speechless
with an excess of quiet pride: she seemed to go off into a sort of
dream, leaning on the counter, saying, very low, Yes, I'd like to
see her face on Christmas morning . . . I'd like to see her face . . .
That I would. . . . Putting away her second receipt with the
greatest of care, she went slowly out of the shop, as if she were
walking straight off the edge of a cloud.

"Funny old stick," said Miss Pierce, writing "Balance,
£3.15." on the parcel.

The next time the woman came in she was embarrassingly
garrulous, and insisted on offering Miss Pierce a cigarette from
an enameled tin case picturing two yellow cockatoos and fastened with a catch which was evidently rather tricky, because
she fumbled such a long time over getting it open. Under the
same frayed Leghorn hat, she looked queerer than ever; her face
was stiff, as if carefully balanced, and there was a streak of
mauvish lipstick on her mouth. She paid only five shillings,
with profuse apologies: "As God's my witness, I'll pay the lot
off at the beginning of the month," she said loudly, raising her
right hand. "As God's my witness . . ." Her hand dropped and

suddenly she smiled, sweetly, sweetly. "For my little girl . . . my little girl," she whispered, evidently to herself. Poor Miss Pierce smiled back fiercely in embarrassment. And suddenly the woman was gone.

The third time she came it was in the morning, and it seemed to the young Miss Pierce that the woman was really much older than she had noticed: she walked so falteringly, the crash shopping bag was much too heavy for her, and her eyes looked red in her bluish-pale face. Had she been crying, perhaps? Miss Pierce thought perhaps the poor old thing had to work very hard at housework; there was a faint smell of methylated spirits about her—she must have been cleaning windows. Four-pounds-fifteen! Why it must be a fortune to her! Miss Pierce wondered if a peroxide blond cashier from the Grand Lyceum was worthy of it. Anyway, the green handbag was another fifteen shillings nearer being paid for.

And that, it seemed, was as far as it would ever get.

Weeks went by, and the woman did not appear; Miss Pierce hid the bag away from the businesslike eyes of Mr. Cano: "What's this?" he would say. "*How* long—?—Put it back into stock. Return the woman's deposit to her. . . ." So the green bag lay waiting behind a pile of hand-tooled leather writing cases.

An intoxication of buying grew upon the town as every day Christmas moved up a notch nearer, and soon the three assistants were elbowing one another out of the way as they smiled, persuaded, suggested, to the timorous, the vacillating, the imperious who came to buy. Miss Pierce really did not even have time to wonder if the woman would come for the bag; her shopgirl's attention was already wrangled into half-a-dozen divisions by half-a-dozen equally demanding customers as it was; there was no small shred left that was not immediately snatched up by someone who had been waiting fully three-quarters-of-an-hour to see a tortoise-shell powder bowl.

But in the fine high frenzy of half-past four on the last Saturday afternoon before Christmas, Miss Pierce was interrupted. "Your customer's here"—one of the other two young ladies prodded her elbow. "—What?" said the girl, dodging the blinding demand of eyes. "The green handbag," said the other, smiling with great brilliance, and diving back.

The harassed girl dodged in and out to the other side of the shop. In the dazed preoccupation that results as a kind of spiritual sunstroke from overexposure to the question and demand of a daylong crowd, she could not recall any green handbag. But then she saw the woman in the battered garden-party Leghorn standing just within the doorway, and of course!—the green handbag, £2.15.0 balance, behind the writing cases. She went forward with a quick smile.

"S'ere . . . ," said the woman, handing out a pound note as if to a blank wall, " 'F you've sorl thabag t'anyone . . . I pay'dfirit and you've got norite t'crooka poorwoman."—Her voice whined through the persuasive buzz of the shop. Harsh fumes surrounded her as rising incense round some image.

Miss Pierce looked at her in astonishment.

Dropping the crash bag, the woman turned to look at it, lying on the floor, as if it were some animal that had just crawled to her feet. She tried to pick it up, but could not. Half bent to the floor, she looked up at Miss Pierce with a sudden chuckle, like a naughty child.

Miss Pierce stood quite still.

"Why'd'you keepm'waiting, whydonchu giviterme," said the

woman with great dignity. There was a red poppy, the kind that charitable organizations give away on collection days, pinned on to the brim of the hat with a large safety pin.

Miss Pierce trembled like a trapped rabbit.

"Youdonwana be'fraiduvme," said the woman with a sudden cunning flash of understanding. "Sorry . . ." She wagged her head, "Sorry . . ."

Miss Pierce burned with guilt. "I'll just get—I mean, I'll see . . . ," she tried.

"Musn be'fraid uvaporeolwoman. Iwan the— the-bag"—she stopped and thought hard—"the-the *green* bag I got f'my daughter. Y'know mydaughter?" she urged, clutching Miss Pierce's arm. " 'Course y'know mydaughter—" She stopped and smiled, closing her eyes. "S'ere," she said, putting down the pound note.

"But that's not enough," said Miss Pierce very loudly, as if talking to a deaf person. "Not enough. You owe two-pounds-fifteen on the bag"—holding up two fingers—"Two-pounds-fifteen."

"Whas' sat?" said the woman, stupidly. Her face grew woeful, sullen. "Don wanagiviterme. Y'don wanagiviterme."

"But you haven't paid for it, you see," said Miss Pierce miserably. Mr. Cano was frowning at her through the crowd; she could sense his one twitching eyebrow, questioning.

"Howmuchwasit?" whispered the woman, winking at her and leaning over into her face.

"Four-pounds-fifteen. You remember."

"Wasit?" she giggled. "Wasit."

"You have to pay another pound and fifteen shillings."

The woman knelt on the floor and felt down amongst the lumps and bulges of the crash shopping bag, collapsed on its side on the floor. At last she got up again. Some anchor in the heart that even the vast swelling uncharted seas of drunkenness could not free her of, pulled at her. Underneath her stiff face, her glassed-out eyes, it was horrible to see that she was alive and struggling. The silliness of being drunk would not come up to save her.

"Iwaned to getit for her," she said. "I *mean'* t'getit for her."

The broken brim of the hat hid her face as she felt her way out. The whole shop was watching, each man from the pinnacle of his own self-triumph.

It had hardly turned back to its own business again when a pale girl, violently white-faced, with the thin pale hair of a slum child, swept tremblingly into the shop. She stood there leaning forward on her toes, shuddering with anger. Just behind her, held leashed by the terrible look of her eye, was the old woman, open-mouthed. The girl's eyes searched desperately round the shop. They seemed to draw Miss Pierce out from behind the counter: she came slowly forward. A flash of angry disgust passed from the girl to the old woman, who blinked beneath it as from a whip.

"Now what is it?" blurted the girl. "What does she owe here?"

"She's paid some, you see," ventured Miss Pierce. They were like doctors in discussion over the patient's prone body.

"Tell me how much, and I'll pay it," the girl cut in violently. Under the pale spare skin of her neck, her heart flew up madly, as a bird dashing again and again at its cage.

"Oh, it's all right," faltered Miss Pierce, avoiding looking at the old woman. "She's not so very much behind in her payments. It's not absolutely necessary that she take the bag now."

Hot bright tears at the recollection of some recent angry scene fevered the girl's eyes. *"Tell me how much it is,"* she whispered fiercely, crazily. She swallowed her tears. *"She* can't pay," she said, with a look of hopeless disgust at the old woman.

"The bag was four-pounds-fifteen. She owes two-fifteen on it."

"A bag for four-pounds-fifteen," said the girl bitterly, so overwhelmed by a fresh welling of furious despair and irritation that her pale eyes filled with bright tears again. She turned and looked at the old woman; her hand sank leaden at her side, as if defeated in the desire to strike. "What next. Always something. Some rubbish. Now a bag. What for—? You people give her things. She's not responsible. I've had just about enough of it.—She ought to be in a home, she should. I can't stand it any longer." The old woman looked out at her from under her eyelids.

Trembling, the girl jerked out two pounds and fifteen shillings in silver and gave it up with a gesture of hopeless impotence to Miss Pierce. Miss Pierce handed to her the parcel containing the green handbag. The girl looked at it for a moment, with an expression of quizzical, sullen disgust. She looked as if she would have liked to hurl it away, as far as her arm could. Then she picked it up, and went out of the doorway.

"Come on," she ordered in a low, dead voice.

And the old woman swayed after her out into the street.

La Vie Bohème

She got off the tram where she had been told, at Minos'
New Tearoom, and looked around her at the streets she didn't
know. Turn to the left past the tearoom and carry straight on.
She crossed the road slowly and recognized in precognition
the windows set with a mosaic of oranges, licorice sticks, and
chewing gum in packets. This was it, then.

As she walked up the street, her eyes ready for the name of
the building, she kept saying over and over to herself snatches
of the conversation she had had with her sister yesterday. She
saw her sister in her white blouse and red peasant skirt coming
in to the exhibition, she felt again the curious suffocating excitement of looking up hard at her and meeting her black eyes
—she heard again the surprised cry "Baby!": her sister's voice,
not heard for eighteen months, so familiar, yet striking her ear
afresh, showing her she had forgotten. And her sister looked
just the same. Just the same. And yet in between she had left
home, quarreled with her parents, married her student *without
any money at all.*—Well, how are you getting on? she had said,
because she really couldn't think what would be tactful to say.
And her sister laughed: Body and soul together, you know.

La Vie Bohème

We've got a little flat—oh very small—minute, not really a flat. —In "Glenorin." There's a balcony.

Live in one room. *Without any money.*—Mother said that, she remembered; kept saying it over and over, until she had felt the awfulness of what her sister was doing. *One room.*— But there, you see, it wasn't one room; it was a small flat, and it had a balcony.

I couldn't believe for a moment that it could be you, Baby.— I was still thinking of you as being at school. . . .

Of course—she had been still at school, when it happened. And her sister never had thought about her much; she was so much younger, and there were a brother and another sister in between. Besides, her sister hadn't ever been a "family" person. She felt the natural ties of affinity rather than the conventional blind ties of the blood.

Come and see me! Why don't you? Come and see my child. —You're not afraid of the family wrath?

That was a compliment. Meeting her at an architectural exhibition, finding that she had grown up, her sister felt perhaps they were of a kind, after all. . . .

With a balcony. Not that building over there? No—wrong side of the street. Besides there were potted plants on the ledge —how her sister always disliked the sword ferns in the bay window at home! It would be something like a studio, inside, she supposed. Warmly untidy. Lived in. God, this room! her sister used to say at home; what a thicket of lace curtains and firescreens and knick-knackery through which to peer out half-seeing at the world. . . .

People drop in. You might meet someone who would interest you. Anyway . . . Her sister always looked so interesting, with her black smooth hair and her contrasting expanses of clear, bright colors; that had always been her way of dressing: as if she had been painted by Gauguin, or even Raoul Dufy.— But why did she persist in this notion, this fancy of seeing her sister against a painted backdrop of an abstract "artist's life." Her sister was not an artist; she was a schoolteacher. And the young student she had married was not an artist; he was studying medicine. Yet her sister brought to mind the black, bright center of a flower, set off within a corolla of the many-colored and curiously distinct petals each resting and overlapping in a curve one upon the other—the pictures she had of an artist's way of life. The simplicity of it—no lounge chairs uncovered for visitors, no halls, no pantries; one room, and in the room, everything. The books that start the ideas; the ideas that start the wonderful talk; the friends who talk. She saw her sister moving amongst all this. . . . Medical student or no medical student. Hadn't her sister's friends—whom she had refused to bring home at all after a while, because her father asked them such banal and stupid questions at table—always been people who wrote, acted or painted?

The building was on the left side of the street and the name was spelled out over the entrance in red cut-out letters, like children's alphabetical blocks. She went in with her heart beating suddenly hotly, looking at the names on the board and reading Mr. and Mrs., Mr. and Mrs., over and over very quickly until she stopped at the name. Second floor. There was a lift, the paint worn off its metal sides so that being inside was like standing in a biscuit tin, and when she pressed the button, it moved off with a belch that drifted into a sigh and died to a stop at the second floor.

Her sister in the red skirt and white blouse . . . She suddenly felt worried and ashamed of home, of that awful stuffy "nice" home that she was sure clung about her, left its mark imprinted on her face and clothes. And her sister would recognize it at once, and smile to herself, curl her lip. She felt very anxious to impress upon her sister that she *knew* home was awful, a kind of tomb overgrown with impenetrable mediocrity; walking along the cold high passage that leaned over the deep well of a courtyard, looking for Number 11, she calculated urgently how she might let her sister know that *she* was not taken in by home.

Number 11 was a green door, like all the others, but there was a knocker on this one, a little black mask with its tongue out. Of course!

Her smile was ready on her face as she clacked the knocker down.

The door opened to the smell of burned milk and bright warm sleepy yellow light from the wide windows; full in her face it came, making a dark outline of dazzle round her sister, standing there with a soapy hand stiff away from her face, holding back a strand of loose hair awkwardly with the knob of her bent wrist. She was wearing the same red skirt and an old pair of creaking leather sandals threaded in and out her toes. She waved her visitor in, talking, shrugging, holding out her dripping hands. On the right wall above the big divan there was a wonderful picture; her eye leaped to it, in excitement! Ah—! An enormous picture: an Indian child, sitting fawn-colored, cross-legged, with her arms round a great sheaf of arum lilies with their white throats lifted. There were bookshelves, sagging; a great pile of papers, gramophone records. A radio with an elongated, slit-eyed terra-cotta head on it. A kind of tall boy with a human skull wearing an old military cap lopsided.

You mustn't mind all this, said her sister, urging her to the divan. I'm in a mess, the washgirl hasn't turned up for the baby's things. Of course you had to catch me like this. She looked at herself as if she wanted to draw attention to her own boldness of not caring.

Feeling rude as a fascinated child, she dragged her eyes away from the picture, vaguely. Oh there, in the corner: a door was open. The tides of light that washed continuously, in deeps of orange and shallows of pale yellow all about the room, stopped there as at the foot of a glowering little cave. Inside she could see only a confused, cellar-like gloom, whitish things hanging quite dead from the lowness of the ceiling, splashes of white, feeble flashes of nickel. If there's anything I hate doing, said her sister, clicking on a light.—There in the flare of a small globe it was a bathroom, hung with napkins sodden on criss-crossed lines of string, a bath and lavatory and washbasin fitted in one against the other, and just room enough for her sister to stand. A chipped enamel pail on the floor held unwashed napkins, and wet ones lay beneath the scum of pricking soap bubbles in the basin.

Oh, go ahead, she said. Don't worry about me.

Her sister's long hands disappeared beneath the scum; she washed and talked, vivacious as ever.

And she sat on the divan looking intensely round the room, looking, looking, whilst she pretended to talk. From point to point her eyes raced; the cushions with brick-colored and white stalking figures like bushman paintings; the woolly white rugs

shaded with stains; the lovely green head of Pan that was a
wall vase and that her sister had had at home, and that there
had been an argument about because her mother didn't like
the wall spoiled with the nail that held it up. There were three
dead anemones hanging out of its mouth. Something was
pressing into her back, and she found that she was leaning
against a big book. She picked it up; whooshed the hundreds
of cool pages falling back smooth and close to solidity: FOREN-
SIC MEDICINE it said on the cover, and beneath it, his name.
She looked curiously at the curves of his handwriting: realizing
that some of the unknown elements of the room were also this
signature.

When she just doesn't turn up like this, her sister was saying, I could wring her neck. In theory, why should another
woman wash my child's napkins for me; but in practice . . .
She gave a little snort of knowing better now.

Can you imagine what mother would say, she said from the
divan, suddenly easily, laughing. They paused: I told you so,
they called out together, laughing. Her sister held up her soapy
hands; she leaned back on her elbow against a cushion, shaking her head. And their laughter faded companionably down.

Her sister had turned back to the basin, letting the water
out with a gurgle. How peculiarly her sister stood, with her
feet splayed out in those sandals, clinging to the floor flatly,
the Achilles tendon at the back of each ankle pulled taut,
strong and thin. . . . The washgirl at home stood just like
that, endlessly before the tub on Monday mornings. . . ?
The recognition came like a melting inside her. She looked
quickly away: sticking out beneath the cushion at her elbow she

saw a baby's knitted coat. With a smile she pulled it out, tugged at the little ribbon bedraggled and chewed at the neck.

The baby's? she said, holding it up.

Oh Lord—give here, said her sister—While I'm at it—

A few minutes later, whilst her sister was drying her hands, the cushion fell off the divan, and she saw a small vest and bib, that had been hiding innocently beneath it. She picked them up; the bib smelled sour where the baby had brought up some milk on it. She put them back under the cushion.

I'll hang them out in the courtyard later, said her sister, closing the bathroom door on the napkins. She stood in the room, pleased, a little uncertainly, pushing back her cuticles.

You know, now that I look at you, I think you've got thinner, or taller or something . . . , she said.

Have I? said her sister, smiling. Yes, perhaps—she smoothed her hips. Now I'll make some tea, and then we can talk.

Can't I go and see the baby? she asked. Her sister had said he was asleep on the balcony.

Oh for God's sake don't wake him *now*, said her sister. Let's have some peace. She went over to a curtained recess next to the bathroom door. Is that curtain hand-woven? she asked her sister, admiring the clay, green and black horses on it. Mmm, said her sister, made by a girl called Ada Leghorn who ate with us—for nothing, needless to say—for five months before she went off to South America to paint.—Anyway— And she pulled it on a little two-plate stove with tin legs and a shelf piled and crammed with pots, boxes of cereal, tins, a piece of polony end-down on a saucer, two or three tomatoes, unwashed glasses misted with milk.

Can I help? she asked.

I think you could wash two cups for us, said her sister.

She got up and went to the little square sink, that stood close against the stove. Out of the breakfast dishes thinly coated with the hard dry lacquer of egg, she found two cups and ran the tap over them. On the ledge at the side of the sink she found a swab, and picked it up to wipe the cups; but it was sodden, and unidentifiable bits of soggy food clung to it. She put it down again quickly, not wanting to be noticed. But her eye wandered back to the slimy rag and her sister's followed it. Her sister made an impatient noise with her tongue: Oh—look at that—she said, and quickly snatched up something the other hadn't noticed until then: a square of newspaper sandwiched over a filling of shaving soap lather, grayish with the powderings of a day's beard. *Never* remembers to throw *anything* away!

He's working so terribly hard, poor child, she said after a moment.

Yes, I suppose so, she said, shyly, drying the cups.

You must come when he's here, her sister said gaily. It's ridiculous—not even knowing my own sister!

Yes! she said enthusiastically, and was suddenly afraid she would not like him.

Do you cook here? she asked—And then the moment she said it she heard with the sharp cringe of regret that it had come out in her mother's voice; she had said it just the way her mother spoke. I mean—all your meals . . . ? she stumbled.

Yes! Yes-s! said her sister loudly, against the splutter of the tap splurting water into a small pot. She planked the pot down on the little stove, taking a lid from another saucepan, much larger, with which to cover it, saying with a short snort of a laugh, Not one of those dinners of mother's at home, that are prayed over and anointed like a sacrifice being prepared for the gods—we eat. Food isn't all that important.

Of course not, she agreed, in contempt of the mother.

Her sister turned round, paused, looking at her, searching: And then we just go out for a really decent meal when we feel like it. —Naturally . . .

I always think of you when we have steak-and-kidney pie, she smiled.

My yes! exclaimed her sister. It was marvelous! The crust! . . . Some day when I've got an oven I'm going to learn how to make it. I'll eat a whole one myself.

They had tea on a tray between them on the divan. Her sister tore open a packet of biscuits. Now! she said.

It's funny to think of you domesticated, she smiled at her sister.

The mechanics of life . . . , said her sister, watching the tea flow into a cup.

Of course, yes, you have to get *through them* to other things, she said, urging her understanding.

Getting through them's the thing, said her sister.

". . . By the time I've got the house cleaned the way I want it, and put three meals on the table . . ." She heard her mother. A familiar phrase of music played on a different instrument.

When he qualifies, said her sister, sitting back with her tea, we're going away . . . to travel. Perhaps to Kenya for a bit. And of course, I'm still determined to go to Italy. We even started to learn Italian. She laughed.—It petered out, though.

We want to go to Italy, and Switzerland. . . . But what we'll do with the baby, God knows. . . . At the thought she frowned, accusing the invisible; put the whole thing away in some part of her mind where she kept it.

Did you see the exhibition of modern Italian art last week? she asked eagerly, ready for the talk. What did you think of it?

Didn't even know there was one, said her sister. I don't know, I don't seem to get beyond the headlines of the paper, most of the time.

Oh, she said. There was an oil that reminded me of that picture of yours—she twisted her head to the Indian child and the lilies.

That's a gouache, said her sister, her eyes on the balcony. She tilted her head. Was that a grumble from the pram . . . ? She looked questioningly.

I didn't hear anything, she said, subsiding back.

I *hope* not, said her sister.

I rather hope he *will* cry, she laughed, I want to see him.

Her sister looked at her very attentively, her eyes held very wide, the impressive, demanding way she had looked at her when they were children, and her sister was the big sister directing the game: Look here, she said, I'm afraid you'll have to see him next time, if you don't mind. I have to go out to give a child a lesson just now, and Alan has to rush back from a ward round to be here with the baby. It's bad enough he has to interrupt his work as it is; if he's got to be here, he's got to get some swotting done at least—and he can't do that if the baby's awake. I try to get him off to sleep and then I pray he'll stay asleep till I get back. So if you don't mind —her hands were trembling a little on the teacup.

Of course not! she protested. I'll see him next time. I didn't know . . . It doesn't matter at all.

No, said her sister, smiling now, friendly, careless, you'll come often.

Did that mean she must go now?

Are you going out soon? she said.

Yes, said her sister, I must get myself tidied up. . . . You can wander round behind me. Then as soon as he comes, I can rush off.

All at once she wanted to go; she must get away before He came. It was quite ridiculous how agitated she felt lest He should come whilst she was still there. She whimpered inwardly to go, like a child in a strange place. She followed her sister distractedly around, unable to think of anything else but her impulse to go. She thought she heard a step; she thought she heard the door, every minute.

Her sister changed her sandals for shoes, went into the bathroom to smooth her hair. The bathroom was steamy with wet napkins; standing there with her sister, she felt hot and hardly able to breathe. I must hang them out before I go . . . , said her sister, her mouth full of hairpins; her eyes were curiously distracted, as if all the time her attention was divided, pulled this way and that. And I should get the vegetables ready for tonight. . . . Her hands fumbled with haste, remembering.

Was that the clang of the lift gate? Her heart beat up inside her. . . . No. You know, I really think I should go now, she said, smiling, to her sister.

Well, all right, then, Baby, said her sister, turning with her old smile, her old slow, superior smile. Next time come in the evening, it'll be more interesting for you. Alan'll be here—

that is, we'd better make it a week-end evening, when he hasn't got to work. . . . But if you wait just another few minutes he'll be here— she encouraged.

No, she said, I've got to go now; I've got to get something for mother, in town. So I'd better . . .

They stood smiling at one another for a moment.

Mother . . . , said her sister . . . God, always something to get for mother. . . . She shook her hair freely, with a little gesture of release; then with long, sure movements, pinned it up.

—Well, I'll leave you then, she said, dodging beneath napkins to the door. With the napkins and the vegetables and the lesson to go to, she didn't say.

And as she turned at the door she noticed something on the bathroom shelf that suddenly lifted her strong sense of depression for her sister; something that signaled out to her that all was not lost. It was quite an ordinary thing; a box of talcum powder. The special kind of talcum powder with a special light sweet perfume of honeysuckle that her sister had always used; that had always been snowed about the bathroom for mother to mop up and grumble over. You still use it! she cried with pleasure—The same old kind in the flowered box! I haven't smelled it since you left!

What? said her sister, not listening.

Your bath powder in those big messy boxes! she laughed.

Her sister's eyes wandered tolerantly to the shelf. Oh *that*! she said. She looked at it: It's just the empty box—Alan keeps his shaving things in it. Fourteen-and-six on bath powder! I didn't know what to spend money on next, in those days. . . . Good-by! she called out from the door.

Good-by, shouted out her sister from the bathroom. Don't forget—

No, I won't, she called back, Good-by!

The lift wasn't on that floor so she didn't wait for it but ran down the stairs and went straight out of the building and down the street and past Minos' tearoom to the tram stop. In the tram she sat, slowly unclenching herself and thinking fool, fool, what is the matter with you? She was terribly, terribly pleased because she hadn't met Him. She was really quite foolishly pleased. When she thought how ridiculously pleased she was, she felt a strong sense of guilt toward her sister. The more pleased, the more strong the pang for her sister. As if her not wanting to meet Him made him not good enough for her sister. Oh her poor, poor sister . . .

Quite suddenly she rang, got off the tram and went into a chemist shop. Strained and trembling so that the assistant looked at her curiously, she bought a large box of the special bath powder. She caught the next tram back to Minos' tearoom and rushed along the street and swept into the building and into the lift. In the presence of the lift she stood stiffly, clutching the parcel. The lift seemed discreetly to ignore her nervous breathing. Out of the lift and along the passage to Number 11, and as she brought down the knocker, it came to her with a cold start—He might be there. Too late it came to her. . . . As it came, the door opened.

Look, said a dark young man—Come in, won't you—just a minute—and leaving her standing, disappeared on to the balcony. She could hear a baby crying; holding its breath and then releasing all the force of its lungs in a long diminishing bellow. In a moment the young man came back. It's all right, he said, with a wave of his hand. He was holding a pair of glasses; his brown eyes were faintly red-rimmed. He looked at her enquiringly.

Good afternoon, she said foolishly.

Good afternoon! he said kindly. Did you want to see me? Or is it for my wife . . . ?

I—I just wanted to leave something—she said—something . . .

He saw the parcel. You want to leave something for my wife, he said helpfully.

Yes—she said—thank you, if you will—and gave him the parcel.

She knows about it, does she? he said. I mean she knows who it's from?

She nodded her head violently. Thanks—then, she said, stepping back.

Righto, said the young man. He was in a hurry. He gave her a brief explanatory smile and closed the door.

She hadn't said it. She hadn't told Him. I'm her sister, I'm her sister. She kept saying it over and over silently inside herself, the way she should have said it to Him . . . And in between she told herself, Fool, fool . . .

Ah, Woe Is Me

Sarah worked for us before her legs got too bad. She was very fat, and her skin was light yellow brown, as if, like a balloon that lightens in color as it is blown up, the fat swelling beneath the thin layer of pigment caused it to stretch and spread more and more sparsely. She wore delicate little gilt-rimmed spectacles and she was a good cook, though extravagant with butter.

Those were the things we noticed about her.

But in addition, she had only one husband, married to her by law in church, and three children, Robert, Janet and Felicia, whose upbringing was her constant preoccupation. She sighed often as she bent about her cleaning, as heavy people do, but she was thinking about the children. Ah! woe is me, she would say, when the butcher didn't send the liver, or it started to rain in the middle of the weekly wash, as if, judging from the troubles in her own life, she couldn't expect everyday matters to go any better. At first we laughed at the Biblical ostentation of the exclamation, apparently so out of proportion; but later we understood. Ah, woe is me, she said; and that was her comment on life.

She worried about her three children because she wanted them to know their place; she wanted to educate them, she wanted the boy to have a decent job, she wanted the girls to grow up virgin and marry in church. That was all. Her own Mission School education, with its tactful emphasis on the next world rather than this, had not made her dangerous enough or brave enough or free enough or even educated enough to think that any place was the place for her children; but it had emerged her just sufficiently to make her believe that there *was* a place for them; not a share in the White Man's place, but not no place at all, either: a place of their own. She wanted them to have it and she wanted them to stay there. She was enough of an uncomplaining realist to know that this was not easy. She was also conservative enough not to ask why it was so difficult. You got to live in this world the way it is, she said.

The things she wanted for her children sound commonplace; but they weren't. Not where she had to look for them.

At first she rented a room for the children in a relative's house in the Location. She paid for their food and went to visit them every Sunday, and the cousin was supposed to see that they went to school regularly and did not wander about the Location after dark during the week; Sarah believed as fervently in education as she feared the corruption of the dark. But soon it became clear that Robert spent most of his schooldays caddying at the golf course—(Why, why, why! moaned Sarah under the disgrace of it—and Robert opened his hand, pink inside like the unexpected little paw of a knowing monkey, and showed the sixpence and tickey * lying there, misted with the warmth of his palm) and Felicia ran scream-

* A South African colloquialism for threepence.

ing about the dark, smoky streets at night, as other children did. It was all right for the others, who were going to be errand boys and nursegirls; but it was not for Sarah's children.

She sent them to boarding school.

Along came the list of things they must have, and the endless low, urgent discussions over the back gate with her husband and the slow passing of folded pink notes and the counting of half-crowns out of a cotton tobacco bag. She spent, not merely a fortune on them—fortunes are things made and lost—but everything she had, her nine pounds in the Post Office, and all of her wages, every month. Even then it was not enough, for the school was in Natal, and she could only afford train fare for them once a year, so that they spent all holidays other than the Christmas one at school, three hundred miles from home. But they were being educated. She showed me their letters; like all children's letters, noncommittal, emotionless, usually asking for something. Occasionally I gave her some sweets to send them, and I received a letter of thanks from the younger girl, Janet, in reply; polite, but without the slightest hint of any pleasure that the gift might have brought. Sarah always asked to read the letter, to see, I knew, if it was respectful: that was the important thing. A look of quiet relief would come over her face as she folded it up again. Yes, she would say, there I know they're being looked after.

When Christmas came I felt ashamed to let her rent a room in the Location for the children for the duration of their yearly holiday, and I told her she could have them with her in the yard, if she liked. She put on her black dress and fringed shawl —she clung to a few old Victorian dignities which were not very serviceable, but were certainly not as ugly as some of the notions picked up by native women from contemporary European vulgarity—and went to meet them at the station, starting off very early, because her legs were bad again, and she could not hurry. She was away all day, and I was rather angry, but when I saw her coming home with her three children I was conscious of a sense of ceremony in her, and said nothing.

They were remarkably good children. I have never seen such good children, so muted, so unobtrusive in their movements, so subdued in their play. Too good: the girls coming to sit silently in the sun against the wall of Sarah's room, the boy sitting with his bits of stick and stone amongst the weeds along the fence. The girls did their washing and crocheted caps of red wool; their laughter was secret, never come upon in the open, like a stream heard gently gurgling away hidden somewhere in the undergrowth. Their smiles were solemn and beautiful, but ritual, not joyousness. The boy didn't smile at all. When I gave him a water pistol some visiting child had forgotten at the house, he took it as if it were a penance. He's put it away in his box, Mam, Sarah smiled proudly. Oh, yes, it's a big thing for him to have that gun, Mam. He feels he's a big man now.

They were not allowed out of the yard, unless accompanied by their mother, or sent on an errand on her behalf. They used to stand at the gate, looking out. Once Robert disappeared for the morning, and came back at lunch time with dust-blurred feet and grass speckling his clothes. Sarah had been complaining all morning: I know where it is he's gone. It's the golf course, I know. It's at the golf course. Her legs were worrying her, or she'd have gone up there after him. In weary martyrdom she gave him a long, hard hiding, but without anger.

He cried and cried, as if in a depression, rather than from hurt.

It wasn't just violent anger followed by wails.

Sarah talked about the child's escapade for days; it was in the three pairs of eyes, turned up, white, to look at her as she came out of the kitchen door into the yard; it rested upon the neck of the small boy with the sun that lay upon his bent head whilst he played.

Sarah was sadly stern with the children, and she was constantly giving them advice and admonition. The smallest transgression set off the steady, penetrating small rain of her sorrow and disapproval, seeping down all over and about the bright spark of the child. Under the steadiness, the gentle soaking persistence of her logic, the spark damped out. I told her that I thought she was perhaps too hard on the children—that was not quite it, but then I could not be clear in my own mind about what I thought might be happening to them—and she thought a moment, and then appealed, with the simplicity of fact: But they got to come against it sometime, Mam. If they learn now they can't do what they like, it won't make them angry later on. They must learn, she said—hard now—they must *learn*.

I think she bored them very much.

They went back to school, away on the train for another year. Who knows what they felt? It was impossible to tell. Only Janet, the middle one, cried a little. She's the clever one, smiled Sarah, she's going to be a teacher. She's in Standard Five already. Though two years older, and physically a well-developed young woman, Felicia was only in the same class. Plans for her were vague; but for Janet—Sarah could never help smiling in the strength of her surety for Janet—there was a place.

They never came back to our yard. During the year, Sarah's legs got progressively worse, and she had to give up her job. She went to live in the Location, and managed to get a little washing to do at home. But, of course, it was the end of boarding school; on her husband's earnings alone, with the food and rent in the Location to be paid for as well, it just couldn't be done. So the children came home, and lived with their mother, and went to school in the Location. She came to see me, troubled, I could see, by the strong feeling that they had lost a foothold; but seeing a check to their slipping feet and seeking a comfort in the consolation that although their education would not be as good, she herself would be able to train them the way they should go. She sat on the kitchen chair as she told me, slowly settling her legs, swathed like great pillars in crêpe bandage.

She did not come again herself. Her legs were too bad. She sent the children—often Janet alone—to see me. They never asked for anything; they came and stood patiently in the back yard until I noticed them, and then they answered my enquiries very softly, with their large eyes looking anywhere but at me. Yes, their mother's legs were bad. No, just the same like they were before. No, she couldn't take washing any more. Yes, they were still at school. I always had the curious feeling that they were embarrassed, not *by* me, but *for* me; as if their faces knew that I could not help asking these same questions, because the real state of their lives was unknown and unimagined by me, and therefore beyond my questioning. Usually there was an orange each for them, and an old dress or pullover that had imperceptibly slipped below the undefined but arbitrary standard of the household. Each time they came, they were—not a little shabbier, exactly, but a little slacker; a big safety pin in Felicia's jersey, a small unmended tear fraying on Robert's pants. Even Janet, in a raggy short skirt that was a raggy short skirt; not the ironed, mended, stiffly respectable, neat rag that she had always worn before. Well, food and clothes were getting more expensive; I suppose they were getting poorer.

A long time passed without a visit from them. I used to ask the other native girls: How is Sarah? Have you seen Sarah? They didn't like her very much. I don't know, they'd say, off-hand. I hear she's sick, her legs are bad.

Sarah's husband isn't working, my girl remarked one day, scrubbing the kitchen table. What, not working? I said. Then how are they managing? *Her* legs are bad, she can't work, said Caroline, shrugging. I know, I said, but they have to eat. The little boy's working, remarked Caroline. He's working in the dairy at the back. She meant he was cleaning up, washing the floor in the handling room.

I asked her to go and see Sarah next time she was in the Location, and find out what I could do to help. She came back and said: Sarah's husband got another job; he was too old for that job he had. Now he's got a smaller job. And is there anything I can do to help Sarah? I asked—Did you tell her? Caroline looked up at me. Her husband's got another job, she said patiently, as if I were incapable of understanding anything told me once.

One Tuesday morning Caroline came in from her ironing on the back porch and said: Sarah's girl's in the yard—and went back to her iron at once.

Janet was standing under the pepper-tree slowly twisting

her bare foot on the stones, and from her stance I thought she must have been waiting there quite a long time. Until Caroline noticed her. Now she said Good Morning, Mam, and came reluctantly to the steps, watching her feet. She wasn't a little girl any longer. The childish round belly had flattened to the curve of hips and the very short, stretched jersey lifted with the quivering new breasts. The jersey was dirty, out-at-elbows. In her very small ears, there were brass earrings with a round, pink, shiny bit of glass in them. She stood looking at me, her head on one side. I hear you've had trouble, Janet, I said, thinking I didn't have to talk to a child, now.

Yes, Mam, she said, very low, and the voice was still a child's voice.

Your father lost his job? I said.

Yes, Mam, she said, shaking her head slowly, like Sarah. There's been trouble.

And Robert's working? I asked.

In the dairy, she said. And looked at her feet.

And couldn't Felicia get a job somewhere? I urged, remembering Sarah's dread of her child acting nursemaid.

She's gone, Mam, said the girl, faintly.

She's what? I frowned to hear better. She's gone to Bloemfontein, Mam, she said, so faintly I could scarcely catch it. She's married, Mam.

Well, that's nice! That's very nice, isn't it? I smiled. Your mother must be very pleased.

She said nothing.

So there's only you at home now, Janet? And you're still at school? Still going to be a teacher, eh?—I was sure that she would smile now, lift up the voice that seemed to be dying away, effacing her, escaping me.

I'm at home, Mam, she said, shyly.

At home?

Yes, I'm home with my mother.—The voice was escaping, struggling to get away into silence.

You mean at home all the time, Janet? I said, in a high tone.

I'm at home with my mother. Her legs are very bad now. She can't walk any more.

You mean you don't go to school at all? You just look after your mother?

Yes, Mam, she said, looking hard at her foot with her eyes wide open. Then she lifted her head and looked at me, without interest, without guile, as if she looked into the face of the sun, blinded.

I said, still in that high tone: Wait a minute, Janet. I've got something for you. I think I've—and escaped into the house. I rushed to the wardrobe, pulled out a dress and an old corduroy skirt and rolled them into a bundle. Halfway down the hall I went back to the bedroom and got five shillings from my purse.

Out in the yard she was still standing in the same position. She hardly seemed to know where she was. I gave her the bundle, saying, Here, I think these will fit you, Janet—and then I held out the money as if it were hot, and said, Give this to your Mother.

Thank you, Mam, she said gravely, and it seemed that she had no voice at all. She tied the money away in a piece of cloth and folded the clothes all over again.

I lingered about the yard, not knowing quite what to do. Caroline was looking at me through the porch windows. Caroline, I called suddenly, Caroline, give Janet some tea, will you?

Caroline never breakfasts until eleven o'clock; it was just time. When I went into the kitchen a few minutes later, Janet was sitting at the table, her face in a big mug of tea, three slabs of bread and jam beside her. I said, All right, Janet? And she took her face out of the mug, and smiled, very faintly, very shyly, with her eyes.

I could hear Caroline talking to her, and presently Caroline came and said: She's going now.

She was standing in the yard again, her bundle in her hand. I came out smiling; I felt better for her. Good-by, Janet, I said. And tell your mother I hope she'll be better. And you must come and tell me how she is, eh?

There was no answer, and all at once I saw that she was making a tremendous effort to control herself, that she wanted most desperately to cry. Her whole body seemed to surge up with the tears that pushed at her eyes. Her eyes got bigger and bigger, more and more glassy; and then she began to cry, her eyes and nose streamed and she cried great sobbing, hiccuping tears.

What's the matter, Janet, I said. What's the matter?

But she only cried, trying to catch the wetness on her tear-smeared forearm, looking round in an agony of embarrassment for somewhere to wipe her tears. She snorted deeply and gulped and could not find anything. There was the bundle, but how could she use that? How could she cry into that?—in front of me.

But what's the matter, my girl, I said. What's wrong? You mustn't cry. What's wrong? Tell me?

She tried to speak but her breath was caught by the long quavering sigh of tears: My mother—she's very sick . . . , she said at last.

And she began to cry again, her face crumpling up, sobbing and gasping. Desperately, she rubbed at her nose with her wet arm.

What could I do for her? What could I do?

Here . . . , I said. Here—take this, and gave her my handkerchief.

The poverty is permanent. Giving material goods cannot make up for the spiritual psychological damage to those not tough enough to otherwise endure it.

oming across the dark grass from the main building to his dark house at eleven o'clock on a Sunday night he stumbled against the edging of half-bricks. End up, all sunk into the earth at the same level, they formed a serrated border along every pathway and round every flower bed in the place. The young boys had laid them with all their race's peasant pleasure in simple repetitive patterns, some memory beneath their experience of rotting corrugated iron and hessian recalling to their hands the clean daub of white zigzag round a clay hut. That would come, he supposed with a smile: they would want whitewash for the bricks.

There were roses growing behind the bricks, tattering the darkness with blacker spangles of reaching foliage. The boys had planted those too. "The man who pulled down prison walls and grew geraniums in their place" —of course the papers had got it wrong. Wrong, all wrong. Whenever things are written down they go wrong. Mistakes are the least of it; by the time they are stamped in print, words have spilt meaning and whatever of truth they have managed to scoop up. Geraniums for roses; that was nothing: but "the man who pulled down prison walls and grew geraniums in their place" —that was a glib summing up that left everything out. As a fact it was true; in the nine years that he had been principal of the reformatory, he had taken down the six-foot walls with the broken bottles encrusted on the top, he had set the boys gardening, he had helped them build playing-fields, begged musical instruments for them. The photograph of him sitting at his desk, dipping a pen. The photograph of the boys sitting cross-legged in the garden, numbers on their khaki backs, gleams of sun on their heads cropped of wool. . . . When did that moment, the moment of the article, of all the articles that had been written about him, all the lectures that had been given in his honor—when did it exist?

As his feet sounded suddenly on gravel, he made a little sighing noise, casting off the bland unreality of it. It left out everything. What had it to do with now, the sleeping darkness of the reformatory behind him, the burning starts of red and flashes of print jittering his inner sight, the quiet of the night veld darkness; the worry that filled all the spaces of his body as his breath did.

This morning he had stood amidst the voices of the boys at church service, this afternoon he had written the draft of a penal reform pamphlet, after supper he had sat with a table full of reports. His nostrils were wide with a pause of concentration, his eyes did not see. His wife sewed at some garment in her lap without looking; he was conscious now and then of the quiet wink of her glasses as she watched him.

All the day, half the night; the worry had been with him all the time. Now the surface of the day had been rolled away, and he was left with the worry, he took it with him as he went up the three steps, over her door mat made of old tire-strips, through the door that gave to his thumb as though the latch had been waiting for his touch. For a moment the night stood in the doorway: the great hard polished winter sky that shone of itself—the nick of young moon was a minor brilliant amongst white sharp stars—without answer above the low heads of the kopjes; where in that humming space was the young boy with the neat head of a lizard? Then the door stood before night; and inside, the dry closed air of the house carried the unspoken question (Have you heard? Any news yet?), the shape of the telephone waited to ring. Here you could not escape the answer coming. . . . The telephone was a nerve, ready to jump.

Somewhere the boy who had lain in the clean discipline of a dormitory and learned so quickly the ritual of the hands and the bent head that made the day pass of itself in work, lay crouched in a hovel of smoke and bright eyes and the smell of breath and beer, and stared through hours at the sluggish possibilities of idleness, rising and writhing in half-discerned murk. Saw desire melt into violence . . . wanting into having. Sat in the cave of hunched faces painted with cosy fear by the light of a paraffin-tin fire, flickered with the torn filth of old newspapers stuffed in corners (newspapers that said stupidly, crime wave . . . robbery . . . old man knifed in the street): and was free. That was the boy's freedom; that was what he had run away to, a week ago. —It was easy . . . there were geraniums, no walls.— It happened a few times every year, always with this same twinge of peculiar pain to the principal: that was what they had to run away to, these young boys; to that; that troubled dreamlike existence of struggle and fear and horror which was what they knew, which to them was freedom. The governing board said consolingly: You mustn't get too discouraged when your system has occasional failures—it has justified itself magnificently in the long run, Collins. And he smiled at them, being accustomed to having patience with people whose understanding is limited to their own capabilities of feeling. Poor Collins, they said to each other—he was a dreamer, an idealist, after all—he's just like everyone else when he's proved wrong. Can't take the blow to his pride.

The boy had been gone now for a week and like others who had slipped from the cool bit of society tasting strange in their young hard mouths, he might have disappeared into the nameless faces of the native locations or he might have been brought back again to lower his head and watch himself watched. But yesterday the telephone had rung and the dutiful voice of the sergeant had said what he had been told to say: That boy that escaped from your place last week—there's been an old woman assaulted and robbed in Jeppe, and the description of the native that did it seems to fit the boy. —Yes, yes— The policeman read slowly through the description again. —Yes, that's right.— Well, that's all, we just wanted to tell you. There don't seem to be any fingerprints, unfortunately. But we should be able to get him. We just wanted to make sure we got the description right. —And the woman, is she badly hurt?— Fractured skull, ribs broken, the lot. He used an old dumbbell that was lying around the kitchen.

The boy with the neat, small head of the lizard, the long small deft hands. As the principal felt quietly along the passage to the bathroom, he saw again, for the thousandth time, the momentary reassurance of a flash of the boy's face, lifted from his desk as you walked in. Like a pain let go, relief came: that boy could never have done it.

He closed the bathroom door with a muted creak so that he

could turn on the light without its pale square opening on the wall in the bedroom where his wife lay. The warm after-scent of a bath met him. He turned on the hot tap gently and the water was drawn like a soft skein over his hand. In the little mirror that sweated runnels of condensed steam from the bath, he saw his face with the nonrecognition of weariness in his eyes. There was a moment of childish comfort, as if, having worried so much, the whole thing was accounted for, expiated. The boy could not have done the thing; not this boy, and he knew boys, had studied thousands of them, every hour of his day, for nine years. It was all right. He had not done it. The description could be anybody, was anybody. It was only that the police happened to have the description of the boy on hand because he had escaped, and so they turned to it first. Whenever they did not have anything to go upon, they fell back on something easy like this; it made it sound as if they had done something, were getting somewhere. "The police are investigating and have the situation well in hand." He knew the police, too, after nine years. Thousands and thousands of faces, all brown, all brown eyes, all thick mouths. That was how the white people of the town saw the black: they were all the same, how could you tell one from another unless he had a scar, or a limp? So if a young boy escapes from a reformatory, and a young boy assaults a woman, it must be the same boy. —He washed his face under the running tap, trying not to make a noise, gasping at the water. And then he found the towel and dried his face, dried the day off his face and left his eyes burning, almost enjoying the relief of their own weariness. A muscle twitched relaxation in one lower lid.

Then he saw her stockings, washed and hung side by side on the towel rail.

As he saw them, the symbol of her routine, the orderly living out of the day which she maintained always, no matter what troubled her, what exile of worry she experienced beside him and with him—for sometimes he told her his worry, and sometimes he did not and she knew it just the same and suffered it quietly and kept her knowledge of it from him—he knew that she was awake in the bedroom. She was awake and worrying. Her hands did the things they had always done in an unconscious effort to keep one sane and quiet reassurance, the safety of commonplace. But the very fact of the reassurance proved the existence of the worry. He could feel her eyes open in the darkness of the next room, staring at a ceiling she could not see, and at once the comfort sucked away out of him and it seemed he had to breathe hard short breaths to relieve the weightiness of his chest. He stood there for a moment with his head jerking and sagging with the intake and release of this distressed breath, and it was all back again: Where was the boy? Had he done it? He had done it. Could he have done it? Was he the kind of boy to do it? With mechanical repetition he enacted the talk with the police sergeant, over and over again. Well, that's all, we just wanted to tell you. We just wanted to make sure we got the description right. —And the woman, is she badly hurt?— He used an old dumbbell that was lying around. We just wanted to tell you. —Yes, yes.— We just wanted to tell you. The cold of the concrete floor was hardening up through his feet as he stood dead still as though the worry were a pain that might pass if he let it, submitted to its spasm and did not give it the incentive of his own attempt to escape on which to tighten its clutch.

His feet were cold as he turned off the bathroom light before he opened the door (she would know from the very meticulousness of his care that he knew there was no sleep from which to awaken her) and felt across the passage into the bedroom. The soft slump of his clothes as he undressed moved like the darkness settling to itself; there was a pause before the long creak of his bed as he let his body down.

Across the strip of rug that separated his bed from hers he listened to her listening for him. She was so still, still with consciousness; stiller than sleep, that deepens and thins, floats and sinks, can ever be. Monday . . . Will it be tomorrow? They've found him. He did it. How can you fight against the time if it is coming, if it is to come; the time of hearing: he did it.

And though she would not let him hear her breathing because she did not want to give it away, the answering conviction of her fear slipped silently out with her soundless breath, and reached him. He did it. Oh did he do it?

But they did not speak. They would never speak. Somewhere below the face of the boy, a pang which had never yet found the right moment to claim attention lifted feebly like an eye of lightning that opens and shuts in another part of the sky. When would there be time to speak to her, to read the face of his wife as he struggled to read the suffering faces of the nameless, the dispossessed whom God made it incumbent upon him that he should spend his life reading?

The face lifted again from the desk. Brown eyes surrounded by a milky-blue rim, the flat flush ears, the sloping temples; the

neat head of a lizard. . . . He studied the face, called it up
again and again, searching.

The night was awake, listening to them.

They had both been asleep a short time when the knock
came at the door. It dinned on sleep like thunder but at the
instant of wakefulness it became a knock at the front door. The
impact of dread, met at last! exploded his blood through his
body like shot. His wife sat up for the light switch. The light
blinded them both. His feet felt over the floor for his slippers
and his arms went into his gown; the knocking was insistent
but not loud, purposeful of the necessity to rouse, but considerate not to shock. His heart beat so slow and strong that every
force of it seemed to swell his veins as if some painful object
much too large for passage were being pushed through. He
went through the house turning on light, acknowledged at last,
behind him, and undid the latch of the door. It's all right, he
was saying, Coming, coming. It was the voice that prisoners
had heard in the condemned cell, the voice that came from
somewhere, never failed him.

Ngubane, one of his assistants, stood there. With a thrill of
recognition, he knew it, the lump in his blood ran fast and
liquid and his heart torrented beats as drops of water fuse in
the rush of a waterfall. He found his glasses in his hand and
now he put them on and there was Ngubane in his neat over-
coat for it had been his Sunday off and he was dressed for
leisure. His own shoulders shielded the light from Ngubane's
face, but he saw the man's mouth parted forward in a kind of
gasp as he pressed in.

Something terrible has happened, burst Ngubane as if the

opening of the door had released the words, and as the principal fell back to let the man in and the light slipped past and lifted the face out of the dark, he saw the astonishing twitch of lost control from Ngubane's nose to lip, blisters of sweat along his eyebrows. It seemed that their panic rose and met, equal. In a trance they went along the passage together, through a door; swallowed; sat down. Their eyes held one another.

I—sir, sir . . . , said Ngubane.

I know, I know, he said passionately. The nostrils of his short strong nose were arched back, two cuts of sorrow held his mouth firm down the sides of his cheeks. His head was lifted in an unconscious gesture to bear. Ngubane, who had seen it before in him, flared his nostrils in sudden tears of gratitude for strength, the strength of Collins. My brother—he was shaking, shaking his head as if to rid himself of what he saw—my brother was killed on the road *now*. I was riding beside him and it happened . . . he was killed.

Your brother?

My brother who was out with me in Johannesburg. My brother Peter the teacher from Germiston. The one you knew —who came . . . The bus didn't see and he was riding on the outside. He was killed, I didn't even see how it happened, he was riding there with me and then he was gone. . . .

Your brother? Collins was leaning forward with his face screwed up with the curious look of questioning closely, almost as if he were irritated with not understanding what the other was trying to say.

Two strings jerked in Ngubane's neck. He nodded till he could speak again. Peter, my brother.

He was killed on the road you say? Killed on the road. . . .
Collins was repeating it to himself as if it were some marvel;
the room, Ngubane, his own voice rising so oddly, seemed to
be sliding rapidly away from him. . . . His head searched a
little for air, his hand lying on its side on the table jumped,
relaxed, faltered.

I'm sorry, he said, Ngubane, I'm sorry. He spoke quickly. His
face was burning hot. He stood up quickly and had his hand
on the man's shoulder. Tell me about it, Ngubane, he said.
Speak of it.

As a child waits for permission to weep, the man put his
head down on his arms and with his nose flattened against the
tweed, let his eyes, showing yellow-white as they twisted up
to Collins' face, slowly fill with a man's hard sorrow.

When the assistant had gone (they had given him something
to make him sleep, words of comfort, and the comfort of promised action in the assurance that tomorrow he must take the day
off to make arrangements for the funeral) the principal and his
wife sat and had a cup of tea in the kitchen. The gulp of tea
down their throats was easy between them. Come on, he said,
and she tried the kitchen window to see if it was locked and
flattened her hands against her dressing gown a moment in a
pause before she went back to bed. He pottered about, locking
up again, turning lights off, picking things up in vague question
of why they should have been left where they were for the
night. Then he came into the bedroom and got into bed. The
two of them sighed as they moved about under their covers,
settling for warmth and sleep.

Then they were still.

For a moment, you know, she said suddenly, I thought he'd come to tell us bad news about the boy.

Well so did I, he said.

She made a little sound that might have meant she was going to say something, or might have been a little sound of sleep.

He lay and the darkness came up to him, the darkness spread out to the edges of his being, the darkness washed away the edges of his being as the sea melts the edges of the sand. But just as it was about to smooth out his head and wash down the pinnacles of his features like a sandcastle, a return of consciousness rose within him and swept it away.

So did I.

It came to him suddenly and it filled him with desolation as startling and wakeful as the thump at the door. It stiffened him from head to foot with failure more bitter and complete than he could ever have imagined. *I'm sorry. I'm sorry. Tell me about it.* The boy is alive so Ngubane is dead. The boy has not done it yet, so tea can be drunk. The boy has not done it so you may lie easy in the dark. A peace can take your mind while Ngubane goes home with his brother's death. If there is room for the boy, there is no room for Ngubane. This conscience like a hunger that made him want to answer for all the faces, all the imploring of the dispossessed—what could he do with it? What had he done with it? The man who pulled down prison walls and grew geraniums. He saw himself, standing up at a meeting, the flash of attention from his glasses as they looked up to him. The silence of his wife, going about her business whilst he worried, nine years he worried, turned from her to this problem or that. If you search one face, you turn your back on another.

He did not know how he would live through this moment of knowledge, and he closed his lids against the bitter juice that they seemed to crush out, burning, from his eyes.

hen he was a child there was the privilege of ownership in going behind the counter and reaching into the glass drawers full of sweets. His small hand, like a little scoop, hung over into the cool, sticky triangles he could not see; the rim of the drawer lifted hard against his underarm. And on his fingers, tiny slivers and splinters of the sugar-stuff clung in facets of pink and green, like broken glass.

But not now. This Saturday he stubbed the toe of his new suède shoes against the deeply scratched varnish of the counter whilst his eyes flickered in automatic reaction to the cars that kept going past outside the window—whhp!—whhp!—whhp!— and he was seventeen and too young to remember. Now he could smell the store too; the smell of furzy woolen blankets, strong soap, cardboard and paraffin, heightened every now and then with the highly personal sweat-smell of an anxious native customer. After the whole week in the cool sweet sterile scent of the chemist shop in town, he could smell it now, and his mouth twitched down at the corner with impatience. He stayed on this side of the shop, where there were the biscuit showcase, the sweet and grocery counters, and a Coca-Cola container with the streamlined red opulence of an omnibus;

on the other side his father moved about the shirts and shoes, the tin trunks and blankets, and the assistants wrapped great brown paper parcels and waited, hand on hip, for the native customers to make their choice. Every now and then the old man looked up, complainingly, the flap of gray skin stretching between his chin and collarless shirt, but he did not seem to see the boy.

Let him look for me, thought his son, let him look. . . .

The cars that went by from the two towns did not stop at the country store; but Saturday was the afternoon when all the people from the small holdings round about came to give their weekly grocery order, and all the natives who worked in the brickfields and on the farms came to do their shopping. Accompanying dogs skittered out of the store before the old man; dust-powdered children planked down their tickeys and stood gasping after drinking their bottles of Coca-Cola at one breath.

But he stood half behind the counter, doing nothing.

His mother, with her long, great breasts that swung softly forward under her apron to rest upon the counter as she worked, served slowly and comfortably, kept unharassed by the habit of twenty-six years. She made a little ceremony of delight whenever she could supply a customer with some item in short supply. "The very last one!" she giggled, holding a rye loaf and waggling it as if in tantalization. And then, with a sweeping generous gesture: "Here you are! I only had six, and here's the last one in the store!"

He stood breaking a match in his fingers, watching her as if she were not his mother. There was one other elderly woman amongst the assistants; slack and heavy too, with a long time of hard work. The other two were the young, plump country girls with bright, coarse faces, small waists, and thick, red ankles bare above their flat shoes, with whom he had played and attended the village school when they were children. Then they had been together, but now with their poor Afrikaans and poorer English, their clumsy hands weighing out mealie meal, their crude pleasure in cheap, shiny earrings for their scrubbed ears, they were shy to remember that they had once splashed through coffee-colored pools after rain with him. And he was forced into patronage by their embarrassment. To think that they had once been able to talk to each other! All these country girls from the poor small holdings were the same; like pumpkin flowers. Sometimes there was something about the openness of them, though, an attraction in their not knowing about themselves, only living and smiling and wanting a trinket or a dress, perhaps. . . . This roused some faintly malicious sensuality in a young man who had played with them as children and now, apprenticed to a chemist in a great city, served, every day, women so different; women who were guarded about by convictions, knowing so much about themselves, and wrapped in their knowledge and the determination to have.

The wide, sun-colored pumpkin flower, with its large-grained texture.

Once or twice . . . His hands gently uncurled against the counter, his eyes softened with sleepiness, as after a yawn or a sigh. Beyond the window and the passing cars on the highroad he was quite suddenly back again in that day, a few weeks ago. There was a rather nice taint of sweet colored soap—dread-

ful in the cake but evidently good on the skin; a special kind
of live warmth in the neck and beneath the arms of Marius
Coetzee's daughter. Freckles on the front of her calves, but no
hairs. She had chewed a grass stalk on the way, and there were
flecks of green on her teeth; she tasted of peppermint.

But he could not taste it again; as soon as he tried to, he
woke to the store.

At once it annoyed him to think that he had forgotten even
for a moment the resentment he fretted against this business
of helping Saturday afternoon in the store. Every Saturday was
worse. He wouldn't say anything, but he'd make them feel it.

His mother was smiling at him, leaning back toward a
woman customer. ". . . seventeen," she was saying. "He's
going to be a chemist." He stared at a chaotically grubby little
boy who was teasing one of the skinny store cats. But she called
to him: "Leo! Come here, son. I want you to meet someone.
. . ." "Fine boy," said the woman enthusiastically. He stood
there, handsome with his young face unpleasant.

"Hand me down the onion pickles for Mrs. Zanter," smiled
his mother. As she filled the paper carton from the jar, she
laughed down into her bosom, eyebrows lifed. "Fancy, you
remember him, eh? You couldn't trust him with the pickles
then. Pickles! There used to be a big tub over near the door,
and he was helping himself every time my back was turned!
Mommy, he used to say, I want a 'tickle'! Give me a tickle,
Mommy. Biscuits he didn't want. . . ."

He felt the hot thrill of surliness curdle in his chest. Not even
looking at the woman, he walked away; he took a bottle out of
the Coca-Cola container and viciously knocked the cap off.

Bubbles pricked back against his throat. Immediately three very small and dirty children whose noses had run and crusted upon their upper lips thrust a jingle of damp pennies and tickeys at him and he had to stand there, serving bottles of sweet drinks to children. A big cattle fly circled his head and kept settling on his lip. More children and natives came in and he kept handing out bottles, kept taking cold, wet, hot, dry, dusty, warm tickeys. He never looked at them; did not speak.

The old man raced past, treading heavily with his heels. "Can't one of the girls do that?" he called, his face screwed up. "You should be over there. They need you. Busy like anything. And you're standing here, taking tickeys!"

And now he was deadly cold, sullen; so filled from head to foot with it that it amazed him so far as he could feel anything but his disgruntledness, that nobody noticed, nobody even saw how distasteful it all was to him. They think it's all right for me, he stoked himself. They think it's quite all right for me here. "Leo," his father shouted, using the telegraphic curtness of comradeship in work, "that red blanket in the window. Get it out. Near the corner there."

To come back to this. To belong to this. He stood crouched in the window with the three-legged cooking pots round his feet, the bright pink dresses hanging on wire hangers about his head, the bottles of brilliantine, yellow celluloid combs and tin jewelry entangled with skeins of thick purple, green and brown wool. In the dead dry air of the window, like the air of a tomb newly opened, dead flies lay sprinkled over everything; he could scarcely move without knocking something over, and as he leaned and strained for the red blanket hooked up in the corner, he lifted his eyes to the smeary glass and met on the other side the gaping faces of native shoppers staring in and the flattened tongue of a child, pressed against the glass for coolness. He added interest to the window display; a few more came to watch him.

Looking out at them with the cold eyes of a snake, he felt he never wanted to speak, ever. He would not speak again to anyone. He did not wish to say anything at all. He saw in his mind his mother and father smiling love and talk at him, and the people whom they knew grinning liking at him, and he saw himself absolutely silent in the face of them. He did not even wish to tell them. The sensitiveness of not even wanting to speak sealed his throat like a lump of pride.

He threw the blanket out into the store and withdrew himself after it. And at once he saw with the light start of the astonishment of actuality, Marius Coetzee and his daughter. Marius Coetzee! There he stood in the store, a big farmer on whose red neck wrinkles drew a map of thirty years' work in the sun. He was half-turned out of Leo's line of vision, and the boy could see his tough hand with the big spread, horny thumbnail, resting on the shoulder of his daughter. But Marius Coetzee was a passionate Nationalist. He neither mixed nor traded with anyone who did not believe as he did, in the Republic, or live as he did, assiduously treating all dark people as his abject servants, resenting his polyglot neighbors—Jews, Italians, Portuguese and English—despising his brother Afrikaners who did not do the same, and never, under any circumstances, allowing a word of English to form in his mouth. Marius Coetzee drove in to shop at the big Nationalist Co-op in the town every week! Why, he wouldn't have bought a sixpence mealie meal in this store.

The Umbilical Cord

Then?

That brown back-of-the-head, like a curly chrysanthemum, that was his daughter with him. That was her.

Oh why had Marius Coetzee come into this store; why, when he never would, ever; when he never had, ever before? Why? Why with his daughter? Not with anyone else, but with her?

He wanted to run over to Marius Coetzee and pull at his arms and make him say why he had come. He wanted him to say: I've come because of—this or that. . . .

He knew why Marius Coetzee had come. His heart, alas, no longer cool and contemptuous, remembered at once that it was only a child, and gibbering, tried to race away. His hand felt back for the door of the window and jerked and slithered it closed. He picked up the blanket.

But when he looked again, the man was still there, his hand on the girl. They did not press to the counter with the other people, but stood back, looking over the heads of the assistants.

Waiting for my father; the logic of each plain conclusion came over him in waves of helpless sickness. He was horror-stricken with the logicality with which he knew the moment was to come; the moment when the now firmly down-closed mouth of Marius Coetzee would be curving in talk like a whip and he would be saying to the uncomprehending old man, looking at him a little impatiently (what does he want of me, this O.B. swine), something has happened to the girl. How would he say it? Not like that. But that was what it would be. Your son, and now something has happened to Marius Coetzee's daughter.

Oh, how he feared her, leaning there on one leg, with the

weight thrusting her round hip out as she waited. She didn't mind, of course. She wouldn't mind anything.

Fool, fool, fool I am—his dethroned self cried inside him—stepping out in insecurity; silly, silly, silly, thinking it's easy, on your own. . . . To have cut loose and found yourself dangling so frighteningly by one thread of skin from the family. To have left yourself almost nothing at all to hang onto of the safe, of the warm, the faithful. Fool, fool, flicking the days by in pictures of the moment, coming and passing, always new ones, and no time to remember.

Not even how many weeks ago it had been. Five weeks? Less?

Marius Coetzee, standing so determined and detached, had made his presence felt in the store. Now, sure enough, he moved forward to be served by the old man. The old man leaned across the counter as if he were waiting to hear: a pocket of sugar or a bag of salt. . . .

Oh, God!

Coetzee's hard voice spoke out hard in Afrikaans to the old man; the girl was listening intently but she lifted her leg bent backward at the knee and was scratching her bare ankle.

There was nothing he could do. He did not want to be near enough to hear. But he could not go away altogether and stop trying to hear.

Now his mother had been called over. She was nibbling a little bit of cheese, as she often liked to. She smiled her good business smile. She nodded, swallowing the last of the cheese. Frowned a little, tongue reaching back into her teeth. Then with a shrug of uncertainty, came out from behind the counter, and—she was leading the girl to the other side of the shop. . . . To the rack, where women's aprons and cheap cotton dresses hung together. They disappeared behind the rack. Across the shop, across his self-despair and fear, he could hear his mother's voice, up and down, exclaiming.

He tasted the salt of the sweat on his lip. And then his mother came out from behind the rack, walking before the girl who was now wearing a bright red raincoat with a hood, and giggling at the cries of praise and admiration which preceded her. "Meneer Coetzee! Look how it fits her! I didn't think I had one left! Just this one, there was; must have been overlooked. I could have sold it over and over. Isn't it lucky, eh dear, just what you wanted. Just the one your daughter wants, Meneer Coetzee. . . ." And she was laughing surprised triumph.

"I'll wrap it up for you," the old man said. "Lena, make a nice parcel for Mr. Coetzee."

His wife called: "Leo! Bring me one of those paper bags— the big ones, eh?"

The old man, who could switch from business serenity to family impatience in the space of an aside, complained at her: "Leo's getting something out of the window. Why don't you get it yourself. He's busy."

He stood, clutching the blanket. He wanted to wrap himself in it; he clung to its thickness of folds as one sobs astonished relief on the shoulder of a friend. He stood there quite still and unseen, whilst Marius Coetzee paid for the raincoat and, hostile-jawed, went out of the store with his daughter beside him, already tearing at the package, unable to bear even momentary separation from her new red coat. Now he had forgotten her completely; there was no after-call of remembered contact with her. She had wiped herself off.

And lightly, lightly his suède brogues went across the shop; he laid the blanket upon the counter. "What parents won't do for children," the old man said, easing the waistband of his trousers. "It shows you. Did you see that? Marius Coetzee hasn't been in here for twenty years. But his daughter sees a raincoat that she wants, and we've got it, and it's her birthday—so, for her, he comes here. Children! You see, even a swine like that, for his child . . ."

The warm, weak happiness that flooded him was difficult to conceal; it was as much a problem to keep it unnoticed as it had been to make his dissatisfaction noticed. He wandered over to his mother at the provision counter. She was busy. He stood just behind her, and quite suddenly he wanted to touch her, but he had not done so for so long that he couldn't.

"Mother," he whispered in her ear. "Pinch me a pickle. A mustard one. I feel like a pickle."

ow is it that no one suspects the power of clothes?
How is it that human beings in the confidence of animacy cannot feel the cold inanimate standing always behind them; the
things they have mastered and made for themselves, standing
behind them. Just behind them, waiting: the machines and the
chemicals and the gadgets . . . and the clothes.

We do not know; we cannot sense the power of things without life. Fear is only of an unknown we believe in; and this
is an unknown we haven't even invented yet. . . . We stir toward
a discovery of it sometimes in time of war, when the missile
often seems to do more and go further than the hand that re-
leases the button could empower, but at parades and confer-
ences later we feel the world belongs to those who can talk, and
power is safe in the human mouth again.

Chairs and tables and walls about us, and the clothes we live
in; how should we think of them as existing outside of us—what
can they do for us, or to us, for we ourselves have made them.
. . . We are so confident of this that we sometimes even wish
wistfully that it were otherwise, we even pretend it is: the adver-
tisements in the newspaper promise that in a dress made by
such-and-such a firm you will lead a new, fuller, gayer life; so-

and-so's ties will make you attractive to women; if you wear Blank's coat at the interview, the prize executive job is yours. . . .

I shudder when I read them.

I remember how, when I was a little girl, my sister and I used to be taken to spend Sunday with my grandmother. Grandpa was there too, of course, but he sat up in a great chair in the corner of the cold little flat, his stiff leg stretched out at an angle, and it was Grannie who basted the chicken and made the apple pie and left us with the bedroom all to ourselves to turn into a dress shop. Most of Grannie's clothes were old, they were all in the dark colors and heavy silks that could only be becoming on a pretty seventy-year-old, and she very rarely bought anything new, unless someone in the family got married. But we never grew tired of her collection, and we sold it over and over again, every Sunday. There was always the same pleasure in opening the pale, satiny walnut doors of the wardrobe and displaying the unchanging stock of limp silks and releasing the faint pleasant smell of Grannie upon the room. Some dresses would have a long white hair, curled bright against a collar or sleeve; carefully picked off and held up against the light, it would spring back into the pattern of Grannie's waved head. Certain dresses were chosen for display models, and, their wooden hangers hooked onto the swan-neck curves of the bedposts, the skirts were spread out over the pink carpet in monkey-ish imitation of the best shops.

There were favorites of course: a brown one with coffee-colored lace that we loved (really *loved* with that softening of adoration which conquers children utterly for all sorts of odd things, seen in shop windows or other people's houses, so that they cry out in anguish: That's mine! I saw it first! That's mine!) and a coat with fur on it that we had had to make a strict rule about, taking turns to sell it.

There was only one dress we were not allowed to sell. Now just leave that alone where it is, Grannie would say, hanging it right at the end of the rail, against the wood—play as much as you like with the others, but don't take that out.

We would not have dreamt of playing with it. I don't think we ever touched it. It was Grannie's best frock. We had seen it, of course, she had taken it out to show to us, but we had never seen her wear it and we knew that it must belong to the occasions of some other world ringed wider round our own, that we would grow up into. That dress was the stranger in the wardrobe; it had a padded silk hanger that was never borrowed or exchanged, and it had never lost its own shape and taken on the shape of Grannie.

We grew up, and the game fell away from us; so gradually, becoming less real, and then—we didn't notice quite when—stopping altogether. We were almost young ladies when my grandmother died, and my mother brought home a few things she could not pass to the hands of others. Amongst them was the dress. What could she do with it? Only keep it. It hung at the back of her wardrobe for years, then on a peg in the cupboard of the discarded and dispossessed.

One day when I was twenty, a native girl walked into our kitchen wearing my grandmother's dress. She had come to see our girl, and she stood there, smiling good-afternoon at me. A sudden excitement thumped up inside me. I burned with recognition of the dress: the dress hanging aloof in my grandmother's wardrobe, and the Game. And in a dissolving flash I had myself again *as I had been.* . . . Then slowly the fusion cooled, I hardened back, away, I was grown up.

The dress was there, coldly, in positive, hard assertion.

I looked and looked at it, and I felt—for the first time, as if something were beginning inside me, a kind of knowing that was fear—the power of the dress. Not just the evocative power—that, after all, had its source in me, in the deep of my own years —but the power to *be,* in a way other than human, to persist, beyond the servant girl who was wearing it and my grandmother who was dead.

That was the first time. And it happened again, I see now, at other times and places in my life: this unexpected tripping up against a trapping of some past scene, a scrap of décor from some old stage, halting me so that I must look up and find myself face to face with an old identity. I, dragged back, entangled with myself again; but the Thing, the shabby pyjamas of a dead lover, the crumpled scarf found down the back of the car seat, the borrowed shirt that was never given back—the *Thing* persisting remote from then or now.

It was a hand shown and as quickly withdrawn. . . . But it was there, all the time.

When, in the sensuality of the mind that suddenly overtakes a group and sets them describing their own feelings, their confrontations with self, I sometimes spoke of the relationship between people and clothes and my own feeling about this, most of my friends protested that the experience was one they recognized in themselves. Oh yes, quite a few of us had felt that way —that most disturbing feeling!—and they laughed, misunderstanding, as probably even I did, the experience itself. For we saw it essentially as a *feeling*, something subjective, from within ourselves. . . . *Feelings* were of enormous importance to us, anyway; they were our cult. We were not exactly Hedonists—we had been born too late for that; its vogue had passed when we were babies—but we had a strong homemade Blakean approach, inclining toward "ruddy limbs and flaming hair" and any valid experience, pleasant or otherwise, rather than insulation.

The novelty of a new, strange feeling was a touch from life; who would refuse it? I, who have always played with my feelings like fireworks, wanting them to sparkle and burst into colored light even if it's *only for a moment,* and there's a dreary smell of sulphur after that one can't escape and that I never remember about—I, certainly, would never refuse the same old beckon of fascination. And when the finger crooked at me again that day I was going to buy my wedding frock, what would I do but laugh in self-congratulation of my daring and originality of code; saying, well, at least it's something completely new for a woman to let a former lover choose the frock she will wear at her wedding to someone else!

I was going along toward the shop in my new sense of peace with myself, when out of a building he came and stopped dead in front of me. "You?" he said.

"Well . . . !"

There was a moment. And then we fell upon one another with the noisy excitement of five years before, for he still looked like a fox with his peaked beard and bright sly eyes, and I half-hoped I was still the young ballet dancer with the Pavlova hair I had been in Cape Town then. There was a kind of thrill of revulsion in being with him again—his untidy trousers, the stains on his fingers—but our time together was so far off now, that I did not need to be afraid of it. We went to finish our exclamations over one another in a teashop, and it was there that we talked our way down to the immediate present.

All the old rather shrill and edgy impulsiveness of his way of living and talking had caught me up again by the time we left the teashop, and when he commanded, with his consciously preposterous laugh, "Look, I'm coming along with you to choose that wedding dress. It'll be a dress if I choose it; baroque mess if you do. . . ." The unfitness of the whole thing caught my fancy and my vanity and I laughed and almost clapped my hands in excitement the way a child does in the craziness of a party game.

So he chose my wedding dress; the blue crêpe dress, the blue in a peacock's tail. I wanted it, of course, I liked the sight of myself wearing it, but he, the artist, chose it for me.

What is there about the dress? I don't know. Not a distinction in the sense of fashion; nor the sleazy investiture of sentiment, the symbol taken for the reality that for a certain type of woman makes a particular dress a "wedding dress." I was not happy or simple enough to regard this frock as my *wedding dress,* yet when I wore it, afterwards, I was conscious of a quality in it. . . . —Of course the first time I had worn it, at my wedding, I had noticed nothing, being too much absorbed in a brief metamorphosis.

I wore it quite often in the first year of my marriage; it was a useful sort of frock for many places. I even remember wearing it once after I had become pregnant and was three or four months with child. Then it became much too tight for me—or rather I became too tight for it—and I did not wear it again for a long time. My son was born a daughter, and left my body changed and rounded with milk and maternity. The dress hung at the back of my wardrobe, like my grandmother's best frock.

But after some months my body was returned to me. I went out little; I had settled down to a second-best kind of response to life that I was aware of without really understanding. I looked for the lack everywhere, even in myself, but I could not find it simply because it *was* a lack—just something not there, rather than something there, and wrong. Every experience was somehow less than one; always a little ridiculous, in the end. One afternoon I found myself walking from room to room, meeting myself in a mirror, standing about. . . .

I got dressed, drove into town and went to see an exhibition of old maps. There I began to enjoy myself *by myself* again, the way I used to. With relief, the mood that had held me lately dwindled into proportion as I walked about, interested, seeing now and then someone I knew and sometimes exchanging an opinion with a stranger in the brief intimacy, like a match struck up, of a shared impression. And then, just as I was leaving, smiling my way through the gently buzzing group round the door, whom should I see in profile, hands behind back, trowel of beard lifted up in uncertainty before an exhibit on the far wall. . . .

With real friendliness and pleasure I excused myself back through the crowd. He was surprised, really glad to see me; we both laughed with that vague astonishment that comes with the unexpected meeting. I was just the person he wanted to see— he'd been going to get in touch with me, because he was trying to get suitable galleries for an exhibition of his pictures up here, and he thought I would know whom to approach. He was a man who—I am suspicious of the term—"lived for the moment"; that is, he was always completely absorbed in the friends, the mood, the philosophy of a current stage in his development, and so it would never occur to him to trade upon a past intimacy—it was *past,* and therefore nonexistent—and the suggestion that I might help him was truly naïve and merely because he knew me and my possible sphere of influence. This was a quality that made him cruel, from the viewpoint of the women in his life, and insincere from the viewpoint of men. Every time one met him, it was as if one met him for the first time. Every meeting was a fresh beginning, uninfluenced, so far as he was concerned, by previous experience of one another: if you had been his mistress last time, you might find yourself a sister this time. If you had been a friend, you might be bewildered to find yourself a lover.

Now he only wanted me to help him arrange his exhibition. I don't think he even remembered how long ago, or where, or under what circumstances we had met last time or the time before. He made the present so intense that you felt a trifle stale for remembering anything of the past. This also had the effect of putting out of mind any conscience I might have had about entering into association with him again, now that I was married. We talked exhaustively of his pictures and the exhibition, and I began at once to think, my mind pleasurably grasping at activity, where and how it could best be arranged.

I came home feeling that I had righted myself inside, that all I had needed was a change in my routine and the stimulation of strangers. Like a child who has recovered from the sulks, I felt oddly comfortable and secure at the sight of my familiar bedroom that I had left a few hours ago. I dropped my hat and bag and pulled off my dress; my old dressing gown was good enough to get splashed whilst I bathed the baby. As I passed through the room again, carrying the child to the bath, I glanced at the things lying on my bed: and saw it was my blue dress. With a curious turn, inside my chest, a momentary beating up of my heart: how odd! And this afternoon had been the first time I'd put it on since before the child was born. And I hadn't remembered that I was wearing it, and he hadn't recognized it as the frock he'd chosen. How staid we must be getting. I gave a little snort, half-stirred, half-amused, and went with my child into the bathroom.

It is difficult for me to write now on that plane of ordinariness; now when my head aches constantly and that pain keeps alive down my left arm. Now, when I sleep so little and dream so violently with dreams so full of words, it's hard to separate what I've thought since from what I really lived.

The light of that bathroom, steamy and scented, with the cheerful noisiness of the water draining out and the gasps and grunts of the baby, the pink light of the bedroom, the tent of yellow light suspended over my chair from the lamp in the study; how strangely they come to my eyes now, like the light of a serene and beautiful afternoon shining far off and difficult to believe in, through the rift in a heavy storm cloud. . . . Over there, the sun must be shining, someone says. . . . The light of all those days, when I moved so unconsciously about, pleasing myself, I find it difficult to see. The glare of the storm in my mind flickers weirdly, lifting into significance much that I hurried carelessly over at the time, and leaving in darkness the "events" that then filled my consciousness.

What concerned me then, what captured my imagination, was the affair that I began again with my friend the artist—yes, it was my doing, I began it; I think I always knew I had almost deliberately begun it: that was part of the fascination, the tightrope that I made of my life and set myself to walk. Keeping my balance with my husband and my baby and security that I clung to so abjectly at one end, and the man and the uncertainty that I had rejected but hankered after still, at the other. Everything else that I did, all the normal processes of living I performed without knowing. The women I spoke to, the flowers I planted, the pots and pans and sewing I touched; I experienced none of it. My whole being was centered on the tightrope, in an excitement of concentration that, in a different person and directed toward different ends, might have produced a piece of music, or an inspired painting.

And now, all that I ignored, that was unimportant background, streaming past in a blur, has taken on significance; the experience itself is the blur. What I keep seeing over and over again is the tent of yellow light suspended over my chair from the lamp; the baby screaming herself red in the bathroom; the pink light of the bedroom; the enameled clock ticking in the sun on the kitchen window sill. And maddening as a neon sign imposing itself against the dark at deadly regular intervals, the picture of my blue dress hanging at the back of the wardrobe. God knows I was not conscious of the blue dress at the time; I don't think I ever wore it. The "affair" was a new thing; it did not require a talisman in the shape of the dress. I would have thought it ridiculous to wear the dress; it belonged to a joke, a friendly joke before my marriage, a time when the relationship between the artist and me bore no hint of the intensity it had since developed.

Yet whenever I try to think back over that time, the dress keeps interposing; I see it hanging there at the back of the wardrobe, all the time. I see it hanging in the exact position, in the particular disposition of folds and creases that it bore on that day much later, only six months ago, when I was to appear at the divorce court, and I went, with the listlessness of habit, to my wardrobe to see what I might wear. What did it matter what I wore? It was an occasion in my life I had not previously reckoned with; a woman never thinks, when buying a dress: now, that would be suitable to wear in court. I was so dazed and appalled that morning; like a child amazed at the pieces of a vase it has broken, looking at the bits on the floor and not believing that the thing is done. . . . I kept pushing dresses along the rack one by one, incapable of sufficient concentration to make the effort of taking one out. And then there it was. Hanging on its special hanger with the belt looped up over one shoulder, and the small round bag of mothballs dangling in the neck. It hung there in the blank assertion of existence. I had forgotten it, but it had not forgotten me. I stood there looking at it, and then I felt it very slowly, examining the stitching and the pleats and tucks and the tiny glass beads, like miniature tubes, round the sleeves. And as I went over it, everything was forced back to me, I remembered myself with the disgust and fear of absolute truth, as I had been for the preceding months. All my concealed motives and self-deceptions spoke plainly back at me. I was suddenly tortured with the desire to put the dress on; yet at the same time the idea of it on my body filled me with a panic of revulsion. I could not escape from the horrible idea, like madness, almost, that the dress was *me;* that I was looking at—myself.

Six months ago. I sit here now and think: only six months back. Surely I cannot be so far from that girl on the tightrope, enjoying herself up there, not afraid she might fall? But no, I am too dizzy now, for adventure. I have been ill, and my legs are wobbly. My illness was not a serious one, nothing out of the way, but it seems to have left something behind it. There is this pain down my arm, flashing through me so bright, it takes my breath away. But I am going to do something about it at last. I have made up my mind to see a specialist. I spoke to my doctor and he recommended a heart specialist and made an appointment for me, for this afternoon. In about half-an-hour's time I must go. That's the best thing to do; find out if there really is anything the matter with me, and then I can be treated, the thing can be put right.

I keep sitting here, and yet it's really time for me to go. I shall be late for my appointment if I don't go soon. I am still sitting here. . . .

Shall I tell you something?

I went to my wardrobe just now to fetch my coat, and I saw the dress hanging there. My attention was drawn to it because it had slipped crooked on its hanger. So I pushed the other clothes that were pressing in upon it aside, and righted its position. As I did so, I noticed curious little marks, all over it. It has begun to rot, at last. Quite suddenly it has gone into little holes, all over, and at the seams the material has become quite thin, and pulled away, frayed. . . .

Irony

The End of the Tunnel

Always midday, and always summer on the road to Lourenço Marques. All through the autumn morning, as they drove, the sun seemed a strong light from the whole sky, no shadows on the warmth but the dark of cypress beside the white light of a farmhouse or a dam bright as a piece of tin; no stone, no softness of red dust, no close grass, no bird's wing unpenetrated by the steady sun. The hood of the car was hot as a helmet; two currents of air fed them through the windows. And the road rose and fell, rose and fell, and they followed its rhythms as if they moved across the body of something that breathed deeply: hills so green and softly folded you could have passed your hand over them rather than walked them; farms spreading from the homestead set white against the slope; patterns of tilled earth, swirl of the plough setting up a wake of earth, fanwise groves of orange trees with their fruit like baubles on a child's Christmas tree. His arm was red where he leaned it on the open window; her leg, turned up under her body, numb a long time now. Once she said: Look, like a late van Gogh. And without turning his head he pulled in his mouth in a slight grimace. It could sometimes happen that the dislike of an artist's vision of something could be transferred to the object itself, so that now his distaste for the artistic cliché of certain van Gogh landscapes robbed him of what would certainly have been his pleasure in the sight of three cypress, changing places gracefully as the road altered the perspective. They were aware of this, of course, as they were aware of so much that they might have left unanalyzed, and valued in one another only what came from the innocent eye. Out of the human silence—the car filled the ears soothingly with speed— he lifted his hand with the watch on the wrist and traced out something along the horizon. She knew it was not for her, it was for himself, and she smiled, also for herself.

When the road lowered itself gently down between the hills and there was a bridge over noisy water and trees that hung, transfixed, above it, she sat up suddenly and he stopped the car. Their senses pricked up like the ears of animals at the scent of water. He got out and she slid across the seat after him and they walked in the sun to the edge of the bridge, stiffly, a faint ringing in their heads, then pleasure in the flex and pull of muscles making them conscious of the unconscious effort of walking. They hung over and looked. He was not the kind of man impelled to throw a stone. She looked for a place to climb down, began to feel along the bank for the foothold of rock, but he caught her guilty smile like an adult interpreting the ingratiating wile of a child about to do the forbidden, and said: Not now. As much as you like later, but now's not the time to stop. And very conscious that she was not a child, in the fact that she could resist the impulse with the adult's knowledge of its unimportance instead of the child's urgent certainty that it will never come again, she came slowly back to the car.

Tiredness settled down upon them again; a physical weari-

179

ness that ached in the bones of her instep, a spiritual exhaustion that made him want to close his eyes. He hoped she would not speak, troubled with the fear, ever-present simply because it was foolish, that something had gone wrong, looking for reassurance from herself rather than from him. But her mind had taken refuge in her body; its bruises had come out through the flesh: she only knew that her feet ached—she pressed her instep with her palm—and her stomach, empty and yet pressing so close to her throat, gagged her. He said, rousing himself: I'll get us to Nelspruit by one. Then we'll go to a hotel and have something to eat and a bit of a break.

I feel sick, she said.

He smiled, he wanted to touch her, to uphold her, but there is a point beyond which it is humanly impossible to draw upon oneself. Love can only signal with earnest eyes behind the hand of depleted nervous energy clapped over its mouth. He drove faster, watching the road, tensing and relaxing his thigh muscle as if the small ease and unease reassured him of the continuance of everyday living, of a time unwinding simply beyond *now*.

The streets of a pleasant town you do not know create the artificial calm of impersonality; you accept the wide level stretch, a country-town street—filled with sun, like a hard beach with the tide retreated and only the sun flowing over the emptiness—a small figure in red scuttling across beside an adult, bicycles twinkling on the edges, the curbstones painted white. Nothing has ever happened at that street corner, no one has ever confronted you, coming out of that shop. A town, abstract, made of low white buildings with people made of faces and clothes, as far from lovers, friends, enemies, as the hypothetical family illustrating an advertisement, or the exclamation marks of paint representing distant figures in a landscape. For the time, *people* exist in an easy moment of oversimplification.

And the town accepted them; a man and a woman, young, with the strained vacant eyes of travelers, with the clothes and the air of strangers. She had suddenly remembered the name of a hotel that someone had once mentioned to her and they drove hesitantly down the street, looking for it. There it was; and because it was white and built round the three sides of a small bright garden where red hibiscus bloomed floridly before shiny uncut grass, they felt it was pleasant.

He jumped out of the car—he had a way of recovering his spirits with a bound, like a dog shaking itself from a sleep. His hair stuck up, thick and almost visibly alive, as growing grass is. To her, who watched herself and him as one might watch the weather in the sky, taking the slightest sign for portent, deciding the hurricane from the quick darkening cloud momentarily covering the sun, it was the complete justification for herself, for him, irrational and therefore certain as no conviction of reason could ever be.

Inside the hotel there was no one about. The reception office was empty; the lounge dim above grass chairs grouped in fours around glass-topped tables. There was the smell of floor polish, the air of a waiting room. She read the notices, CHILDREN NOT ALLOWED IN THE LOUNGE, A DANCE WILL BE HELD IN THE PALM COURT EVERY THIRD SATURDAY AT 8 P.M. ADMISSION: 10/6. HOTEL GUESTS: 5/–. Above double glass doors curtained in net there was another: DINING ROOM. He had been touching the pollen-thick stamens deep inside some unfamiliar lilies that stood in a florist's silvered basket, and now he went over to the doors and rattled at them enquiringly. At once an Indian with tired obliging lines appeared, his serving jacket half buttoned in sign of off-duty, and told them that lunch could not be served before one o'clock; the electric clock on the wall gave a little jerk to twelve-fifteen.

They were rather put out. She seemed to feel herself swaying slightly, with the motion of the car, where she stood. "It doesn't matter really. I want to go to the chemist and get some aspirin. And I must tidy up—"

"The cloakroom is along the verandah to the left, madam."

They went out again into the sun and crossed the street to the chemist. Seeing herself in the mirror behind the counter her tiredness seemed intensified to nausea again; it was impossible to think or feel beyond such tiredness. And the thought made her anxious: this was not the way it should be . . . but even the thought slipped through the slack of tiredness. The assistant looked to him to pay, seeing men and women as husbands and wives, and husbands responsible for their wives' purchases. And he already had his hand in his baggy trouser pocket, dredging up silver from notes with the suggestion of uncertainty and surprise, as if he were not sure whether there would be money there or not. Of course they had been into shops together many times before (where had they talked but in teashops and along the streets amongst the press of other people, remembering just before it was time for her to go that there was some purchase in the surface conduct of her life that she had forgotten, soap for the house or shoe polish for her husband) but now the small act was significant, it was the translation of the private, the personal into the language of the world. It was at the same time an achievement and a surrender, the sweet spurious comfort of acceptance, and the exchange of the reality for the symbol.

"What do you want to buy?" he was saying. "Do you want something else?" But there was nothing she wanted, even to please him. She was conscious of her hair rubbed into tangles against the car seat, her paleness.

In the cloakroom at the hotel (it was obviously the one meant for casual guests at dances, there was a little shelf beneath the one mirror—wan as a pond on a gray day—round which the paint was stippled with fingerprints in lipstick) her consciousness of her face was confirmed. She looked unfamiliar and rather plain. She washed in cold water without soap and dried her face as best she could on a handkerchief. She put on her cream and powder and painted her lips and her face emerged like the pale blur of a print turning clear and definite in developer solution. When it was done she realized suddenly how she had concentrated on it; how important could it be, weighed against all he knew of her, all he saw when he looked at her, the hardness of her face in obstinacy, the calm secret sleeping face the morning after love, the steady, seeking face of a child, more constant than any, always there, behind them all, beginning of them all?—That is how love is blind, not the way the platitude would have it: blind to the attractive smooth surface that does for others. Knowing this, she marveled, humoring herself ironically, in what small busyness her insight was swept aside by a quasi-magical ritual in which, for the duration of its performance, she could be as believing and absorbed as any seventeen-year-old factory hand.

When she got back to the lounge he was sitting near the basket of flowers with his arms resting curved along the chair arms. He said: I've combed my hair—as if he had just performed some great service for her. He had the sincerity which can be perfectly naïve without appearing incongruous coexistent with intellect. It irritated some people, charmed some, was on the roster of reasons friends had used to try and dissuade her. Now for this once and by this one woman he was loved for it, because for her it was also a little saddening, as of an innocence of the heart that surely cannot last. His deep joy in her being there that suddenly broke through in his face was about to release both of them, to give them back to one another as they had been, beyond guilt or reproaches, before the explanations and the legal quibble and the practical arrangements;—they were about to speak, it was coming—when a man came in through the reception office and looked at them as he passed to a door on their right.

He was in the room and yet he was not. They could hear him moving about, and some unidentified sounds rather like a fingernail being run over moiré silk. Almost at once he came out again, and, like a fanfare in his wake, a popular song opened in nasal blare. It filled the empty room peopled by chairs with a kind of shock, as if voices had spouted out of a dreaming sea, or a drunk man had started shouting in a hushed theater.

The man stood a little way off, waiting for some effect.

"That's more like it, isn't it? We're not really so dead around here." With his hands on his hips, he came smiling to them. He stood there certain of their pleasure, a man with the young-old face of a film star, the tanned face lined very slightly—it might be the sun, it might be laughter, marking round the eyes—the

clipped mustache, the good teeth a little yellowed, again perhaps nicotine rather than years, the loose silk shirt and tropical
trousers slung flatly round his hips to emphasize a lack of
paunch. He carried his youth with the conscious air of someone
who has already lost it.

For an impossible moment all three of them were listening to
the song.

It seemed to hold them down in their chairs listening to it.
He stood with his head a little on one side, his eyes cocked sideways. The girl smiled with nervous compulsion. There would
be no help from the young man, who had no notion of appropriate social formulae, who, when he could not be himself,
lapsed into selfish and unrepentant silence.

"You hear a lot of this one up your way?—Jo'burg?" said the
proprietor.

"Yes!" she said, with the ridiculous lying enthusiasm with
which one answers a child who has asked whether one drinks
milk, or believes in Santa Claus. She could have managed quite
well had she been on her own, for she had a gentle dishonest
facility with people, but in his presence she embarrassed herself, with his eyes she saw herself capering. *leap about gay /frolicsome*

"They do them to death, don't they? But this is a catchy
thing, all right. Soon as people come in of an evening, it's on.
I'll have to send up to Johannesburg for another record of it,
soon, it'll be just about worn through." He had let himself down
onto the edge of the adjoining table, resting on the palms of his
hands. He paused a moment, regarding them with a half-smile,
easily. "You've been fixed up?" The question was man-to-man
rather than in the way of business, and addressed to the young

man in the unquestionably accepted code that practical matters are for men. He could not escape answering. He said coldly, in his beautiful voice: "Thank you. We are waiting for lunch."

The voice was apparently unexpected; she saw the older man looking at him, as if for the first time, probably indeed for the first time, for this man with his slightly tarnished air of sexual gallantry would think it unmanly to notice another man. Now he looked with a faint growing air of distrust at the unimportant clothes, the intense face; perhaps here was one of those curious beings, a man who wouldn't play snooker, who wouldn't care about golf, who wouldn't be one of the boys in the bar, and yet they are men all right, when it comes to women. . . . But the record had ended; he listened for the click of the change mechanism; heard it with a slight nod.

"This one's my wife's favorite." He grinned intimately to himself. "Whenever she goes up to Jo'burg, she buys what she likes, and whenever I go, I get what I like; always remember which ones I've bought, even a year or so afterwards. She's just been up, a week ago. Only came back on Friday. Every time she comes back she's got herself a new hair-do and I have to guess what to look for when the train comes in. This time she went up in the car, though, it gives you more of a chance to get about. Do you help your husband with the driving?"

"I like to look out the window in peace." She was even a little strainedly playful, keeping it up.

"The bell's behind you," said the young man to her suddenly, as if he had just entered the room. "I should like something to drink."

"Sure thing—you get dry on the road. Where you going?

Lourenco? Good place—" He leaned gracefully to the bell before she could reach it, then, as if without thinking, pulled out a chair and sat down with them. Grrl.

An Indian with his little round tray came in for the order.

"Sherry. I'll have a sherry," she said. The young man nodded: "And a beer."

"What about you—you'll have something with us—" she said.

The man smiled carefully charming, impressing his regret at the loss of such a pleasure: "No—I never do with guests, you know—a matter of policy. You mustn't be offended. If you start it with one, you've got to do it with all. Like when we have dances here, you know, I never see my wife, she dances with one, she's got to dance with the lot."—he laughed and she laughed with him—then he shrugged it off with a lift of the eyebrows— "I don't mind. I like to see other people admiring her, as a matter of fact. I like her to dress well and keep herself attractive. And though I say it myself—well . . ." He sat back and drummed his fingers on the chair a moment, sizing up whether they were worthy of such a confidence or not. Then he leant forward and opened his mouth with a short indrawn breath before he spoke: "Do you know that we've been married eighteen years in April and we've never had a word? We've always been able to *talk* to each other; so many married couples got nothing to say after the first six months. Sometimes we wake up at night and lie there talking for hours. We can tell each other anything. Anything." He was looking straight at them, triumphant.

"Unusual," she repeated stupidly. "It's unusual."

"That's the trouble. Most people can't. We don't live in one another's pockets, we each go our own way, but it's all open. I know she goes out with fellows when she's up in town, and why not? There's nothing in it, it's all above board. It's simply a matter of . . . trust, that's it. . . ."

"Confidence," she supplied, out of a habit of offering the right word when someone hesitated. She knew that was the right word. Confidence; it was what her husband in his fatherly endless understanding had had in her. For some people it meant dances, parties, for others, concerts, exhibitions; but really it was all the same thing. She and the hotelkeeper's wife, who went out with fellows, on the parole of confidence, confidence at first so loyally and gratefully used (she would say she likes a good time, I would say civilized people must have individual liberty) and in the end thankfully snatched as pure opportunity. She struggled against this picture of herself, ranged beside the hotel-keeper's wife. It seemed that they stood grouped together and the woman turned to her with a smile of complicity and she stiffened, fought against it, but some other part of her, unemotional, insistent and unmoved by pleading, tears and indignation, held her to it. She looked across at her lover. Head down, the stain of the sun beginning to show along the ridge of his nose, his was the tempered flesh of the *religieux,* who does not feel gibes, jeers or the silent mocking of commonplace because he has too much faith to see even momentarily, his belief as others see it: simply one of a thousand crackpot cults from Jesus to Yogi. But he had known it would not be so for her. She would doubt herself with every doubt leveled at her, she would have misgivings with every misgiving of an old, hard, jealous world, scratching and whining over what it has never had for itself. You must understand, he had told her, that everyone, everything will be against you, in principle if not in person. The face of an unknown woman taking her child to school will be a reproach to you. And another time: . . . hurt everywhere, because you're running counter to laws to which your own moral nature subscribes. People will try to punish you, you'll try to punish yourself—you understand? If we're to get out of this, it'll have to be backwards, against the light, on our hands and knees, through a long dark tunnel.

"Love," the man was saying, "so long as you love each other, that's what I always say. Keep on loving each other and everything's O.K." He sank back in his chair with a furtive, admiring air, his hand lifted in a staying gesture. His voice had dropped, as if to avoid frightening the approach of some pet animal. "There she is," he said slowly. "That's her, there—" The flap door of the reception desk rose and snapped down again behind a tall bold-bodied redhead who walked across the foyer and out of the front entrance, looking straight before her and smoothing her blouse down into the waist of her skirt. As she pushed the silk in, she held a breath high in her chest to make room, and her breasts rose in their shape and fullness. Her heels chattered down the steps, her red hair swung.

"We've got a daughter of sixteen." It was pronounced in smiling anticipation of astonishment.

She said it. "You simply wouldn't credit it."

The man accepted it as his due in the right coinage. Like the softening influence of a paid bill, it expanded his interest toward them. He looked at them a moment, the young man with his unfathomable face, drinking beer with the concentration of a bird, the girl who had put down her glass and paused with her hands on her knees, as if she was about to say something that

189

she would never say, ask herself some question she could never answer.

He stood up. "You two haven't been married very long, I don't suppose."

She looked as if she had not understood what he had said, and then her eyes went slowly to the wedding ring on her finger. She wore it still, out of superstition of, rather than respect for, the law. She had put it on because she was not yet finally legally freed of her marriage, and there was the feeling that she must not damage, by anticipating its accomplishment, the life beyond it which was to come. She was fully aware of the hypocrisy of this reasoning, but that did not release her of its compulsion. She saw her lover looking at the ring, too. The ring had been a sign, signifying quite the opposite to what one might expect. When she had worn it at their meetings it had come to mean that he had nothing to fear; she was free of the marriage in herself, and was conscious of only the legal semblance of the bond. But when she had come without it, he knew by the unadorned hand that the old ties seemed to her to have reasserted their validity, and because the marriage was still alive to her in her heart she did not need its symbol on her finger. And on the presence or absence of this small ring had hung the balance between so much hope and pain.

A slow expression of delight came over the man's face as he interpreted the pause. It seemed that already, in the quirk of his mouth, he was telling yet another "honeymoon couple" story to the men in the bar, to the red-haired wife who would laugh in the superiority of her full-blown sex.

"Well never mind. You just remember"—his hand rested a moment on the young man's chair in a masculine hint—"so long

as you love each other, it's O.K. I'm talking from experience."
With a backward smile, he was gone into the dining room.

At lunch he said: "You're droopy, Theresa." It was character-
istic; his word, his snorting accusation. He had never treated
her as she was used to being treated, as the creature whose mood
must be accepted as the key to which the moods of others must
be pitched in hushed respect. As she looked at him, firmly but-
tering his bread—he did not care what he ate or when but
always ate with concentration—she felt again that awful rush of
pleasure, possession and unbelief, the divine unbidden lunacy
that came to her in spite of the fact that she didn't believe in it;
that she knew must wear out; that she knew nothing in life,
nothing in the cherished resources of the mind, could equal.
She loved him so much that love carved him out in relief from
the room of human and knife-and-fork chatter, the past when
he had been different and the future when he would be
changed, and he became the whole world lifted clear of time.
Out of weakness and incongruity, she, who never cried unless
there was not even the witness of a mirror, saw the outlines of
the crockery turn wobbly with tears. As he tucked a piece of
roll into his cheek he looked up and saw her, unable to eat, looking before her with big glassy eyes. He saw not so much the
tears as the pathetic attitude of her shoulders, as if, by keeping
quite still, they were trying to excuse her.

Suddenly he became very gentle to her, he almost fed her, he
helped her through the meal and through the faces of other
people with a special kind of restraint and sanity. He had always
shown great tenderness toward her, but this was something different, something she had never known in him before. When

they were in the car again and the town was behind them she told him—it was an unburdening almost in the physical sense, she wanted him to lift it from her mind, to carry it for her— the humiliation she suffered so idiotically, since her intelligence accepted it as merely superficially true and quite unimportant, at the slightest evidence that her behavior in their relationship could be casually bracketed with that of other women. Even as it all came out—the hotelkeeper's wife and "confidence," the sham, the vulgarity—above all the vulgarity—she knew the answers that were there for her. There was that unmoved, unvanquished part of herself that knew the answers: you have had the courage to take what you want, but now you want to be a good girl into the bargain. And there's a snobbery in you that doesn't like the thought that a woman who doesn't know anything above the level of her breasts might have exactly the same emotions as a woman who holds all the beauty of the world in her head.

But he didn't say them. He didn't say any of them. She sat there with her eyes fixed on him doglike for comfort, asking for comfort, and he gave it to her. In her downcast insistence she was demanding it of him, and he was giving it to her. None of his penetrating intuition, none of his sharp logic; only comfort, soothing. Soothing. That was what he was that he had never ever been before. And yet it was familiar to her, she clasped it to her with the closed eyes and the wriggling sigh of a child handed a familiar toy. She watched the fields go by with half-interest and the tension in her chest dissolved like a physical melting.

She leaned slightly against his arm. It's all over, she thought, we're out, we're free, it's really happened.

The End of the Tunnel

And then suddenly her mind turned on her. Soothing. That was how her husband had been to her, gentle, comforting, like a father. . . . Dismay threatened her with panic.

I'm going to make him just the same, she thought, *I shall change him into just what I've always had.*

Protest and dismay tingled through all her veins as though she had just taken some fiery drink. She threshed about wildly within herself for an escape, but there was no way out of this prison walled by her own skin and guarded by the alarm of her own nerves. With the sharp breath of confession already drawn into her mouth, she turned to him, appealing—and stopped herself, and in time, and sank back against the seat slowly and began pleating, fold on fold, the material of her dress.

The Defeated

My mother did not want me to go near the Concession stores because they smelled, and were dirty, and the natives spat tuberculosis germs into the dust. She said it was no place for little girls.

But I used to go down there sometimes, in the afternoon, when static four o'clock held the houses of our Mine, and the sun washed over them like the waves of the sea over sand castles. I felt that life was going on down there at the Concession stores: noise, and movement and—yes, bad smells, even—and so I would wander down the naked road, with the hot sun uncomfortably drying the membrane inside my nose, seeing the irregular line of narrow white shops lying away ahead like a jumble of shoe boxes.

The signs of life that I craved were very soon evident: rich and careless of its vitality, it overflowed from the crowded pavement of the stores, and the surrounding veld was littered with sucked-out oranges and tatters of dirty paper, and worn into the shabby barrenness peculiar to earth much trampled upon by the feet of men. A fat, one-legged native, with the patient detachment of the businessman who knows himself indispensable, sat on the bald veld beside the path that led from the Compound, his stock of walking sticks standing up, handles tied together, points splayed out fanwise, his pyramids of bright, thin-skinned oranges waiting. Sometimes he had mealies as well—those big, hard, full-grown ears with rows of yellowish tombstones instead of little pearly teeth—and a brazier made from a paraffin tin to roast them by. Propped against the chipped pillars of the pavement, there were always other vendors, making their small way in lucky beans, herbs, bracelets beaten from copper wire, knitted caps in wonderful colors—blooming like great hairy petunias, or bursting suns, from the needles of old, old native women—and, of course, oranges. Everywhere there were oranges; the pushing, ambling crowds filling the pavement ate them as they stared at the windows, the gossips, sitting with their blankets drawn close and their feet in the gutter, sucked at them, the Concession store cats sniffed at the skins where they lay, hollow-cheeked, discarded in every doorway.

Quite often I had to flick the white pith from where it had landed, on my shoe or even my dress, spat negligently by some absorbed orange-eater contemplating a shirt through breath-smudged plate glass. The wild, wondering dirty men came up from the darkness of the mine and they lay themselves out to the sun on the veld, and to their mouths they put the round fruit of the sun; and it was the expression of their need.

I would saunter along the shopwindows amongst them, and for me there was a quickening of glamour about the place: the air was thicker with their incense-like body smell, and the sudden rank shock of their stronger sweat, as a bare armpit lifted over my head. The clamor of their voices—always shouting, but so merry, so angry!—and the size of their laughter, and the open-mouthed startle with which they greeted every fresh sight: I felt vaguely the spell of the books I had read, returning; markets in Persia, bazaars in Cairo. . . . Nevertheless, I was careful not to let them brush too closely past me, lest some unnamable *something* crawl from their dusty blankets or torn cotton trousers onto my clean self, and I did not like the way they spat, with that terrible gurgle in the throat, into the gutter, or, worse still, blew their noses loudly between finger and thumb, and flung the excrement horribly to the air.

And neither did I like the heavy, sickening, greasy carrion-breath that poured from the mouth of the Hotela la Bantu, where the natives hunched intent at zinc-topped forms, eating steaming no-color chunks of horror that bore no relation to meat as I knew it. The down on my arms prickled in revulsion from the pulpy entrails hanging in dreadful enticement at the window, and the blood-embroidered sawdust spilling out of the doorway.

I know that I wondered how the storekeepers' wives, who sat on soap boxes outside the doorways of the shops on either side of the eating house, could stand the breath of that maw. How they could sit, like lizards in the sun; and all the time they breathed in the breath of the eating house: took it deep into the recesses of their beings, whilst my throat closed against it in disgust.

It was down there one burning afternoon that I met Mrs. Saiyetovitz. She was one of the storekeepers' wives, and I had seen her many times before, sitting before the deep, blanket-hung cave of her husband's store, where a pile of tinsel-covered wooden trunks shimmered and flashed a pink or green eye out of the gloom into the outside—wearing her creased alpaca apron, her fat insteps leaning over her down-at-heel shoes. Sometimes she knitted, and sometimes she just sat. On this day there was a small girl hanging about her, drawing on the shopwindow with a sticky forefinger. When the child turned to look at me, I recognized her as one of the girls from "our school"; a girl from my class, as a matter of fact, called Miriam Saiyetovitz. Yes, that was her name: I remembered it because it was ugly— I was always sorry for girls with ugly names.

Miriam was a tousled, black-haired little girl, who wore a red bow in her hair. Now she recognized me, and we stood looking at one another; all at once the spare line of the name "Miriam Saiyetovitz," that was like the scrolled pattern of an iron gate with only the sky behind it, shifted its perspective in my mind, so that now between the cold curly M's and the implacable A's of that gate's framework, I saw a house, a complication of buildings and flowers and figures walking, where before there was nothing but the sky. Miriam Saiyetovitz—and this: behind her name and her school self, the hot and buzzing world of the stores. And I smiled at her, very friendly.

So she knew we had decided to recognize one another and she sauntered over to talk to me. I stood with her in the doorway of her father's store, and I, too, wrote my name and drew cats composed of two capital O's and a sausage tail, with the point of my hot and sticky finger on the window. Of course, she did not exactly introduce me to her mother—children never do introduce their mothers; they merely let it be known, by referring to the woman in question offhand, in the course of play, or going up to speak to her in such a way that the relationship becomes obvious. Miriam went up to her mother and said diffidently: "Ma, I know this girl from school—she's in class with me, can we have some red lemonade?"

And the woman lifted her head from where she sat, wide-legged, so that you couldn't help seeing the knee-elastic of her striped pink silk bloomers holding over the cotton tops of her stockings, and said, peering, "Take it! Take it! Go, have it!"

Because I did not then know her, I thought that she was angry, she spoke with such impatience; but soon I knew that it was only her eager generosity that made her fling permission almost fiercely at Miriam whenever the child made some request. Mrs. Saiyetovitz's glance wavered over to me, but she did not seem to be seeing me very clearly: indeed, she could not, for her small, pale, pale eyes narrowed into her big, simple, heavy face were half-blind, and she had always to peer at everything, and never quite see.

I saw that she was very ugly.

Ugly, with the blunt ugliness of a toad; the ugliness of seeming not entirely at home in any element—as if the earth were the wrong place, too heavy and magnetic for a creature already so blunt; and the water would be no better: too subtle and contour-swayed for a creature so graceless. And yet her ugliness was without repellence. When I grew older I often wondered why; she should have been repellent, one should have turned from her, but one did not. She was only ugly. She had the short, stunted yet heavy bones of generations of oppression in the Ghettos of Europe; breasts, stomach, hips crowded sadly, no height, wide strong shoulders and a round back. Her head settled right down between her shoulders without even the grace of a neck, and her dun flat hair was cut at the level of her ears. Her features were not essentially Semitic; there was nothing so *definite* as that about her: she had no distinction whatever.

Miriam reappeared from the shades of the store, carrying two bottles of red lemonade. A Shangaan emerged at the same time, clutching a newspaper parcel and puzzling over his handful of change, not looking where he was going. Miriam swept past him, the dusty African with his odd, troglodyte unsureness, and his hair plastered into savage whorls with red clay. With one swift movement she knocked the tin caps off the bottles against the scratched frame of the shopwindow, and handed my lemonade to me. "Where did you get it so quickly?" I asked, surprised. She jerked her head back towards the store: "In the kitchen," she said—and applied herself to the bottle.

And so I knew that the Saiyetovitzes lived there, behind the Concession store.

Saturday afternoons were the busiest. Mrs. Saiyetovitz's box stood vacant outside and she helped her husband in the shop. Saturday afternoon was usually my afternoon for going down there, too; my mother and father went out to golf, and I was left with the tick of the clock, the purring monologue of our cat, and the doves gurgling in the empty garden.

On Saturdays every doorway was crowded; a continual shifting stream snaked up and down the pavements; flies tangled overhead, the air smelled hotter, and from the doorway of every store the high, wailing blare and repetition of native songs, played on the gramophone, swung out upon the air and met in discord with the tune of the record being played next door.

Miriam's mother's brother was the proprietor of the Hotela la Bantu, and another uncle had the bicycle shop two doors down. Sometimes she had a message to deliver at the bicycle shop, and I would go in with her. Spare wheels hung across the ceiling, there was a battered wooden counter with a pile of puncture repair outfits, a sewing machine or two for sale, and, in the window, bells and pumps and mascots cut out of tin, painted yellow and red for the adornment of handle bars. We were invariably offered a lemonade by the uncle, and we invariably accepted. At home I was not allowed to drink lemonades unlimited; they might "spoil my dinner"; but Miriam drank them whenever she pleased.

Wriggling in and out amongst the gray-dusty bodies of the natives—their silky brown skin dies in the damp fug underground: after a few months down the mine, it reflects only weariness—Miriam looked with her own calm, quick self-possession upon the setting in which she found herself. Like someone sitting in a swarm of ants; and letting them swarm, letting them crawl all over and about her. Not lifting a hand to flick them off. Not crying out against them in disgust; nor explaining, saying, well, I *like* ants. Just sitting there and letting them swarm, and looking out of herself as if to say: What ants? What ants are you talking about? I giggled and shuddered in excitement at the sight of the dried bats and cobwebby snakeskins rotting in the bleary little window of the medicine shop, but Miriam tugged at my dress and said, "Oh, come on—" I exclaimed at the purple and red shirts lying amongst the dead flies in the wonderful confusion of Saiyetovitz's store window, but Miriam was telling me about her music exam in September, and only frowned at the interruption. I was approaching the confusion of adolescence, and sometimes an uncomfortable, terrible, fascinating curiosity—like a headless worm which lay shamefully hidden in the earth of my soul—crawled out into my consciousness at the sight of the animal obviousness of the natives' male bodies in their scanty covering; but the flash of my guilt at these moments met no answer in Miriam, although she was the same age as I.

If the sight of a boy interrupting his conversation to step out a yard or two onto the veld to relieve himself filled me with embarrassment and real disgust, so that I wanted to go and look at flowers—it seemed that Miriam did not see.

It was quite a long time before she took me into her father's store.

For months it remained a vague, dark, dust-moted world beyond the blanket-hung doorway, into which she was swallowed up and appeared again, whilst I waited outside, with the boys who looked and looked and looked at the windows. Then one day, as she was entering, she paused, and said suddenly and calmly: "Aren't you coming . . . ?" Without a word, I followed her in.

It was cool in the store; and the coolness was a surprise. Out of the sun-naked pavement—and into the store that was cool, like a cellar! Light danced only furtively along the folds of the blankets that hung from the ceiling: crackling silent and secret little fires in the curly woolen furze. The blankets were dark somber hangings, in proud colors, bold and primal. They hung like dark stalactites in the cave, still and heavy, communing only their own colors back to themselves. They brooded over the shop; and over Mr. Saiyetovitz there beneath, treading the worn cement with his disgruntled, dispossessed air of doing his best, but . . . I had glimpsed him before. He lurked within the depths of his store like a beast in its lair, and now and then I had seen the glimmer of his pale, pasty face with the wide upper lip under which the lower closed glumly and puffily.

John Saiyetovitz (his name wasn't John at all, really—it was

The Defeated

Yanka, but when he arrived at Cape Town, long ago, the Immigration authorities were tired of attempting to understand and spell the unfamiliar names of the immigrants pouring off the boat, and by the time they'd got the "Saiyetovitz" spelt right, they couldn't be bothered puzzling over the "Yanka," so they scrawled "John" on his papers, and John he was)—John Saiyetovitz was a gentle man, with an almost hangdog gentleness, but when he was trading with the natives, strange blasts of power seemed to blow up in his soul. Africans are the slowest buyers in the world; to them, buying is a ritual, a slow and solemn undertaking. They must go carefully; they nervously scent pitfalls on every side. And confronted with a selection of different kinds of the one thing they want, they are as confused as a child before a plate of pastries; fingering, hesitating, this or that . . . ? On a busy Saturday they must be allowed to stand about the shop endlessly, looking up and about, pausing to shake their heads and give a profound "OW!"; sauntering off; going to press their noses against the window again; coming back. And Mr. Saiyetovitz—always the same, unshaven and collarless—lugging a blanket down from the shelves, flinging it upon the counter—and another, and then another, and standing, arms hanging, sullen and smoldering before the blank-faced purchaser. The boy with his helpless stance, and his eyes rolling up in the agony of decision, filling the shop with the sickly odor of his anxious sweat, and clutching his precious guitar.

Waiting, waiting.

And then Mr. Saiyetovitz swooping away in a gesture of rage and denial; don't care, sick-to-death. And the boy anxious, edging forward to feel the cloth again, and the whole business starting up all over again; more blankets, different colors, down from the shelf and hooked from the ceiling—stalactites crumpled to woolen heaps to wonder over. Mr. Saiyetovitz throwing them down, moving in jerks of rage now, and then roughly bullying the boy into a decision. Shouting at him, bundling his purchase into his arms, snatching the money, gesturing him cowed out of the store.

Mr. Saiyetovitz treated the natives honestly, but with bad grace. He forced them to feel their ignorance, their inadequacy, and their submission to the white man's world of money. He spiritually maltreated them, and bitterly drove his nail into the coffin of their confidence.

With me, he was shy, he smiled widely and his hand went to the stud swinging loose at the neck of his half-buttoned shirt, and drew as if in apology over the stubbled landscape of his jaw. He always called me "little girl" and he liked to talk to me in the way that he thought children like to be talked to, but I found it very difficult to make a show of reply, because his English was so broken and fragmentary. So I used to stand there, and say yes, Mr. Saiyetovitz, and smile back and say thank you! to anything that sounded like a question, because the question usually was did I want a lemonade?, and of course, I usually did.

The first time Miriam ever came to my home was the day of my birthday party.

Our relationship at school had continued unchanged, just as before; she had her friends and I had mine, but outside of school there was the curious plane of intimacy on which we had, as it were, surprised one another wandering, and so which was shared peculiarly by us.

I had put Miriam's name down on my guest list; she was invited; and she came. She wore a blue taffeta dress which Mrs. Saiyetovitz had made for her (on the old Singer on the counter in the shop, I guessed) and it was quite nice if a bit too frilly. My home was pretty and well-furnished and full of flowers and personal touches of my mother's hands; there was space, and everything shone. Miriam did not open her eyes at it; I saw her finger a bowl of baby-skinned pink roses in the passing, but all afternoon she looked out indifferently as she did at home.

The following Saturday at the store we were discussing the party. Miriam was telling Mrs. Saiyetovitz about my presents, and I was standing by in pleasurable embarrassment at my own importance.

"Well, please God, Miri," said Mrs. Saiyetovitz at the finish, "you'll also have a party for your birday in April. . . . Ve'll be in d'house, and everyting'll be nice, just like you want."— They were leaving the rooms behind the shop—the mournful green plush curtains glooming the archway between the bedroom and the living room; the tarnished samovar; the black beetles in the little kitchen; Miriam's old black piano with the candlesticks, wheezing in the drafty passage; the damp puddly yard piled with empty packing cases and eggshells and banana skins; the hovering smell of fish frying. They were going to live in a little house in the township nearby.

But when April came, Miriam took ten of her friends to the Saturday afternoon bioscope in celebration of her birthday. "And to Costas Café afterwards for ice cream," she stated to her mother, looking out over her head. I think Mrs. Saiyetovitz was disappointed about the party, but she reasoned then, as always, that as her daughter went to school and was educated and could speak English, whilst she herself knew nothing, wasn't clever at all, the little daughter must know best what was right and what was *nice*.

I know now what of course I did not know then: that Miriam Saiyetovitz and I were intelligent little girls into whose brains there never had, and never would, come the freak and wonderful flash that is brilliance. Ours were alabaster intellects: clear, perfect, light; no streaks of dark, unknown granite splitting to reveal secret veins of brightness, like thin gold, between stratum and stratum. We were fitted to be good schoolteachers, secretaries, organizers; we did everything well, nothing badly, and nothing remarkably. But to the Saiyetovitzes, Miriam's brain blazed like the sun, warming their humbleness.

In the year-by-year passage through school, our classmates thinned out one by one; the way seedlings come up in a bunch to a certain stage in their development, and then by some inexplicable process of natural selection, one or two continue to grow and branch up into the air, whilst the others wither or remain small and weedy. The other girls left to go and learn shorthand-and-typewriting: weeded out by the necessity of earning a living. Or moved, and went to other schools: transplanted to some ground of their own. Miriam and I remained, growing straight and steadily. . . .

During our matriculation year a sense of wonder and impending change came upon us both; the excitement of coming to an end that is also a beginning. We felt this in one another, and so were drawn together in new earnestness. Miriam came to study with me in the garden at my house, and oftener than ever, I slipped down to the Concession stores to exchange a book or discuss work with her. For although they now had a house, the Saiyetovitzes still lived, in the wider sense of the word, at the store. When Miriam and I discussed our schoolwork, the Saiyetovitzes crept about, very quiet, talking to one another only in hoarse, respectful whispers.

It was during this year, when the wonder of our own capacity to learn was reaching out and catching into light like a veld fire within us, that we began to talk of the University. And, all at once, we talked of nothing else. I spoke to my father of it, and he was agreeable, although my mother thought a girl could do better with her time. But so long as my father was willing to send me, I knew I should go. Ah yes, said Miriam. She liked my father very much; I knew that. In fact she said to me once— it was a strange thing to say, and almost emotionally, she said it, and at a strange time, because we were on the bus going into the town to buy a new winter coat which she had wanted very badly and talked about longingly for days, and her father had just given her the money to get it—she said to me: You know, I think your father's just right. —I mean, if you had to choose somebody, a certain kind of person for a father, well, your father'd be just the kind you'd want.

When she broached the subject of University to her parents, they were agreeable for her to go, too. Indeed, they wanted her to go almost more than she herself did. But they worried a great deal about the money side of it; every time I went down to the store there'd be a discussion of ways and means, Saiyetovitz slowly munching his bread and garlic polony lunch, and worrying. Miriam didn't worry about it; they'll find the money, she said. She was a tall girl, now, with beautiful breasts, and a large, dark-featured face that had a certain capable elegance, although her father's glum mouth was unmistakable and on her upper lip faint dark down foreshadowed a heavy middle-age. Her parents were peasants; but she was the powerful young Jewess. Beside her, I felt pale in my Scotch gingery-fairness: lightly drawn upon the mind's eye, whilst she was painted in oils.

We both matriculated; not so well as we thought we should, but well enough; and we went to the University. And there too, we did well enough. We had both decided upon the same course: teaching. In the end, it had seemed the only thing to do. Neither of us had any particular bent.

It must have been a hard struggle for the Saiyetovitzes to keep Miriam at the University, buy her clothes, and pay for her board and lodging in Johannesburg. There is a great deal of money to be made out of native trade concessions purchased from the government; and it doesn't require education or trained commercial astuteness to make it—in fact, trading of this sort seems to flourish in response to something very different: what is needed is instinctive peasant craftiness such as can only be found in the uneducated, in those who have scratched up their own resources. Storekeepers with this quality of peasant craft made money all about Mr. Saiyetovitz, bought houses and motorcars and banded their wives' retired hands with diamonds in mark of their new idleness. But Mr. Saiyetovitz was a peasant without the peasant's craft; without that flaw in his simplicity that might have given him checks and deeds of transfer to sign, even if he were unable to read the print on the documents. . . . Without this craft, the peasant has only one thing left to him: hard work, dirty work, with the sweet, sickly body-

smell of the black men about him all day. Saiyetovitz made no
money: only worked hard and long, standing in his damp shirt
amidst the clamor of the stores and the death-smell from the
eating house always in his nose.

Meanwhile, Miriam fined down into a lady. She developed
a half-bored, half-intolerant shrug of the shoulders in place
of the childish sharpness that had been filed jagged by the rub-
rub of rough life and harsh contrasts. She became soft-voiced,
where she had been loud and gay. She watched and conformed;
and soon took on the attitude of liberal-mindedness that sets the
doors of the mind slackly open, so that any idea may walk in and
out again, leaving very little impression: she could appreciate
Bach and Stravinsky, and spend a long evening listening to
swing music in the dark of somebody's flat.

Race and creed had never meant very much to Miriam and
me, but at the University she sifted naturally towards the young
Jews who were passing easily and enthusiastically, with their
people's extraordinary aptitude for creative and scientific work,
through Medical School. They liked her; she was invited to
their homes for tennis parties, swimming on Sundays, and
dances, and she seemed as unimpressed by the luxury of their
ten-thousand-pound houses as she had been by the contrast of
our clean, pleasant little home, long ago, when she herself was
living behind the Concession store.

She usually spent part of the vacations with friends in
Johannesburg; I missed her—wandering about the Mine on my
own, out of touch, now, with the girls I had left behind in the
backwater of the small town. During the second half of one
July vacation—she had spent the first two weeks in Johannesburg—she asked me if she could come and spend Sunday at my

home, and in the afternoon, one of the Medical students arrived at our house in his small car. He had come from Johannesburg; Miriam had evidently told him she would be with us. I gathered her parents did not know of the young man's visit, and I did not speak of it before them.

So the four years of our training passed. Miriam Saiyetovitz and I had dropped like two leaves, side by side into the same current, and been carried downstream together: now the current met a swirl of dead logs, reeds, and the force of other waters, and broke up, divided its drive and its one direction. The leaves floated clear; divergent from one another. Miriam got a teaching post in Johannesburg, but I was sent to a small school in the Northern Transvaal. We met seldom during the first six months of our adult life: Miriam went to Capetown during the vacation, and I flew to Rhodesia with the first profits of my independence. Then came the war, and I, glad to escape so soon the profession I had once anticipated with such enthusiasm, joined the nursing service and went away for the long, strange interlude of four years. Whilst I was with a field hospital in Italy, I heard that Miriam had married—a Doctor Somebody-or-other: my informant wasn't sure of the name. I guessed it must be one of the boys whom she had known as students. I sent a cable of congratulation, to the Saiyetovitzes' address.

And then, one day I came back to the small mining town and found it there, the same; like a face that has been waiting a long time. My Mother, and my Dad, the big wheels of the shaft turning, the trees folding their wings about the Mine houses; and our house, with the green, square lawn and the cat watching the doves. For the first few weeks I faltered about the old life, feeling my way in a dream so like the old reality that it hurt.

There was a feel about an afternoon that made my limbs tingle with familiarity. . . . What . . . ? And then, lying on our lawn under the hot sky, I knew: just the sort of glaring summer afternoon that used to send me down to the Concession stores, feeling isolated in the heat. Instantly, I thought of the Saiyeto-vitzes, and I wanted to go and see them, see if they were still there; what Miriam was doing; where she was, now.

Down at the stores it was the same as ever, only dirtier, smaller, more chipped and smeared—the way reality often is in contrast with the image carried long in the mind. As I stepped so strangely on that old pocked pavement, with the skeleton cats and the orange peel and the gobs of spit, my heart tightened with the thought of the Saiyetovitzes. I was in a kind of excite-ment to see the store again. And there it was; and excitement sank out at the evidence of the monotony of "things." Blankets swung a little in the doorway. Flies crawled amongst the shirts and shoes posed in the window, the hot, wet, sickening fatty smell came over from the eating house. I met it with the old revulsion: it was like breathing inside someone's stomach. And in the store, amongst the wicked glitter of the tin trunks, be-neath the secret whispering of the blankets, the old Saiyetovitzes sat glumly, with patience, waiting. . . . As animals wait in a cage; for nothing.

In their delight at seeing me again, I saw that they were older, sadder; that they had somehow given themselves into the weight of their own humbleness, they were without a pinnacle on which to fix their eyes. Whatever place it was that they looked upon now, it was flat.

Mr. Saiyetovitz's mouth had creased in further to the dead folds of his chin; his hair straggled to the rims of his ears. As he spoke to me, I noticed that his hands lay, with a curious helpless indifference, curled on the counter. Mrs. Saiyetovitz shuffled off at once to the back of the shop to make a cup of tea for me, and carried it in, slopping over into the saucer. She was uglier than ever, now, her back hunched up to meet her head, her old thick legs spiraled in crêpe bandages because of varicose veins. And blinder too, I could see: that enquiring look of the blind or deaf smiling unsure at you from her face.

The talk turned almost at once to Miriam, and as they answered my questions about her, I saw them go inert. Yes, she was married; had married a doctor—a flicker of pride in the old man at this. She lived in Johannesburg. Her husband was doing very well. There was a photograph of her home, in one of the more expensive suburbs; a large, white modern house, with flower borders and a fishpond. And there was Miri's little boy, sitting on his swing; and a studio portrait of him, taken with his mother.

There was the face of Miriam Saiyetovitz, confident, carefully made-up and framed in a good hairdresser's version of her dark hair, smiling queenly over the face of her child. One hand lay on the child's shoulder, a smooth hand, wearing large, plain, expensive diamond rings. Her bosom was proud and rounded now—a little too heavy, a little overripe in the climate of ease.

I could see in her face that she had forgotten a lot of things.

When his wife had gone into the back of the shop to refill my teacup, old Saiyetovitz went silent, looking at the hand that lay before him on the counter, the fingers twitching a little under the gaze.

The Defeated

It doesn't come out like you think, he said, it doesn't come out like you think.

He looked up at me with a comforting smile.

And then he told me that they had seen Miriam's little boy only three times since he was born. Miriam they saw hardly at all; her husband never. Once or twice a year she came out from Johannesburg to visit them, staying an hour on a Sunday afternoon, and then driving herself back to Town again. She had not invited her parents to her home at any time; they had been there only once, on the occasion of the birth of their grandson.

Mrs. Saiyetovitz came back into the store: she seemed to know of what we had been speaking. She sat down on a shot-purple tin trunk and folded her arms over her breast. Ah yes, she breathed, ah yes. . . .

I stood there in Miriam's guilt before the Saiyetovitzes, and they were silent, in the accusation of the humble.

But in a little while a Swazi in a tobacco-colored blanket sauntered dreamily into the shop, and Mr. Saiyetovitz rose heavy with defeat.

Through the eddy of dust in the lonely interior and the wavering fear round the head of the native and the bright hot dance of the jazz blankets and the dreadful submission of Mrs. Saiyetovitz's conquered voice in my ear, I heard his voice strike like a snake at my faith: angry and browbeating, sullen and final, lashing weakness at the weak.

Mr. Saiyetovitz and the native.

Defeated, and without understanding in their defeat.

A Commonplace Story

nce a music teacher, always a music teacher, her mother had said. But really, it had seemed so much nicer than working in a shop or an office all day. There was something refined about being able to say, "I have my mornings to myself, you know." When her sister had gone off to count change up in the little brown cage above the counters of the draper's shop, she could sit on the stoep in the sun, doing a bit of sewing; it wasn't until after school came out, when she'd already had her early lunch, that the pupils began coming at regular half-hour intervals.

She had started off thinking she might do a great number of things with her "free time," but actually the five mornings were nibbled away doing household shopping for her mother, or tidying out the cupboards; the vague promise of them evaporated, and was soon forgotten. Her profession—as she liked to think of it—was quite uneventful. Twice a year the pupils took examinations, and once a year, at Christmas time, she held a party for them, with "best frocks" and jellies and jujube sweeties that her mother said were "quite good enough." She gave lessons every afternoon from two till six, except Saturdays, when she taught in the morning. And before she was married she had a theory class on Mondays and Wednesdays, but now that was changed to Wednesdays and Fridays because Monday was washday.

It was very useful that she "had her music" and she could continue teaching after she was married. She was twenty-eight and a tall, pale, freckled girl with a naturally glum expression which was unfair, because she was good-natured, and she married the only man who ever asked her: a silent, small-featured fitter who had worked on the mine with her father for some years. He had been married before, and he had a permanently subdued nature, as if something had once weighed on his mind and left a dent there. He went off to work on a motor-bicycle at six o'clock each morning, wearing his old working clothes and a worn blue cap, and he came home at half-past four every afternoon dirty and quieter than ever, and his wages were not enough to pay for the rent of the small rough-cast house, the installments on the furniture, and the food. So it was most convenient that Agnes had her music.

The wooden board with "Miss Agnes Bretherton, A.T.C.L., Teacher of Pianoforte, Theory and Harmony" painted on it, was removed from her parents' garden to her own front gate. There it hung, year in, year out as from two to six each afternoon the procession of children passed in and out clanging the gate behind them. The gate screeched as they opened it, clanged as it shut; she meant to ask her husband to oil it, but somehow it never got done, and as the gate grew older and rustier, the screech became shriller: still, it served to mark off one lesson from the next; when she heard it—eeeeeeee-ch-k-langg!—she lifted her hands from the treble end of the piano, where beneath her habit-firm fingers the voice of the piano said emphatically what the faltering voice produced by the pupil was mumbling a few octaves down, and rising from her chair, marked the Czerny study with two ticks and the date at the end of the bar. "Practice that for next time, dear."

And that lesson was over; and another was ready to begin, as the next small girl clattered up the steps.

She had two babies; her long, sapless body soon returning to its wintry sparseness after this brief flowering. People thought it amazing the way the babies slept through the afternoons, while scales climbed up and down the air, and pupils trailed in and out the house. Really there was nothing remarkable about it; the unvarying pattern of sound had rocked the mysterious seas of the womb in which they had lain; they were born into a world where the same scales and studies and nocturnes hung about on the edge of sleep. They slept; in the next room the metronome tock-tock-tock-tock-ed and the afternoon sun spattered in through the shrunken lace curtain and touched the bent head of the struggling pupil and the wispy, patient head of the teacher. In the winter, a round, three-footed oil stove stood near the piano, giving off a slight, sickly heat to warm the short, stiff hands of the children and the bony, earnest hands of Agnes—Agnes had always been ashamed of her hands; the spatulate thumbs, the square, bluish nails, the unpleasantly dry skin, so faded round the nails.

And in the summer, in the dreadful torpid no-time of afternoon heat, the sun breathed hot breath through the green blinds that kept him out, and the room swam in hot and dazzling semi-dark. The white teeth of the piano gleamed through; and the succession of small, sweaty, inept fingers left watermarks of dirt upon them. The metronome ticked like a beetle. A trapped bee droned round the ceiling: *and* one-and-two-and-*three*-four, one-and-two-and-*three*-four, went Agnes' voice. The sun hammered at the blinds. . . .

Released, the child broke out into the summer afternoon, lay on the grass, lifting her arms to the shade, letting the breeze trickle down inside her clothes. But back in Agnes' living room the next child was wriggling onto the warm piano stool; now;—one, two! one, two!

Slowly the sun drew away from the day, the pale sky was cool; the earth rested; in gardens round about hoses hissed the smell of water into the air. Her husband was in his shirt sleeves in the yard, wiring a rabbit hutch, the two little boys trotting about him, faces streaked with red sand. Through the windows came the endless sound of the piano, that they did not hear. The gate clanged behind the last dazed pupil; a chip of a star opened in the pink sky.

Agnes went into the bathroom and wrung out a cloth to wipe the keyboard. The room was exhausted; the poor shabby carpet trampled with dust, the vase of roses deathly pale and scentless. She lifted one white bloom; its head dropped, limp. She felt that she scarcely breathed at all; she sat there. After a few minutes she discovered that she had forgotten to turn off the metronome; it was still going tock-tock-tock-tock.

Of course, she wasn't always going to teach. Sometime, she would give it up. But that time was always coming; it was never here. There were doctor's bills to pay for the children; she and her husband had reproduced themselves too faithfully: the children were not robust, the younger boy small and whining, the elder tall and with a face so like his mother's that it really did seem that nature had given way to malicious impulse. Looking at him with his glum, pale face, so odd on a child, she realized for the first time how plain she herself was. It came to her like a statement, through the face of her child.

Her husband's position did not improve. He was a painstaking, dutiful worker, but it was obvious that no one would think of promoting him. They did not expect it: she did not expect it of him, and he did not expect it of himself. He was in the clutch of drabness; the strongest enemy to fight, in the end.

Once every few years they went away for a fortnight, down to the sea, but there was a notice in the paper, and in the back of her mind, all the time: ". . . Music Studio will re-open on January 15th." The pupils lay in wait for her. When they grew up, or went away to school, or stopped learning to play the piano, smaller brothers and sisters were old enough to begin. Five-finger exercises, notes with one tail, notes with two tails. . . . The small house seemed to belong to the pupils; never to be quite free of them, for their feet had worn a thin path across the orange-and-brown living-room carpet, from the door to the piano, and the legs of the dining-room table were nicked and scratched where their feet swung against it whilst they were doing their theory. The powdery dust marks of their small broad feet permanently freckled the stoep; the squeaky gate sagged on its hinges from too many joyous pushes. It seemed that carelessly, guiltlessly, the day-by-day, year-by-year procession of children innocently wore away her life; powdered her down, she who was so brittle and sapless, unable to renew herself. . . .

Like a fragment of twig, falling in interrogation upon a stagnant pool, a faint stir threatened in her life.

A Commonplace Story

The mothers of three pupils wished their children to take music as a subject for matriculation, and came rather dubiously to see her about it. At first she felt trapped. She knew that her own knowledge was faded and inadequate, but she feared for her reputation should she admit herself unqualified. Then the idea came to her that perhaps she herself might take lessons, from some master in Johannesburg, and mark in fresh bold ink the faint penciled remnants of counterpoint still lingering in her mind. So in the face of the suspicious mothers, she timidly asserted, yes, she would be able to prepare the children for matriculation, and she made arrangements to take a weekly lesson from a well-known teacher in Johannesburg.

It would cost three guineas a month for the lessons, but after all, it was spending money in order to make it: she felt quite a little businesslike thrill at the thought. On the Friday morning of the first lesson she put on her costume and a pink knitted silk jumper and her navy felt hat, pinned the felt posy her mother had given her one Christmas on her lapel, and clanging the gate behind her, went off to the station. She felt as nervous as a schoolgirl; the posy bobbed on her thin chest as she breathed with a flutter. She sat in the train, waiting for it to jerk off, and the hot sun brought out the leather-smell of the carriage seats. She realized suddenly that the particular smell of the house was away from her; a faint clinging smell of soup, dusty sheets of music, and the orange juice smeared round the mouths of the two little boys. . . . She was out of it.

But once she was in Johannesburg and she had had the lesson and was walking about uncertainly, spending the half-hour between trains which was to be her own in the luxury of window-gazing—the whole thing dwindled colorless and flat. Leaden, the little adventure sank to the bottom of her stagnant life. She could not support the newness, the change; she was "out of it," out of the child-battered house, the dusty garden where nothing grew, the smell of piled music and soup and oranges. But was there anything left of her? People passed this way and that in the street; women, glowing the warm self-absorption of the cared-for, came into the tearoom where she sat drinking a cup of coffee, women who talked and laughed and met one another and made plans. People came face to face with her, crossing the street, and they did not see her. She wandered about, uncertain as a ghost. In a strip of mirror in a shop window she came face to face with herself, and saw with a shrug the incredible dreari-ness of her appearance. A dead tree standing on through sum-mer after summer, whilst the green leaves of other trees fluttered and jostled about it. That pale face where even the freckles were faded, that ridiculous old felt hat, the costume that hung, the ugly flower that didn't look right; the glum expression she was always surprised to see because she didn't feel it, inside her. She was as dry as a stick; and she knew it. She was nothing at all. Nothing, except when she sat in the chair at the treble end of the piano, leading the pupil's blurred tune with her own clear, loud hand, and counting the time in an encouraging voice. It was a shock to her; all these years she had gone on, unquestion-ingly. And now she knew that there was nothing left of her. She discovered the treadmill she had patiently walked for years. A music teacher! That was all. A music teacher! And for how long? For always, until the hands stopped playing and the voice didn't count any more; and so the music teacher joined the rest of her that had died so quietly and slowly that no one noticed. . . .

A music teacher! Until she died.

And quite suddenly she was dead.

On the journey home, the train gave a horrifying shudder, jumped the lines, and thundered over on to its side. A confusion of glass, solid wood and a steel luggage rack struck her as she was flung beneath it to the floor.

When she found herself she knew she was dead. She sat quietly on a sort of knoll, and the thought came to her: I shall not teach music any more. She lay back and closed her eyes. And presently they came to fetch her, and she was brought before a council. "Well, what would you like to do?" they asked kindly. "What sort of work would you like to do here?"

She looked bewildered. What . . . ?

"Here you may do what you wish, any sort of occupation you feel yourself fitted for. There are no square pegs in round holes. You continue your life usefully, but doing whatever you are really fitted for. Economic necessity vanishes."

She tried to think of something she might do. Paint? Cook? Act? Be a lady of fashion? As if she could. Be a typist? There was nothing she could do, nothing she knew. . . .

"Well . . . well, you see I'm a music teacher . . . ," she said, very muffled.

"Ah? Good. Very well," they smiled, "of course that can be quite easily arranged"—and ticked her name off the list.

Once a music teacher, always a music teacher, said the gossipy, informative voice of her mother.

Waking up in a public ward at the hospital (her husband had thought they really couldn't afford a private one) she did not remember she had dreamed she was dead. She had been slightly concussed by the accident, but was unhurt. Her good little husband sat on the edge of a chair, holding his working cap in his hands, watching her face.

She gave him some instructions about the house, told him what to do for the children; she would be home in a day or two. He took it all in very earnestly; he was a nice enough little man, and worried about her, in the shamefaced, unemotional way of his kind. "All right," he said. "I'll be up again this evening."—And he tiptoed creakily to the door. There he stopped, turned uncertainly, and said: "Oh, about the pupils—they'll be turning up. What am I to tell them?"

There was a pause. Her eyes were closed.

"Tell them," she said, not opening her eyes, "tell them I'll take them as usual on Monday."

Monday Is Better Than Sunday

The smell of kippers browning in butter brought morning to the flat. The young ones lay late in bed on Sundays but the old master was about the bathroom already, stropping his razor with the slap! slop! slap! of a horse trotting sharply in the street below. "Lizabeth!" he bellowed. "Get my breakfast! Have it ready." His slippers thumped up and down the passage. He stood in the kitchen doorway, pinkly shaven, stomach protruding in his white bowling trousers: "Where's my breakfast?"

Elizabeth carried into the dining room—that, closed against the morning, held last night's liver and cigar smell—the butter and sea scent of kipper, the orange juice, cold and bright in its glass, and the two large squares of brown toast. Out she went again, walking quietly in someone else's shoes, her sullen head in its blue knitted cap.

"Lizabeth!" the voice choked with impatience. "Where's the tea?" She took the teapot off the stove and brought it to the table. He grunted.

"Why don't you see that the milk's hot? Why do I always have to tell you."

She felt the jug and then went out.

Soon she heard him, bustling and aggressive in the bedroom,

his wife's voice coming up from the pillow: "What's it, Daddie?"—"Blooming girl—does not listen. If I've told her once—"

On his way out, she heard him at the flowers in the lounge; a rustle of red gladiolus petals curled like tongues for want of fresh water, snap of the smooth, crisp straight stem. "Elizabeth!" he said as he passed to the front door. "Put water in the flowers, eh?"

"What baas?"

"You must put water in the flowers. You don't do it. Give them all fresh water." He stood looking at her out of his small, restless eyes like the little eyes of a big animal, bison or rhinoceros, always uncertain whether or not to charge; but he could think of nothing else. He grunted and left.

Elizabeth took the fowl out of the refrigerator and began to clean it. Out of the cold white corpse—the skin puckered in a pattern, as if stitched where the feathers had been plucked—came the red guts in her brown hand. Blood flowed, alive and cold from the refrigerator, over her fingers, over the old wide yellow wedding ring that had grown its place into her finger as a hoop of wire, tied round the trunk, makes itself part of the tree.

There was the long-drawn sigh of the lavatory being flushed, and then the missus appeared in the kitchen doorway, blinking in her checked dressing gown. She was a fair woman with thin hair slipping the curlers on her pink scalp, and as she was much alone and no one talked to her very much, her mouth always moved a little, soundlessly, around the things she might have said. She looked slowly round the kitchen and then went back to the bathroom.

Elizabeth shook the pan in which the crumbly butter from

the kipper had coiled into a surface like thin ice over the liquid beneath, and taking two more of the plump fish from their grocer's wrapping, dropped them in.

The sizzling brought the missus back. Yet she did not like to say what she had come for. She opened the refrigerator, moved something inside it, and then shut it again. She wandered over to the stove. "Who're these for, Elizabeth?" she whispered; her voice was always the quietest, softest possible.

"It's for the young baas and the little missus," explained Elizabeth boldly, letting the volume of water from the tap run through the fowl.

"But they're not ready yet," said the missus, wanting to have it explained. "They're not up yet?"

"I did think they were," said Elizabeth, tucking the fowl's wings into position.

There was a moment's silence.

"They're still asleep," said the mistress, sibilant with concern. "Still in bed . . ."

There was no answer but a spurt from the pan. She turned and left. She went to knock timidly on her son's door, and when there was no answer, timidly entered. But the bed was empty of him, sagging empty of his shape as a glove from the hand that has filled it. She found him in the bathroom. "The girl's made your breakfast, son," she said. "Tell Adelaide to hurry up. Everything's cooked and ready."

"But good God, what for?" he said, the faded animation of the night before lying like the shadow of his beard upon his face. Toothpaste foamed at his mouth. He spat. "Del," he called, "you can have your bath afterwards—we've got to have breakfast now."

Her hair hung heavily on her shoulders, her thickly white hand hung heavily on the porridge spoon; it was too early for her to talk, and he held the Sunday paper in one hand and fed himself dabs of porridge with the other.

Elizabeth came in and took away the porridge plates.

"She doesn't say good morning," said the girl. "Fool she is," he said, reading. "Just goes and makes breakfast whether anyone's ready for it or not." The more he spoke of it, the more it irritated him. "Doesn't bother to ask; just goes ahead and does it."

The girl, who wanted to be liberal and to recognize her personal conception of the equality of servants and masters, but didn't quite know how to convey this expansion of the spirit, tried to think of some explanation, but couldn't.

In came Elizabeth.

"But I don't eat kipper," cried the girl, prodding the beige fat fish steaming tenderly beside the egg on her plate.

"Go on—. It's nice for a change," he said, still reading.

"I never eat kipper," she said, looking at it on her plate.

Elizabeth stood there with her tray, offering no solution, giving no reaction; merely waiting to see what was to be done.

"Here," he said, "I'll take it." He flipped it onto his plate, then said with dismay, "No, I can't eat all that.—You can have it, Elizabeth. I'll leave it for you, eh?" And he put it aside.

"Thank you, Elizabeth," said the girl, when the tea was brought in. She felt beholden to her. But Elizabeth's dull-black face accepted nothing.

After breakfast the bath water ran, the young people went in and out, the girl carried her pots of cosmetic, her hair nets and pins and combs from mirror to mirror. In the room she had left, shoes met in social groups on the floor, stockings snagged on Elizabeth's hard hands as she lifted discarded clothes from the bed in order to make it. Down at the bottom a hot-water bottle, now cold as a jellyfish, wore a knitted cover of orange wool. Elizabeth threw it out, made the bed, folded the pajamas. She was screwing back the lids on cream jars and lotion bottles so that she could clear the table to dust, when the young one came in, dressed and emerged into her daytime self now. "Oh!" she murmured self-reproachfully; but it seemed too late to do any tidying up herself—she only got under Elizabeth's feet. Picking up her book, and taking a bottle of nail varnish as an after-thought, she fled.

In the dining room the table was still laid and the missus sat quietly in her dressing gown, drinking a cup of tea.

Elizabeth went from bedroom to bedroom, stretching, bend-ing, sighing; lifting each crazy, sprawling bed by the scruff of its neck and sobering it to square neatness.

The young girl passed along the passage and heard her, talk-ing to herself as she scrubbed out the bath; "D'you know what," she laughed, coming to kneel beside the young man on the sofa, like a child bringing some treasure to be shown. "That girl's a bit queer. She's saying Oh Jesus! Oh Jesus! all the time she's doing the bath."

They went out on to the balcony and sat with their feet up in the sun whilst the paper blew and crackled in their hands. The visitors came; there were cries, laughter, the front door opened and closed, children, full of the excitement of being newly arrived, skated the rugs. The voice of dinner began to rise in the kitchen, too; a blare of hissings when Elizabeth opened the oven to baste the chicken, the mumble of gently boiling water waiting for the vegetables.

"Elizabeth? Would you make some tea for Boss Albert and Miss Nellie, please," stated the young girl politely.

There was another knock at the front door. Adelaide answered it, and when she came back to the balcony again: "Who's that?" asked the young man. "Someone to see Elizabeth," she said. "No other time, of course, but now, when she's cooking."

The young man and the girl ran in and out, busily hospitable, for clean glasses, the lemonade opener, some ice. Elizabeth was bulky; they dodged round her, bumped one another. "Oops!" said the young girl, with a sudden smile. Elizabeth opened her mouth a little, showing three big teeth alone in an empty gum.

Shouts of laughter washed up from the lounge and balcony. Smoke wandered through the air; ash speckled the carpets. In the kitchen the sound of cooking rose to a crescendo, and Elizabeth whipped cream. With the bang of the door and the thump of his woods dropped in the hall, the old man was home. His big face tucked with pleasure, he swung the children into the air, went into the lounge like the ringmaster entering his circus. "Stuffy," he frowned. "What's the matter here? Why don't you open the windows?" A woman smiled beautifully and wrinkled her nose: "It's kipper," she said. "I could smell it as soon as I came in."

The old man went from window to window, swung them open, grumbling briskly. When he had finished he stood a moment; "The flowers"—he clapped his hand to his ear—"Oh my God, those flowers!"

227

"I thought I told you to do the flowers?" he accused Elizabeth over the cooking pots. She did not answer; went on stirring the white sauce. "Why didn't you do it?" he demanded. Again she did not answer for a moment, pouting down into the steam from the pot. "I was busy," she said at last, noncommittally.— "Well, she *was* busy," said the girl Adelaide, coming in at that moment with the empty ice dish. And again saw Elizabeth's face, turned steadfastly away from her, and felt again that ridiculous sense of rebuff.

Elizabeth took another look at the chicken, almost done now, pushed the vegetable pots aside to keep warm, and took the extra leaf for the dining table from behind the kitchen door. Whilst she was laying the table the old missus came tentatively in and, trying not to look at the old blue skirt and man's pullover, whispered: "Don't forget your white cap and apron, eh, Elizabeth? You know the master likes you to wear your apron. . . ."

The radio was on now, above the voices. The old man turned it up for the news. Sshhh . . . The voice blared through the flat. Elizabeth turned and bent, came and went in a breathless routine; stove; sink; table; refrigerator; assembling the dinner. Gravy sizzled; cauliflower slithered on to its dish; Elizabeth went into the dining room and shook into life the silly little laugh of the cut-glass bell.

And they all came in to dinner. The chairs scraped in and out, the children changed places three times; they talked and laughed and no one had remembered to turn the radio down. The old man carved, the knife squeaking through juicy chicken flesh—and a potato shot off the dish and made a greasy patch on the tablecloth.

Elizabeth, you haven't given Master Peter a serviette.

Elizabeth, slice a lemon and bring it.

Elizabeth, another spoon.

The cheese that's wrapped in paper at the back of the refrigerator.

Bring some ice, please.

Elizabeth, why did you let the sauce go lumpy?

Bring a fresh tomato for Miss Vera.

When they had left the litter of the table Elizabeth put the drumstick and the pile of potatoes and the stump of cauliflower that was her dinner into the left-over warmth of the oven, to share later with her husband, and plunged to her elbows in the washing-up. The old man went to lie down, the others sat about in the blue haze of the lounge, smoking and talking. And by the time Elizabeth had put away the dishes and cleaned the rim of grease and food from the sink, they were waiting for tea. Once again the kitchen added its voice to the voices, and the kettle hissed and frothed at the lid for attention whilst Elizabeth filled tarts with jam and buttered the scones.

And when tea was over they sat around amidst the flagging talk and the forgotten cigarettes and realized that Sunday was almost gone again, ebbing with the heaviness in their stomachs and the red sun cut into red-hot bars by the railings of the balcony. Monday was coming. The freedom of Sunday wasn't freedom after all, but only a routine-dictated time of inactivity. They were waiting for Monday, that they hated; and that was the distaste, and the disappointment of it: Monday was better than Sunday.

No one remembered to call Elizabeth to clear away the tea-things. She stood in the passage a moment, her thick, set lips slightly open. Then swiftly and quietly, she closed the front door behind her so that it only clicked faintly, as a person clicks his tongue in a sleep, in response. The cold clear breath breathed out through the cement lungs of the city met her on the open corridor, seven layers above the tiny cement courtyard buried away below like the smallest of the Chinese boxes. Up she went, on the spiral back stair clinging like a steel creeper up the side of the building. And at the top, there was the roof, with something of the remoteness, the finality of all mountaintops. All around the sky was pink, streaky, and further away than ever. A thin shadow of smoke aspiring like a kite from the chimney of the boiler room asserted this. The gray row of servant's rooms, one-eyed each with its small square window, looked down at the gray pebbles that covered the roof.

There was no one about. Bits of torn paper and empty lemonade bottles huddled against the balustrade. Elizabeth drew her foot out of her shoe and scratched the sole, hard and cracked with all her childhood of walking on hot bare earth, against her ankle. Beneath and around, as far as she could see, there was block after block of the city, nothing but spires and jutting rectangles of cement, deeply cleaved by black streets, and faintly smoking. Here and there, like a memory stirring, the fleck of a green tree.

Elizabeth stood looking down over it for a minute, and was lonely.

*A*nd what's the old girl like?" he said, thinking.

"What a hag," said Marks.

"Bad?" He leaned against the washstand, his eyes following the other from the bed to the suitcase, from the suitcase to the bed: like watching a game of tennis.

"Ah-h man," Marks stopped, drew up his face as if to cry. He stuffed in a pair of dirty socks; pushed down a hanger that kept elbowing out.

"That's good news," he said.

"A hag," said Marks, "I'm telling you."

"So the old girl's a terror," he said, without moving from the washstand, as a young man with a red, nubbly face came in, carrying a portable radio.

"Who's that?" Badenhorst asked with an intense grin of curiosity.

"Who do you think?" He looked at him with the level appraisement of the long suffering.

"Sister Dingwall?" asked Badenhorst innocently. Communication with him must always be preceded by a restatement of facts already assumed, and as well known to him as to everyone else. It was a kind of ritual one must go through with him.

"No," he said. "The other one."

"You look out with her, I'm telling you," said Marks happily.

"Well, if that's the case, I wish I were you, and finished, instead of beginning. How many did you get, anyway?"

"Fifteen." Marks was having a last look in the wardrobe drawer; he banged it back.

Badenhorst said from where he crouched half under a bed, trying to plug the radio in: "Did you get a lot of babies, Marks?"

"I just said. Fifteen."

"Hell! We've got a long way to go, eh? Once the first one's over I won't mind so much—what do you say?"

He said from the washstand, "I'll tell you when the first one's over."

"Don't forget, you must be there when the head's born; if you're not, it's not your catch and you don't get any credit for it. She'll tell you there's plenty of time—she'll always tell you that—and then the moment your back's turned, the kid pops—and there, you've missed it.—Look, I'll leave these for you chaps"—passing the rickety wicker table on his way out, Marks picked up a pack of cards—"But look, bring them back with you . . . ? You can give them to me at Medical School." And he stood a moment, raincoat over his arm, suitcase pulling down one shoulder, looking back at the big bare room with the four well-kneaded beds like grown-up cradles beneath their canopies of dirty mosquito netting; the wardrobe with the spotted mirror; the rain-stained ceiling, the unopened suitcases, the bleary window; the young man with the pimple-scarred neck squatting on the floor; and the other, leaning back against the washstand with the broken door. Marks smiled to be leaving them to it.

In the morning, coming out of the hotel on the way to the hospital he passed the only painted portion of the hotel—a white, square room with a door marked "Bar" and a smaller door marked "Off-Sales Dept."—and came out on to the road and saw the sea, lying away down there below and the flying boats resting on it like dragonflies. Climbing the slope between the sea and himself was a confusion of waving cranes, ships, warehouses and rail tracks that was the docks. The flying boats glittered at him for attention. But it was all a long way off, like seeing someone's mouth opening and shutting urgently, but not being able to hear. He trudged on up the hill to the hospital.

There was the red-brick, institution gateway, staying and supporting the usual institution waiters; the people who are always there, outside prisons, hospitals and public homes, waiting for news or for visiting hours. Two Indian women sat bundled up against the wall, their black hair steely in the sun, and an ancient couple, dried and creased as only Indians and mummies can be, squatted with their knees up to their chins in the gutter. Two little Indian girls in yellow silk fluttered about, very shy, uttering decorous, suppressed cries when they caught one another, and a native baby, resting his paunch on the ground between his outstretched legs, watched them in silence. The Zulu watchboy, cotton reels pushed through his ears, sat on a small soap box, straining at his serge uniform. Seeing the white coat, he wheezed respectfully and tipped his cap.

The hospital was red-brick, old and new, wings and separate buildings, double and single story, this way and that on top of the hill. Round the corners the wind whirled grittily into his face; he found the Maternity Section, fly-screened like a big meat-safe, and going inside, walked through a long ward full of surpriseless eyes, laconically watching, or not seeing him from the rows of humps beneath brown blankets.

In the Beginning

The little plump brown nurse led him along the corridor. She called him "doctor"; he smiled to hear it, and began to get himself ready. Outside the door he knocked at once and went in.

Sister Dingwall was looking up straight at him and he could see that so far as she was concerned she had seen him hundreds of times before; she was sent two new medical students every fortnight. He introduced and explained himself, relieved and surprised, as usual, to hear how respectful and quiet he came out in the presence of authority. She asked questions and told him what was expected of him in a plain, cold Scots voice, looking into his face with what would have been insolence, curiosity or interest on the part of another person, but was in her so entirely disinterested that it could be taken for nothing but what it was: a desire to make herself plainly understood. When she looked down at her report, her mouth locked in at the sides and she tightened her nostrils; when she lifted her head her eyes stared straight back, dark and deep-set, not by beauty, but by time and a masculine sensibleness, from beneath rough and shaggy eyebrows whose long hairs swept in a kind of wavering grandeur of line from the frown-niche above her nose. She had no lips and her false teeth were ugly and too regular, like a row of mealies.

He followed her to the delivery room, the theater, the nursery, and when she left him in the cubicle of the student doctor's duty room, he stood twirling and untwirling an end of cotton round the button of his white coat, wondering what he had expected. Something more positive, certainly; something he could have related. She was too impersonal even to make herself unpleasant.

Badenhorst's *Manual of Obstetrics* was lying on the table.

What had she said as she went out? "Now's the time when you want to use your eyes and ears and common sense." But she said it neither as encouragement nor warning: it was merely a statement of disbelief in the existence of such qualities. He thought of this with a mild flash of irritation.

—And her face, disappearing round the door, with that peculiar loop of hair, streaky black and gray, pulled out under her veil onto her forehead, yearning towards those eyebrows, like the pictures of his mother in the 'twenties!

After three days it had replaced all aspects of living, for them. From eight in the morning until twelve at night they moved between the labor wards, the delivery room and the nursery: the door opening on women crouched on their haunches in the concentration of birth pains; on the steam and warm bloodiness cut by the flash of steel instruments lifting wicked crocodile mouths out of the sterilizers; on the squirming surface of the new-born—real people lying row upon row in canvas hammocks, with live red mouths squared for continuous demand. In between times they sat waiting in the duty room, with the cockroaches and the cups of tea and chunks of sugary "shop" cake. Even when they trudged back down the hill to the hotel to sleep, the extension telephone on the wicker table tied them to the smell and sight and sound of birth. They talked of nothing else; their ears shut out all temporal sound, attuned to the delicate drum of the fetal heartbeat approaching from the other world. Their jokes were of birth; "position is everything in life" they laughed, discussing, discussing. Where was the head? Was that the knee? How was the child lying? And the riddle of the world was the mother's belly—all the day and night-long succession of bellies—over which their hands passed and the concentrate culled from the *Manual of Obstetrics* pondered: half-knowledge, half-instinct, like the hands of the water diviner.

The mental and muscular concentration of the women giving birth magnetized them; they were part of it, too. What else was there? What did other people do, who were not busy with this business of birth? It did not seem that other things could be happening at the same time.

When the first one was over, he felt emotional, as if he could have cried, or grinned foolishly. It was a most beautiful child he held, more beautiful because it was brown, and in a newly made creature, not two minutes old, the scrolled, wide native nostrils were marvels of intricate craftsmanship, so much more skillful than the smudgy nub of a white baby's nose, and the half-inch long black curls, sudsy with *vernix caseosa,* made the baby look as if it had been interrupted in the midst of a shampoo, and made him want to laugh with pleasure at the cheek of it! He bathed it and cleaned up the mess; Sister Dingwall walked in and out. He wanted someone to say: there, it wasn't so bad was it?—so he smiled at her, in a kind of self-deprecation.

"It won't always be as easy as that," she said, staring straight back at him. "Don't go thinking yourself an obstetrician on the strength of that."

True, it had been a multipara who gave birth with the practiced confidence of experience; it had been a normal vertex presentation. But others that followed were nearly all complicated in some way, and the effort and fear of his own inept hands which they involved made the reconstruction of them in memory as separate experiences impossible; they soon became merely different aspects of the one thing: birth—and even the first lost its emotive significance.

"Did you tear her?" became Badenhorst's obsession.—It was a point of medical honor, and also, between them, a rivalry, to try and deliver a primapara of her first child without tearing the inflexible and narrow passage of her body. Badenhorst had torn three badly. He had torn one. What added to the pre-existent difficulties of both their and the patient's inexperience in these cases, was the rule that no anesthetics might be given in any but operable emergencies. The pain of the woman was flustering, hard to bear with. "At home in their kraals or their dirty shacks they'd have it a lot harder," said Dingwall, always standing by. She would walk over to the woman, and bending her stiff, rooster-breasted body, take the brown naked shoulder in the grip of her hand with the nurse's big, leather-strapped watch turned face-inwards authorizing it, and shout into the woman's face: "Come along now! That's enough of that! That's enough noise. Quiet now, d'you hear me?"

"If she keeps on with that, slap her face," she said once, noting on her watch that it was teatime, and opening the door.

"—Well, did you tear that kid?" Badenhorst looked up from the cake crumbs on the duty-room table.

"No. She's all right.—Miserable little baby." He sat down in his birth-smeared mackintosh apron, looked for a cigarette.

"What do you expect? Did you see her age? Fifteen years old."

"Babies for babies."

"I'm surprised you didn't tear her," said Badenhorst.

"No, I managed," he said. He knew that Badenhorst would go out presently to ask the native staff nurse if he had.

"My God, she is a hag," he said, sickened.

"Dingwall?" asked Badenhorst. "I was talking to her last night."

"I didn't know she could talk."

"Neither did I. She's been a midwife for twenty-seven years."

"That doesn't make her any the sweeter, I'm afraid."

"Imagine how many kids she's seen pop! Imagine how many she's bathed."

"She should have tried having one herself. It might have made her a bit more human."

"She never got married," said Badenhorst with a shrug.

"Who would marry her, for God's sake. . . ."

"Oh, she mightn't have been so bad, twenty years ago."

They looked at one another and laughed.

"That bit of hair," he said, laughing. "That bit of hair. How I'd like to stuff it back under her veil."

"I'll go and make tea," said Badenhorst, taking his feet off the table, and went out to ask the staff nurse whether the Indian girl had been torn.

Little touches of antiquity; the juxtaposition of her acquired scientific knowledge to the instinctive creative knowledge of the peasant women patients; her official authority in a domain where woman's is the natural authority of birth: these things turned their reaction to Sister Dingwall's snubs, the human rebuff of her coldness, the draining of their confidence through her expecting nothing of them, toward ridicule. There were only two ways to turn; one was into dislike, the way Marks had gone, the other was into ridicule.

She became "Ding-Dong" to them; when they heard her insistent voice in a long monologue of blame against one of the native staff nurses, they lifted their heads and smiled. "Ask not for whom the bell tolls . . ."

They discovered that she collected stamps—for her father in Scotland—in her off-duty time. "Twenty-seven years of multi-colored babies; lording it over young nurses; sneering at medical students; and stamp collecting for fun: no wonder she's turned into a starched despot." They could hear her particular stiff, measured stalk down the corridor. "There she patrols"— Badenhorst jerked his head toward the door.

She was a little deaf, but like that of so many people, hers was a selective deafness, and she heard what she chose. Yet she had the stare of deafness; that look coming up straight at you, as you stood palpating or examining—or was it merely the look that told you that you didn't know, flatly and plainly. . . . When you asked her advice or help on a case, she gave you that look again, and always, without a word, went ahead with the appropriate manipulation. She always *knew* when you would be coming to her; it was in the set of her mouth, when you did come.

"Every time I deliver a baby for the rest of my life, I'll see that face of hers with the mouth pulled in with self-control at my idiocy and that bit of hair straggling out," he exaggerated. "She's an irritating old cow," sulked Badenhorst.—She had a way of catching the corner of her underlip in her teeth, and pursing out the top one like a horse, whilst she swiveled her foot on the old-fashioned waisted heel of her white shoe and looked away, each time he tore a case.

In the evening he went to Sister Dingwall and said: "Do you think it's all right if I leave the case that's just come in, whilst I go for supper? I don't want to miss her, though."

"You should know by now," she said, lifting her eyebrows and looking down at her accounts.

"—Don't go, Doctor," the little staff nurse took him aside in conspiracy. "The baby it'll come when you're gone."

He went back and examined the woman again. She smiled at him, said something in Zulu that he didn't understand.

Badenhorst was having his first evening off, so he couldn't call him. He went back to Sister Dingwall. "Sister, there's a possibility that the woman's going to have twins."

"Who says so?" She was counting out soap into a box held by one of the staff nurses. The little brown nurse turned her eyes, white, in fearful appreciation, wanting to smile.

"Well, I think so," he said.

He stood there.

"All right," she said, dismissing him.

A few minutes later she came into the ward. He was persuading the patient, who, like many native women, wanted to get out and squat on the floor, to remain in bed. A pain came on, strong and pulling, and Dingwall stood waiting for it to pass before doing her examination.

As soon as the woman had struggled out of the current to rest again, he became full of the excitement of explanation; did not know what to show the sister first. "Listen," he said quickly. "Two hearts, I'm certain. It's plain isn't it? It's unmistakable—

I think. And then here—if you get your hand here—that's one head, eh? And then feel down here—that's another, I'm sure that's another." He watched her face as she examined, waiting.

"Yes," she said. "You're going to have twins." It was the first time she had ever made anything approaching a joking remark. He wanted to laugh, was afraid to, lest after all, in the distortion of his excitement, he had mistaken her tone.

The woman had borne four children, and the rhythm of birth developed quickly in her. Soon the first child was born, lying small and glistening wet, a very light yellow-brown in his gloved hand.

"Fine child," said Dingwall, showing her mealie-cob teeth.

"Not bad," he said admiringly. He felt he must do whatever she told him. He thought of Badenhorst, sitting in a cinema, not knowing about his twins.

"Well, what are you waiting for now?" she said.

He twitched his cheek to work his mask into a more comfortable position: "I don't quite know . . . ," he said, but felt confident.

"Well you're not going to stand there and let her relax and have labor start all over again from the first stage, are you?"

"No," he said. "Now for the other one, I suppose." The woman's body still gaped, unlike the aftermath of a single birth. "But I can't see the head at all," he said, looking up from examination.

"You can't see anything," said Dingwall. "If you're going to wait to see the head come down then you're going to have her in labor again, right from the beginning."

"Oh, of course," he reproved himself.

"Here," she said, handing him a pair of forceps. "Give the

bag of waters a nip—one little pull will be enough to break it. Just go carefully—guide the forceps along your hand: put your hand in first."

Of course he knew that was what he had to do. He had read about it time and again. After the birth of the one twin, remove the bag of waters and the second child will follow at once, in the path opened for it by the first, without further labor.

He turned back to the woman, waiting, like a cave; forceps in his hand. Slowly he inserted the forceps. But where was he? Inside the woman's body he felt only darkness, softness, and did not know. His hand crept along, but what? Where? The forceps were so hard he was afraid of them. It seemed that his hand could recognize nothing, nothing that he knew in his mind as a landmark of anatomy. He felt distressed, and a yellow dancing spot of concentration went in and out in front of his eyes. He was holding his breath.

He struggled on and said nothing, and Dingwall said nothing: he knew she must be thinking that he was getting on with it. The idea agitated him feverishly, made it impossible for him even to think what he was doing; like running and knowing that there is someone just behind you and yet being afraid to look and see how near, lest you give yourself away. At that moment he felt something, with the steel tip of the forceps; the start went right through him, the way he started sometimes in bed, just as he was going off to sleep. Not wanting to, not wanting to, he opened the forceps a very little and closed them on the object, the bag of waters.

But what if it was the uterus?

What if he pulled down the whole uterus?

It couldn't be. It must be the bag of waters.

Water ran through his whole body, flooded all his arteries and made him light, light, all through. His hand opened of itself; with the obedience of the lifeless, the forceps let go. He drew out his hand and the forceps, straightened his back, and felt that he was smiling at Sister Dingwall, felt his face smiling at her in he could not imagine what way, but unable to do anything else with it. "No," he said, still smiling, and shrugged his mouth.

He knew that he stood there, unable to stop the smile.

She came, bent her starched rooster-breast over the woman, took the forceps from him and inserted them, along her hand. Through her face, concentrated under the stiff loop of hair, the mouth locked in, he watched her searching. Then he saw her mouth unlock, it was half-parted, in chance, catching at a breathless moment of uncertainty; and she shut her eyes—shut her eyes tight, and tugged.

It was astonishing, the sight of her; the set, preserved body, the face that had decided its expression long ago in 1920, the neck that always knew and never hoped or feared: all screwed up, trusting to luck like a child wishing hard at a lucky dip bin. . . .

In a moment she held the child; born into her hands.

Coming out into the late night and walking round the building with the secretive grating roll of the stony path beneath his steps, the evening throbbed back through him as blood thumps slowly, reliving effort, after exertion. Mechanically, he lowered his eyes ready for the wind; it came, in a gritty burst at the corner, blurring the light from the sea. He smelled dust, then the sea. The boat lamps bobbed and swung, far down. Out the hospital gates and down the hill, the wind pushing him from behind, his feet striking the road jogged him pleasantly, making him go faster.

In the big empty room at the hotel, he slowly took off his coat and emptied his cigarettes, matches and keys out of his pockets. He kept thinking about her all the time, seeing her. He saw her looking up at him with that look, with her mouth down. He saw her back disappearing authoritatively down the corridor. He remembered the stamp collection, the old father, sitting under a plaid rug somewhere in Scotland. He saw her smiling, the mealie false teeth holding your attention, the loop of hair carefully arranged. Twenty-seven years in that place! Never anything else! Days and years of other people's babies. The stamp collection and the old father, for fun.

He was sitting on his bed, shoes off, and he looked up and saw himself in the narrow wardrobe mirror opposite. He was alone in the room with himself, with himself looking at him. He looked back, shoe in hand. Red, crinkly hair, that very pale skin of the red-headed, and the ugly shadows that freckly people get beneath their eyes. The eyes were light, on guard with an expression he did not feel. And the mouth, the glum mouth, set in the line of a disappointment he did not even remember.

Why, *I* look different from what I am, he thought suddenly, that is me, but I don't know it. And also that is not me, and other people don't know it.

And he lay back on the bed, wanting to be still with the novelty of understanding.

DATE DUE

NOV 21 '63			
DEC 10 '63			
JAN 6 '64			
DEC 10 '86			
MAY 10 '86			
GAYLORD			PRINTED IN U.S.A.